Death by Chocolate

By the Same Author

Sleeping with the Fishes

Death by Chocolate

TOBY MOORE

VIKING
an imprint of
PENGUIN BOOKS

VIKING

Published by the Penguin Group

Penguin Books Ltd, 80 Strand, London WC2R ORL, England
Penguin Group (USA) Inc., 375 Hudson Street, New York, New York 10014, USA
Penguin Group (Canada), 10 Alcorn Avenue, Toronto, Ontario, Canada M4V 3B2
(a division of Pearson Penguin Canada Inc.)
Penguin Ireland, 25 St Stephen's Green, Dublin 2, Ireland
(a division of Penguin Books Ltd)
Penguin Group (Australia), 250 Camberwell Road,
Camberwell, Victoria 3124, Australia (a division of Pearson Australia Group Pty Ltd)
Penguin Books India Pvt Ltd, 11 Community Centre,
Panchsheel Park, New Delhi – 110 017, India
Penguin Group (NZ), cnr Airborne and Rosedale Roads, Albany,
Auckland 1310, New Zealand (a division of Pearson New Zealand Ltd)
Penguin Books (South Africa) (Pty) Ltd, 24 Sturdee Avenue,
Rosebank 2196, South Africa

Penguin Books Ltd, Registered Offices: 80 Strand, London WC2R ORL, England

www.penguin.com

First published 2005

I

Set in 12/14.75 pt Monotype Dante
Typeset by Rowland Phototypesetting Ltd, Bury St Edmunds, Suffolk
Printed in Great Britain by Clays Ltd, St Ives plc

A CIP catalogue record for this book is available from the British Library

ISBN 0–670–91488–6

For Hugh Willis

Acknowledgements

Thank you to Tony Lacey, Peter Straus, Rowan Routh, Richard Collins and, especially, Zelda Turner. I am also grateful to Raffaella Baruzzo, Neil Beckett, Michael Troxler and Dr Stuart Lewis.

Control is an awful flop,
We like it.
It can't stop what it's meant to stop
We like it.
It's left a trail of graft and lime,
It don't control worth a dime.
It's filled our land with vice and crime,
We like it.

Popular song

Food is sex with condiments, right? If you can't have a burger smothered
in chocolate, blocked arteries, cancer of the bowel, at least one catheter
and diabetes by the age of ten, just what is this life for?

Racy James at the Comedy Store, Manhattan,
recorded shortly before his second arrest on obesity-related charges

I

She wasn't obviously f*t, but they pulled her over anyway. Strong seemed anxious to write a ticket, even if it meant leaving the squad car and choking on expressway fumes. Meeting Cupid Frish on that day, when a cold wind was blowing in from the east and raging through leafless trees, felt random.

The strange new summers when ice cracked underfoot were hard on Health Enforcement agents; everyone was wrapped up, even those within permitted weight limits. Sometimes it was the face, especially on men with double-burgered cheeks, hanging jowls or absent jawlines. Women hid excess below the line of sight around the thighs. The academy had a class on facial indicators. But, in the end, after a few years on the job, agents developed an instinct.

Devlin watched his partner saunter to the Porsche, a gun-grey Ecoslayer 988 with UV filter canopy. It had drawn up smartly when they flashed and let the siren whoop.

Strong curled a finger for the driver to get out. August. Shit weather. A big black fly smashed into the Chevy windscreen, mesmerized by some pointless autism to do it again and again. 'Shit,' Devlin said, finally hitting it dead with a rolled copy of the *Post* to put it out of its misery.

The woman was brunette. Young. Strong had trouble with other women, even on their first day together, when they waved down one heaving great plates of useless matter in Brooklyn. Strong had surprised Devlin by being insulting, which was against regulations. The only permissible reaction was pity, no matter what visual provocation came from the guilty of size. It was in the regulations. Even when they pulled over real arbuckles, the ones with a six-thousand-calorie a day habit, Devlin was always polite. Yes sir, yes ma'am. No prejudice. He liked to think it was just good manners.

Devlin saw the small, pink-laminated weight licence exchange hands.

What? Maybe five-seven, 120 pounds. Too relaxed not to be in her permit range. There didn't look to be an ounce of f*t on her. She had polished, thin legs; the sort that looked straight out of *Good Eating* magazine, and high cheekbones. Maybe Strong was right. There was a good eye to go with that bad mouth, Devlin had already conceded.

He was ahead in the game they played to pass time on the long patrols and liked to call it a gender edge, one that came from sizing up women since tenth grade. It was a dollar for every false stop. Strong was down four bucks that month and it was only the fifteenth.

Devlin smiled. She looked disappointed after the brunette had stood on the fergie. He saw his partner take out the callipers, department issue, to measure body f*t on an upper arm. Left or right, it didn't matter. Devlin noticed the metal ends all but touch. Not a breath could have squeezed between them.

'Another buck, sister,' he said, yawning and rubbing a hand through his short-cropped, dark hair as Strong came back to the driver's side, staring at the licence. 'Just admit you're wrong. Come on, it's real. Nobody likes a sore loser.' He gave a warm, friendly laugh.

She ignored him and swiped the card and they both looked at the screen, gamblers watching the reels fall: Cupid Frish, 280 Montcalm Avenue, Apt 510, Hoboken, New Jersey 20032. Weight allowance: 119 pounds. No endorsements, no medical exemptions.

'She's no breacher, I'm telling you.' Devlin looked out of the windscreen to give himself a second opinion. She was still tall and thin, leaning against that gleaming I-Got-Money machine and ignoring the cold, holding her face defiantly to the weak sun. They said it would snow later. He'd learned to live with climate change; it was climate unreliability that stuck in his craw. 'What was her body-f*t index? I'm guessing twenty-four, twenty-three?'

'Twenty-three,' Strong replied. 'I'm searching anyway, okay.'

'Fearless, truly fearless. And all because you just can't handle surrendering George Washington's face. You're tight.'

But the words sounded more false than funny because Devlin already knew that Strong was generous, except to him, and it was a puzzle. The unit had Strong Nights. They were infamous. She'd stand beer shots at Finnegan's, the bowling alley next door, each round tightening the bonds. She was single. Devlin was single. But he was a single father. She went out. He went home. There was some line she didn't want to cross with him, although they were rubbing along and, as Devlin kept telling himself, it had only been a few months. They just needed time together and he was a patient man.

It was certainly good to be working outside the city, to have distractions. Devlin had been arguing with Sylvia, and the apartment was a charnel house of slights and bruises and that difficult age, fifteen going on twenty-five. He knew she was using.

'I'm trained,' he told Strong. 'She had silver foil in her backpack and I wasn't snooping. Okay, I was. But I'm a parent, so poking around is part of the job.'

'Cut her some slack, man,' Strong had said, laughing gently. 'Didn't you ever break a rule?'

'Not this kind, no. Anyway, you need every edge you can get to keep ahead in the war against teenagers.'

'I don't know who put it there,' Sylvia had said, sullen and angry when he'd confronted her with the evidence: small, brown crumbs, powdered and cheap. He'd tasted earthy flavours, the vegetable f*t they mixed with street brown, the tip of his tongue dabbing cautiously. He winced immediately. It was obvious. She probably bought it in Washington Square, off some dealer shuffling nervously from foot to foot before looking around and pulling the contraband quickly from a hidden recess; flapping both arms across his chest to keep warm and diverted while she sniffed the goods.

'And, anyway, you shouldn't go through my things like I'm one of your shit brownheads,' she shouted back.

'Don't use language on me,' he'd said, putting on the voice he reserved exclusively for shit brownheads who used language on him. 'Jeez, sweetheart, you know what'll happen if you get caught.'

She looked defiant and wounded and drew a hand through long, blonde hair streaked a violent mauve.

He pressed home the attack. 'How does health tribunal and eating rehab every Saturday for a year sound? Good? I don't think so.' Saturday, that holiest day in the teenage calendar. Bad. Her head dropped slightly. The battle was over before it was won, not that he enjoyed the spoils of war or wondering when this desert in their relationship, a place without contours and shade, would ever be crossed.

Sylvia had good grades, which Devlin tried to keep as his steadying horizon. Most parents didn't mind and used themselves. The suburbs buzzed to swinging gorge parties by the hot tubs, passed around brown and turned up Hendrix. But most parents weren't agents. Raiding food smugglers and weight abusers by day and watching a daughter use didn't seem a good fit. The law was the law and Devlin thought it would be a crazier world if people could still do what the heck they liked with their bodies. Not that he was political. It was just plain common sense. The President was right. Somebody had to pick up the tab, take responsibility. Food was a final frontier, she said in her inauguration address. Out of control.

He blamed the school. If only the job paid more then he could have sent her private, away from the city and temptations that seemed to be its sacrament. She was impressionable and they grow up fast, but sometimes not fast enough. He knew her friends experimented with cheeseburgers, despite federal advertising campaigns, and it gnawed at his gut.

So, Devlin found himself whistling an unhappy tune, playing back snatches of life and wishing there was some guidebook to show for all the centuries of human evolution, at least a chapter on dealing with teenagers. It was Support Your Cranky Partner Day, he decided, suddenly needing some air and pushing open the car door.

'Hi.' Devlin flashed his special, one-hundred-dollar dating grin, as Strong began rummaging through the back seats. Frish looked his six-foot frame up and down, like a seasoned loss adjuster, and smiled loose change back through lips glossed a deep mahogany, a turn of collagen that said: do your best, you look shapeless, city-payroll cheap. He stared at her, sensing it. Strong concentrated on the search.

Frish was wearing a light blue, curve-hugging dress, the sort that said This Season. Her fur-trimmed white leather coat looked expensive. Devlin was in blue and unfashionably flared. His padded jacket cut just the wrong side of well and a white shirt, one of a bargain consignment from Chang Hwa's tailoring store in China-town, was strictly No Season. No Money; the words almost stitched across the breast pocket.

There were trademark 'uh-huhs', as Strong checked off a mental list: spare-wheel recess, loose linings, hollow compartment. She ran through it all. Even used the scanner. Not a blip. Frish smiled, knowing. Devlin waited and wondered: what kind of name was Cupid anyway? Given or business?

'I used to have a fish called Cupid when I was a kid,' Devlin lied pleasantly. 'Damned if it didn't die from overfeeding, all swollen and puffed. A terrible thing to happen. Ugly.'

'Yeah?' she replied, eyes staring upwards, drawn to a sight more interesting, a cloud. 'Probably suicide. Fish are funny about the company they keep.' She turned and winked at him, then glanced away and began tapping her foot, humming softly, teasing some ballad. It never worked on Strong, who was methodical as well as insubordinate.

'Tell me, on a scale of one to ten, how do you rate my roadside manner?' Devlin asked.

She stared at him. 'Am I allowed a fraction of one?' She laughed softly to herself and looked calmly back at the sky.

It didn't take long. Three boxes in a compartment hidden under the arm rest in the passenger door. There must have been thirty pounds. Devlin whistled theatrically.

'It's for personal use,' Frish said in a soft drawl before a question was asked, cool as thermidor-protected brown.

'Three boxes?' snorted Strong. 'You must be one sick puppy.'

'I got withdrawal issues, abused childhood, self-esteem problems and a long drive.' She was measured, bored, counting off the list one long finger at a time. 'Heading to the Keys tomorrow. Catch some rays to be a rich, cho-co-late for the fall,' she emphasized the C-word, looking at Devlin for a rise. Vivid, crystal-green eyes stared, level and motionless and she drew a tongue slowly over her plump, red-glossed upper lip. He didn't wince. 'You must need to see the doctor's certificate.' She held it out in a practised way.

Devlin took it, feeling Chang Hwa's shirt sticking to his back itch and irritate. The certificate looked genuine, right down to the flashy, indecipherable signature and the translation underneath: Howard DeLosso MD, Obesiatric Specialist. He handed it back and sniffed the box.

'Pure? Maybe some ganache?' He peered at the label. It was covered in florid, excitable curly words that mystified him because foreign words had never made it to Eminem High, Jefferson City. But he'd already guessed they could be summed up in just one: expensive.

'This looks good treatment, Ms Fresh. You've got taste and excellent health insurance, I can tell.'

'It's Frish, like fish, but with an r.' She rolled the word into a tiger's growl. 'Practise it at home. Anyway, like I told you, it's for personal use. Gift from abroad. An admirer.' She tapped the box and ran a finger along the biggest lettering, tracing its twists. 'That's French, by the way, in case you was wondering.'

'Not enough to lose sleep.' Devlin handed the box to her and walked back to the Chevy.

'Hey, ganache means stupid,' she shouted after him, laughing. 'Did you know that?' But Strong lingered. They were talking.

'Come on,' Devlin shouted through the open window, irritated by the soundless conversation. A sudden wind buffeted the car and blew papers around inside. He thought guiltily about the third piece of bread he'd toasted and honeyed for breakfast. Another two hundred calories consumed. On the radio they were saying that some islands in the Pacific had disappeared overnight, huge tidal waves wiping everything away. Four thousand people dead. They were fighting again in the Middle East over that dwindling, spindled Nile. An international convention was meeting in Geneva to work out what was happening with the weather. A tactical nuke had gone off in a bus terminal, so a little place in Central Asia with more name than territory was spinning around the planet, now all molecules and United Nations resolutions. Two hundred extra calories. Devlin knew he had to get a grip, manage the stress of his new job.

'Neat car,' Strong said, turning the ignition as they watched Frish pull away.

Devlin swallowed an amphetamine ('Marlboro Country: Where The Appetite Suppressant Is'). He didn't know it, but the next time he was going to see Cupid Frish, she would be unwrapped and the taste would be lingering, like the bean they pick from the Criollo cocoa trees north of Caracas. That is, if US marshals didn't find the crops and napalm them first.

2

In the twenty-first century of Our Lord, Christ the Fit, it was illegal to be f*t in most states, except Louisiana and Alabama, where they clung to chicken-fried-deep-fullest-f*t-cream-sodden-gumbo-dunkin'-mall-waddling lives as if their eternal souls depended on such graces. Chocolate, brown to just about everyone, was banned outright after Congressional hearings deemed it too tempting, mind-altering and f*ttening to be tolerated in a civilized society trying to live within Weight Control.

The Thirty-Eighth amendment to the Constitution, passed despite opposition from states rights groups, tightened the screw, making it a federal offence to 'transport or sell' a range of other processed foods. People deep-froze full-f*t ice cream in the months before it hit the statute books and tried to trade Hershey Bars on eBay; ignoring the second district federal Court of Appeal ruling with a coy code, wanting bids on twenty-five grammes of 'brown pleasure'. There was plenty of illegal eating. The cheese supposed to be going as aid to Africa and Asia fell off trucks all the time. It was the same with sugared drinks.

The quest for lo-cal brown was the holy grail for scientists at Pfeizer and Wellcome, especially since every kid with a chemistry set was finding cures for cancer.

Smugglers, the professionals anyway, faced the stiffest sentences, up to fifteen years if the quantities of brown were high enough. Plenty of people still took the risk. But it was serious prison time for repeat offenders, rehab for the least.

Over the border in Mexico, factories retooled, producing full-f*t burgers loaded with salt to satisfy a maddened underground American market for dangerfoods. Even the Chinese switched from fridge magnets and missiles to salted snacks, export grade, most of it smuggled through Canada.

Enforcement had burning pits for contraband they found hidden in cars, pickups and trucks. The air in El Paso smelled so much of barbecue, the old sort, that they said you could taste over-done meat in the southern winds blowing through scrub and dirt where farm towns used to be. At least guided smelling tours were booming; work for the old cowboys and ranchers.

President Bryant was elected on a Control ticket, pure and simple. The people had spoken. They wanted lower health-care premiums for eating clean, tax breaks for approved diet plans and fitness club memberships. The Health of America coalition she put together with food fundamentalists had proved unbeatable. It wasn't hard. Schools or f*t? Money in your wallet or f*t? 'Gross or great?' as it said on the posters.

Tolerances were low because treating the obese was costing $180 billion a year, money that Bryant suggested should be diverted to fighting pollution, or helping relocate New England from its ruined coastline and constant assault from a spitting, aggrieved sea.

It wasn't just diabetes; even the military was affected. Route marches had become route drives; in automatics. People stopped making love because it was too much effort. They watched the video instead and hoped their South American maid would have a spare bambino for adoption. 'Everyone's still having the candlelit dinners, three or four courses,' reported the Kinsey Institute. 'Then they go home and sleep. If this trend continues, the United States population will decline by 15 per cent over the next thirty years.'

But guilt was bad politics. 'You are not to blame,' the President told rallies through the Midwest, in those towns where they were most to blame; the great waddling humonsters with chapped, sored thighs and innocent, porcine faces who sought salvation from the fever of food.

'You are victims of corporate greed. There is no excuse. They lied. It was addictive. I will give you back your bodies. I will give you life.' There were always roars at this point, because they liked being given things, the humonsters, such as a free apple pie with a main course; even life.

Global warming was also vexing in the Midwest, more than she dared admit or could do anything about. It was forcing up electricity prices and driving people off the barren, waterless lands. Genetically modified wheat was unionizing in Missouri, demanding rights, for heaven's sake. Thick snow in summer, Florida flooding every five minutes, islands disappearing under the sea in the Pacific, bobbing up again in the Caribbean. And the budget was a curse. There was never enough money; that was the only constant in political life. It should be carved in stone over the hermetic weather bubble protecting Capitol Hill from the spin cycle of seasons.

Mid-terms were only six months away and campaign strategists were in panic over priorities. Where was the promised health-care reform? She hadn't even begun to think about the new national fault line, southern states threatening to take northern ones to court, claiming f*t segregation was illegal.

She owed her victory to the Great Crash of Twenty-Nine, a fortuitous tragedy. Fifteen overweight diners at a Wichita Burger King were killed, crushed by debris and each other after an upper floor collapsed. The local coroner had given the now historic verdict: death by weight. Burger King was found guilty of 'reckless feeding'.

The appeal to traditional values that she championed rang across the conservative Midwest, harnessing anger at rising health-care costs, those the disciplined thin knew they bore to care for the profligate f*t. Everyone carried the burden of obesity in their premium payments. It was the perfect political pincer. She promised grants for playing fields and swimming pools, a new national lottery for fitness equipment in schools, Jane Fonda on Mount Rushmore. Eating fundamentalists, particularly the Anti-F*t League, joined her campaign. So did anti-globalization protesters. It was passionate, heady and populist: a promise of life and beauty, while trees in the mountains wept leaves in spring, lakes became kaleidoscopes of impurity and flowers refused to bloom under mauve, pungent and toxic skies.

'Why should fit, thin people pay for the excesses of those who, albeit through no fault of their own, have fallen to diabetes, weak hearts and chronic breathing problems,' Eleanor Bryant told them in Missouri. 'Why should you pay for people to look bad?' she asked the Fashion Society annual in New York.

But she was having difficulty persuading her Mexican counterpart to ban production in his own country.

As Luis Suarez pointed out, gently, during their first summit in Cancun, it wasn't illegal to eat chocolate in Mexico, a place where many people struggled to eat at all due to the dramatic reduction in American beef imports.

The summit banquet had included, in addition to unnecessary flirting by the taciturn and married Mexican, an egregiously large number of dishes involving mole, that molten chocolate and chilli fusion too risqué even for the eateasys. It was a pointed gesture and did not go unnoticed.

President Bryant delicately scraped hers to one side. Nobody was getting photographs of her breaking the law. She told the Secretary of State on Air Force One as they flew over Tijuana that they should reply in kind, treating Suarez to the blandest lentil cutlets the White House kitchens could devise when the time came to return the hospitality.

Beneath them, the United States was bingeing and dieting, torn between consumption and denial. It was only natural, social commentators said reassuringly. The Pilgrim Fathers had arrived at Plymouth Rock with no food at all and begged off the locals, before killing them, to go through a similar catharsis.

Celebrities endorsed this and that f*t-reduction treatment, aversion therapy and chocolate patches. A school in Oregon banned F*ts Domino, Hot Chocolate, Big Pun, Barry White and Chubby Checker from music classes, claiming they were 'incitements'. The National Association for the Advancement of Colored People said this restriction was pure racism. 'What about white Mama Cass? Meatloaf?' they demanded. The case was still working its way to the Supreme Court.

Slim was the most popular name for boys, according to the *New York Times* annual survey of registered births. Flow, which evoked notions of a body in control, was most favoured for girls.

*

II

In Manhattan, Bishop Instructor Heston Gotfelt knotted the waist-band string to jogging pants, laced his trainers, slipped on a tight black Lycra vest and adjusted his white dog collar before leaving the hotel room for breakfast.

It was Friday. He paused at the full-length mirror and patted his stomach. Flat as an altar top.

There was still a hint of high-school football star: erect but rolling, wide shoulders tapering to a narrow waist that measured the same thirty-two inches it had in his linebacker prime.

The face, which was severe and impiteous, unlined and tanned, seemed wiser than its forty-four years. He dyed his hair, adding a startling, cruel raven to its darkness. As in life, there was no room for grey and Gotfelt had known this instantly when he saw the twisted, weak, wizened strand, ashen and dismal, lurking in the lustre of his ponytail. He was plucking his eyebrows at the time and meditating on the purity of an apple, a single green apple blushed lightly with red.

It had been expected. His father was grey at forty. But that had little to do with genetics, more with taking a hallelujah show around the dirt halls of North Dakota and preaching religion to listless farmers with lice in their heads and indifference in their souls. He never made a dime and died at fifty-three, exhausted and broke, bitter and confused. God had called him, but forgot to pick up the tab.

Look at the son, Heston Gotfelt would think to himself: the scholarship boy who made it to business school off the back of physical speed, dormant for most of those early, overweight and miserable years when every calorie was his solace and comfort. Consumed, but never burned: he had lived the American nightmare.

Heston Gotfelt the third, as he styled himself despite the absence of a first or second, soon became more religious corporation than preacher; progenitor of a money-making machine with its own cable television channel pumping out the nourishment of faith, christhefitspeeddating.com for the lovelorn, and a permanent future in the form of the University of Christ the Fit in West

Virginia. Mere multimillionaires had hospital, museum wings and tame members of Congress. True success meant an institution, a perpetual-motion machine of largesse and tax write-offs.

Gotfelt was also a best-selling author, thanks to the writers he employed. The Oscar for Best Original Religion was kept in a small recess above his private altar, beside a shelf of early Heston Gotfelt weight-loss cookery tapes ('Call 1-800-LEANER. Christ was fit for you; are you fit for Christ?'). They sold four million copies in less than two years. A population greedy to swap pounds for cheaper health insurance and anxious to keep within the laws puffed to the bookstores, but mostly they ordered online or over their vidphones. Sitting.

In the breakfast room, heads turned and he felt the fuel of awed, curious eyes surge through his veins, following his every step to a table with views over Central Park. Vanity for the Lord, he reminded himself, only for the Almighty All Lean. He sought little for himself, except to ensure that his religion did not end up like all the others – just another Vegas lounge act.

Somebody would always ask, hesitantly, for an autograph, invariably before he unfurled his napkin. He would sign with a powerful flourish and comment on the physique of the supplicant, approving if possible, encouraging if plainly not. It was important to give. The gates would then be opened and others would approach, respectful; the waddling, struggling masses or the proudly toned. He could have eaten in his room, but it helped to feel sins radiating off others to salve his own, which were restless more than ever.

'Good morning, Holly,' he said as his assistant approached. People rarely intruded when Holly Fareham, tall and purposeful, was in his orbit. She was twenty-nine, thin and comfortably within her weight limits. All his staff submitted to random tests. It was written into their contracts. She had never failed one. Not even after Thanksgiving, a favourite time for Weight Watchers to tour with their fergies.

'What's the schedule?' he asked before she sat down.

He trusted her judgement, although it was not the curvaceous brain with a Harvard degree that first attracted him. Not that he ever tried a seduction of this practical blonde, secretly enjoying the denial, a little piece of everlasting Lent. It never occurred to him that she might not be interested, which she wasn't.

'Good morning, Bishop.' The smile was firm and professional as her hands opened a small computer. 'I've loosened up the schedule, as you requested. You've got CBS this afternoon, Ricardo and Julie.'

'Which one?'

'There's more than one?' She was momentarily flustered. 'I'm sorry. I'll find out.' She brushed a hand through her short hair. 'The camera crew will come here. It's a fifth-anniversary segment. Should be routine. He, sorry, or they, may ask about the Louisiana state court ruling on weight limits being unconstitutional. We pushed the mayor back to eleven so that you can be filmed running around Central Park in an hour. You're preaching tonight: the Jewel Health Club on West Fourth. Limo from here at seven-fifteen. I've told the local Instructor that it'll be abdominal crunches and running machine. The communion will be green salad, capers, tomatoes, spring onions, portobello mushrooms, all tossed in a light mustard vinaigrette. There's a new movie about brown addicts in Brooklyn that Marketing want to congregation-test.'

Gotfelt nodded but had felt his stomach tighten involuntarily at mention of the mayor. John Finch was proving less than grateful, despite the block of votes secured for him by the Church at the last election. 'Has he moved at all?' Gotfelt asked, a forkful of scrambled egg white with parsley hovering beneath his mouth.

'No, says it's a police matter and that he can't interfere, much as he's sympathetic etcetera, etcetera.'

'Like hell,' snorted Gotfelt. 'Finch hasn't the spine God gave him. Get me his assistant, what's-his-name?'

'Tom Lonergan?'

'Get Lonergan. Tell him that if his man does not act, I shall go on the seven o'clock news. I'll unleash a backlash at the next elections that neither will forget. Be firm, Holly. This is intolerable and I want them to know it.' Gotfelt sounded pained and exasperated. 'I'll need a briefing note on Louisiana, by the way. Just the usual: rates of diabetes, heart disease, that *Newsweek* piece about how much selfish eating costs taxpayers.'

Eateasys. Dens of coagulant vice and f*t tolerated by the political establishment; secret doors through which the weak and unControlled passed to satiate themselves on cheeseburgers and grease-sodden fries, anything in flagrant breach of the Production Code for meat product and f*ts. They gorged on yielding brown of every conceivable texture and hue, soft and running, hard and commanding. Brown. He felt dizzy, guilty and mildly aroused. A big, thick slab of it in three dimensions spun on an invisible axis, sticky and smooth, before he regained his composure.

There were hundreds of eateasys in this city. He could all but smell them: hidden in backrooms, cellars and secret office suites; down alleys and in dank places; secret worlds of culinary debauchery. More opened every day, it was said. Their existence made a mockery of the law. Worse, they made a mockery of him. Each was a personal affront.

They were the principal reason he was in New York, to drive the message home with Finch, discreetly if possible, publicly otherwise. Finch played populist but it was Gotfelt who secured his election, pulling out the self-serving suburban vote, just as he had done for the President.

The new Constitutional amendment was his reward from her; but it was unpopular and if New York rebelled, the rest of the country could follow. Opposition must be stamped out, but he was optimistic. Had he not successfully smote the most famous eateasy of them all, Dumptys on Sunset Boulevard? Busted when it was heaving with Hollywood A-listers filling themselves with saturated, dripping Mexican burgers, twisting their worry beads and muttering kabbalah mantras. They'd all been weighed at the scene. Dozens failed. Pounds over! The court cases were more free publicity. He was on all the networks and cable news channels commenting from the Los Angeles county courthouse steps.

These things were always easier in California, where people took no persuading about the sin of f*tfulness, worshipping thin long before he came along and deified it into something tax deductible.

The western Church was carefully tailored to incorporate tarot card readings and meditation, a whole research department existing to mix and match faiths. It was important to keep belief fresh for daytime talk shows by spicing its content with found mystical texts, such as the Book of Indulgence, one of several texts secretly devised to keep the Church of Christ the Fit West in a state of novelty.

Gotfelt could understand the South: backward, poor, sullen and suspicious. But Manhattan. Maybe it was the long cold summers and some instinctive need to store f*t? But probably it was just New York fuckyouness.

Massachusetts might have been hard, but proved easily flattered when chosen as the place 'where history began again'. Joe Regard was responsible for publicity and that was his idea. What a night. Throwing McDonald's quarter-pounders into Boston harbour at the very start of the campaign to get the Thirty-Eighth passed. Those pimpled saps behind the counter didn't know what hit them.

'Surrender all of your burgers now, in the name of God,' Gotfelt had thundered to the sallow youth with a vacant, misangled boy-face.

Loaded cameras stared resolute, rows of black holes perched on squinted faces. Reporters, notebooks cocked, were primed to witness the historic encounter between global junk and Christ the Fit.

'Regular or large fries with that?' the youth had asked, hesitant and smiling shyly. 'Hi, Mom,' he waved awkwardly at a television camera.

There were low sniggers around him. Gotfelt quickly raised his hand. 'Let this be the end of what is consuming us from within,' he roared.

Supporters rushed behind the counter, seizing frozen and cooked meat, whooping and hollering and flinging them into black bags, smashing the teats off drink machines, but leaving pickles, lettuce and tomatoes. 'Off-message,' Regard had counselled.

The servers stood by, mute, nobody willing to take a hit for Big Mac. Not on minimum wage, anyway.

'Boston Burger Party', the *Globe* newspaper headline called it the next day. 'McDonald's To Sue Over "Outrage"' was buried deep in the text beneath, its plea for freedom to choose lost to the excitement and novelty of crowds filling themselves on free, dry-roasted tofu bakes and unsweetened apple juice, all of which the Church provided. Nobody was thinking about rights. Everyone was too busy toasting lower health premiums, promised on the spot by Empire Blue Cross Blue Shield to those signing f*t food waivers and committing to exercise routines. The McDonald's behemoth was humbled.

Fireworks lit that night sky as burgers were hurled into the still, dark waters of Boston harbour. It was a dramatic touch, calculated by Regard to ensure that witnesses always recalled fun, not the start of a campaign to deprive them of pleasure. It worked. Even humonsters turned up, drawn by the smell of processed flesh, little realizing what strictures they would soon face.

'Remember, they launched the fourth Gulf War with a telethon,' Regard told Gotfelt as they watched. 'This is show business, too.'

3

Luther Atom had been following his own morning rituals. Namely: sipping a nuclear-powered espresso, eating a croissant, arguing with his chef and checking the sports pages.

'Palm oil,' Henri Bouche almost spat the words. 'No more. I simply refuse.' He hurled a baking tray at the far wall.

'Shhhh.' Atom scrunched his thin frame as if that alone might absorb the cacophonic rage of metal against bare brick. Certain noise carried, even with army-issue insulation acquired from the supply corps, extra insurance for his underground of syrups and saturates.

A basement wasn't enough any more. Not with the odour detectors. But he paid people, had the right kind of clientele. Hotshots covered his back, military technology his front. Rich criminal attorneys with bright lies and sharp suits rubbed shoulders with their clients after hours. Everybody passed through Atom's, although no sign outside announced its existence. The most famous eateasy in Manhattan enjoyed its notoriety by word of mouth alone. A chain of guilt and dependence tied all the customers, guaranteeing a low profile and no advertising costs.

The theme was burger bar from the last century, its walls simple, bright colours; idiot reds and yellows predominated. Big clown figures based on designs kept on permanent display at the Met seemed to act as supporting columns for his saturnalia. The tables were anchored to the floor and the chairs were anchored to the tables. Architectural historians still pondered the central mystery that they enshrined: did people steal them?

The kitchen was in a second, neighbouring building equipped with high-speculation odour dousers. Air vents sucked whatever was left from the smell of bilious, bubbling animal f*ts through to a third property, unknown to its baffled owners or the health specialists trying to understand their unusual olfactory symptoms, and then into a capillary system of shafts before opening near the A, C and E subway stop tunnel at Fourteenth. Northbound. The food itself arrived on a shorter route along a conveyor belt the width of an air-conditioning duct.

If there was a raid, the kitchens were supposed to have time to dispose of burgers, chocolates and cheeses before being discovered. But if there was a raid, Atom would have words with Tom Lonergan.

Above, in his other restaurant, Atom championed mean cuisine. Zagats had given him four stars. The Health Commissioner himself and his pale, hairless assistant were regulars, usually choosing cheese-free cauliflower cheese, egg-free quiche or ratatouille. When Atom told the commissioner that the ratatouille was, naturally, without rat and was met by a stony stare, he knew that this was not a man with any kind of humour and had shrugged.

But on this day Atom was left wondering, not for the first time, whether the skills of his cook were worth the attendant volatility. He only needed the standards after all: brown, burgers, pepperoni pizzas, hotdogs. Nothing fancy. Rich or poor, everyone craved the same. But Bouche kept insisting on a bloody, lean steak with a light sauce of mustard seed and peppercorns, a dish from the old days in Montmartre, wherever that was. Lite, anyway. 'I don't know Henry,' Atom had said. 'Where's the edge? Don't see the call for it.'

'Bien sûr, Monsieur Atom. But I 'ave reasoned on that. I will use only the f*ttest steaks, the richest of creams. And,' he winked and paused for effect, 'I now will add the finest brown. From Ecuador.'

Atom had negotiated a compromise and 'burger au chocolat extra supreme' came to anchor the menu. But he wasn't paying for Ecuadorian brown. Most of his customers couldn't tell the difference between a powder-dry Trinitario from the West Indies and a ground-down Hershey made from ordinary Forastero bought off some bench-living low life.

But Bouche still made hell if he felt like it. 'I am being keeled here, keeled by offul cooking.'

Atom turned a page, oblivious.

19

'The art of the kitchen is like a violin. You must practise all the time, always harder pieces, or it goes. Poof.'

'Sure, Henry babe,' Atom sighed. 'But your bank account is not exactly being killed. Very much alive, I'd say. And you know they don't call palm oil tree lard for nothing. It makes food taste good, comprendi?'

'The word is comprenez in my country, not comprenday,' Bouche corrected, exaggerating the final word. 'And where is my creativity? I trained classically under Hubert de Savarin.'

'Whatever. The fact is, friend, there's no call for that kind of material here. People pay a lot of money for what they can't get, see? That's the American way. It isn't about having it all, it's about trying to have it all. The Constitution says we pursue happiness. If we ever got it the whole place would grind to a halt. There'd be no point,' his grim laugh echoed. 'Anyway, I'm not running no eating improvement courses. Leave that to the seminaries and colleges.' Atom did, privately, consider himself a divine on the deeper value of Food, especially brown. 'They don't want goodness, see. They get enough of that shit up there,' he said, pointing to the ceiling, the streets above and the heavens above them.

He put an arm around the shoulders of his head chef. 'Listen, what's the point in having the best cooks in New York unless I got them making hotdogs?'

'Pah,' Bouche exclaimed, but the sting had been drawn, as it always was, by a flambé of flattery. 'I need to spread my wings, that is all. To fly. I am artiste.'

'Yes, you are,' Atom agreed fervently, reaching for his balloon of brandy and thinking of a few other, less flattering, qualities.

'Every chocoburger that I construct contains a piece of my soul, my very essence,' said Bouche, patting his chest dramatically, proudly.

'Don't it just,' replied Atom equably, already back with the 4.20 at Saratoga and thinking, anxiously, about his gift to the mayor and when it might win, ensuring his favoured status with the administration. He didn't want Finch as an enemy. The very idea made him shiver.

It was nearly midday. The first guests would be arriving soon, making their way to the bar in his official restaurant and asking for 'a vegetable feast, hold the mayo', which was their key to his magic kingdom, its border post a side room designed to resemble a hotel reception. Some were always nervous and excited, like truant children sneaking a peek; others stayed cool and calm.

A hostess would emerge, rather dramatically, from behind the concealed door, a bookshelf, to lead them down textured rubber steps to the real Atom's, a place rank with eating decadence where everything was rumoured to be available. They would be scoped first, retinal scans to confirm identities from reservations made a month in advance, time for Atom's team to carry out background checks.

Women would clutch the arms of male escorts, who always tried to look composed, as if they diced with their diets every day.

There was no written menu for legal reasons. The young hostesses would, instead, insinuate ingredients into wicked options. Everything revolved around a firmament of dissipating burgers, big pumped-up sixteen-ounce beef patties, and desserts debauched with brown 'from around the world', but really from the Albanians in Rhode Island. Where they got it from, Atom never asked. He also offered a full bar and drinks came in the old measures.

There were no rules, although a rigorously enforced dress code ensured that a certain decorum was maintained: jackets and ties for the men, no jogging wear for the women and heavy petting only between midday and 2 p.m. Music played through hidden speakers and couples could dance to all the hits, songs about kids popping brown, drive-by shootings, love, ozone depletion.

The wilder Lucullan banquets, most Thursdays, offered a rite from Guatemala, where tribes mix cocoa with spices to alter consciousness, raise awareness. Other nights would infuse the brown with stimulant guarana from Brazil to feed the Bacchanalia. In the mornings, cleaners picked up the complimentary syringes, discarded after giving palpating users a hit of insulin before they risked the streets and lurking Health Enforcement agents.

Atom had toyed with offering sex – there was certainly room in the labyrinthine red-brick caverns to install a brothel – but decided against.

'Too ordinary,' he told the visiting papal nuncio. 'I know in Italy it's still the thing. But here it's food, see. You can get sex anywhere in New York. It's cheese and chocoburgers and pure brown that get the juices spouting.'

Atom looked at his watch. They needed to get the supplies stored. Calming down Bouche had wasted half the morning.

'Hey, Henry, you need more full-f*t C and brown. I put an order in last week. Should be out back.'

'I check,' said Henri, who had been gorging mentally on his bank account. It was true, he was making a fortune. Soon, he would take it back to Paris and open Henri's. Kings and queens and presidents would abandon their weatherpod palaces for his orgies of taste and sensuality. There would be Michelin stars, media stars, Hollywood stars; beautiful women with proper European curves. He was still dreaming when he saw the reclining sculpture on the long, cedar refectory table where he tested new ingredients, often seasonings from the Far East with which to flavour the hand-crafted burgers. His jaw dropped and he squinted. Chocolate.

It was quite exquisite, extraordinarily lifelike, to scale even, and lay on its back, arms resting by the side, vulnerable and gorgeous. The detail was astounding; breasts perfectly formed, nipples and areolae highlighted with delicate lines, dots, ridges and shadows. Such attention. The pose was restful, not suggestive. Her face was simple and honest, a white chocolate, translucent, and the eyes were bright. The small nose had deep, almost natural nostrils. 'Rodin en chocolat,' he said softly, clapping his hands together like a pleased child. It must be a present. From Monsieur Atom himself, no doubt. How unexpected. Magnifique. Superbe.

The chocolate alone must have cost $30,000. He should be careful, of course; his weight certificate renewal exam was in two weeks and they were always tough on migrant chefs.

But he reached, hesitantly, to break off a piece. His hand hovered over the nose and lips after he drew it lightly along the arm, feeling the dulled matt of brown. He was tempted to stroke between the legs, but laughed to himself, embarrassed by his lewdness. Nervous.

'Non, non,' he said, shaking his head, tongue protruding, expectant. He held the lower half of the left ear lobe and began to bend, expecting to hear that familiar, firm crack of pure brown.

The scream was unusually powerful, reaching the restaurant above. Waiters quickly claimed a problem with the rice boiler and Atom leapt out of what little skin he had, racing to the store, head bent against the slipstream of his own motion.

Henri Bouche stood immobile, white as the hat on his head and pointed, wordlessly, at the shape on the table, dark brown except for a small exposure of pink ear lobe. His mouth moved, a marine creature puzzled and outraged to find itself ashore.

Atom walked slowly around the form, staring intently. One hand was on his chin, as if studying a museum piece, an exhibit. He was drawn in particular to the sightless emerald eyes.

Their last sight had been of a haired monster, some giant creature with a quizzical face that stared down. Impassive. She was puzzled and nearly laughed, but died instead. Her last memory, as she slipped into unwilled oblivion, was of a children's party in Odessa. She was six and running away with the parcel, hiding behind heavy, age-scented curtains in her grandmother's bedroom and tearing at the paper, layer after layer, searching for the prize that was her due because it was her birthday.

'She has to go,' said Atom. 'There's no room for you to work.'

But the gases that powered Bouche were inert as he stood transfixed by the human delicacy in front of him.

'Hey,' said Atom, clicking his fingers. 'Earth to Henry.' Christ, French chefs. 'Ain't you ever seen a corpse before, back in France?' He sounded genuinely surprised.

'Non,' muttered Henri indignantly. 'Sous chefs don't just leave them lying around, you know.'

'No? Well, see, the important thing here is that a dead body's the same as a live one, only more amenable.'

'Comment?'

'What?'

'Exactement. Comment? What?'

'Meaning we got to get her out of here. She isn't moving on her own, my friend, and I can't exactly call the cops.'

Henri winced, protesting that he could not touch her.

'Jesus eats! A minute ago you were ready to make a meal of her.'

'That was when she was a brown feast, not a –'

'– broad en croûte. Yeah, I know,' Atom interrupted, lighting a joint and wishing his tobacco supplier hadn't been caught. 'Well, I'm not telling anyone else. It's just you and me, buddy. The fewer people who know about this the better.' He drew a long line of smoke into his lungs. 'We'll move her tonight, when the heavy gorgers have gone. Keep this place locked, okay? And we should put her in the cooler.'

Atom looked hard at the face and checked for signs of identification. There was none. No clothes, money, wallet, bag or jewellery. Not even a ring. It was a good job and a shame about the brown.

He broke off a corner near her toe and examined it. 'No bloom, no cracks. This is good shit, Henry,' he said, absently putting a piece in his mouth. 'Ecuador? That would be my guess.'

He held out a small section.

Bouche winced. 'I could not possibly.' He rubbed his hands together as if to purge an unpleasant residue. 'It would be like cannibals.'

'Suit yourself.' Atom tested it on his tongue, eyes closed in concentration, mouth opening slightly to oxidize the softening matter for enhanced flavour. 'Roses, definitely. Arriba bean. Ecuador, I'm certain. Very pure. Scrape it off, will you? But leave her covered where it matters.'

They were all objects of veneration, including those who paid Atom 15 per cent to work the floor, picking up the gentlemen and occasionally, ladies. And dead women should always have their clothes on. He was old-fashioned that way.

Henri nodded. 'But 'ow did she get here?' he asked quietly.

There was only one public entrance, through the restaurant. The other was a guarded secret, involving a neighbouring building and his suppliers, the Bartek twins. Atom, who couldn't help but admire a hit of considerable taste and style, knew that somebody with moulds, refining equipment and brown to waste was responsible. It sent a chill through his knotted frame, but he wasn't going to risk another French scream. 'Probably just kids.'

4

They were still there. F*t people. In the shadows. He could always sense them. 'Chocolate sellers are dealing openly, brazenly, in Washington Square,' said Gotfelt, urgency and shock seasoning his tone deep and tallowed. 'And no wonder. There is not a police officer in sight, I am told. This cannot be tolerated.' He sipped the strong, black coffee and stared at Finch, who stood, hands clenched behind his broad back, looking through the windows of City Hall.

Twenty-three floors below, life was a distant hum of deals and doubts, deceits and delights. A gilded ormolu clock ticked on the mantelpiece, echoing slightly off the polished, panelled walls. The silence between the two men seemed a test of wills. Gotfelt under-stood it as a weapon and moved his mind to other rooms, but not the locked one where brown was stacked.

Finch blinked first. 'Well, Heston, it's like this. I can appoint a chief of police and I can sack a chief of police, but while he runs Police Plaza, the conduct of law enforcement is his business or he'll complain, very noisily, about political interference. You understand that, surely? I can only set priorities and make noises from my bully pulpit.' Finch turned and hoped his pleasant, pleading face, the one he deployed for the elderly, cable news and schoolchildren, would work on Heston Gotfelt.

'You know, I got a city workers' strike to deal with here and it's twenty below. The police are stretched taking on ambulance duties, clearing trash. The rats are practically applying to open restaurants. Give me time.'

'Mr Dessler, please remind me of those figures,' Gotfelt asked a young aide, raising a hand imperiously. Dessler seemed relieved to have a task and opened his briefcase, eventually finding the single sheet of paper it contained.

Gotfelt knew the numbers by heart, but this was more powerful.

Dessler cleared his throat and began reading, his tone an accountant-flat monologue, firm but respectful. 'Sixty-seven per cent of Church groups in the New York metropolitan area report illegal eating activity in the last three months; that's a rise of 4 per cent on the same quarter last year.'

He paused. Gotfelt allowed his dark eyebrows to knit as if at some painful torment. 'Go on,' he said.

'Of those chapters, more than half noted chocolate, wrappers lying around playgrounds, outside schools and other public spaces.'

Gotfelt looked at Finch and intoned quietly, pausing between words to drain them of outrage. 'Around playgrounds. Outside schools. Is this law and order now? Is this the example that the most important city in the country sets the nation?'

Finch clenched his right hand into a fist and imagined it into a twenty-two-pound dead weight designed specifically to crush the skull of Heston Gotfelt. 'I can't vouch for your numbers, Bishop,' he said, tight and constrained.

'You doubt them?' Gotfelt raised a mocking eyebrow at such precocity, and from someone merely elected to office.

'Not at all. We just don't have resources to gather those sort of statistics. But even if true, they can only be a partial picture. I must tell you that the New York Police Department, in cooperation with Health Enforcement, has broken seven burger-smuggling cartels this year. In addition,' he paused, reaching for a paper of his own, 'twelve eateasys have been closed in the last six months alone –'

'Out of what, say, two hundred or so operating in the five boroughs?' Gotfelt interrupted easily, ostentatiously looking at his watch. 'Is that the time? Let's make it two hundred and twenty eateasys.' He collapsed and rebuilt a steeple from his fingers. 'Forgive me. Perhaps I exaggerate.'

'Bishop – Heston – You know how committed I am to Control. Nobody more so. F*t is an abomination, a terrible drain on our resources, a bane to taxpayers, a killer of our young; unpleasant to look at, too. We're all agreed. I stood by you during the first Anti-F*t League marches. Didn't I make fresh water available free

27

in schools to every child under ten? Didn't I mark my inauguration with a prayercise at your church on Fifth Avenue?'

But Gotfelt was unmoved. He understood utterly the fickle loyalties of politicians, their tribal bonds and venal opportunism. These were not men of principle, but of moment; they were callow and untrustworthy.

His own intelligence people had warned about Finch. There were rumours of personal visits to eateasys in Brooklyn and Far Rockaway, out of sight of cameras and Church activists, where he was said to scavenge for votes and mock the faith. I'll finish you, Gotfelt had sworn to himself then, as Christ is my fitness. But that was for another day.

'And I am grateful for your support Mr Mayor – John. You have, indeed, been a staunch ally and,' he hesitated to position his knife carefully, 'you were rewarded with the votes my people gathered for you, votes delivered in the expectation of a public crackdown on those who defile the standards, who refuse to take Control of their bodies.'

Finch felt sweat beading on his temple, pools of salt and tension. Elections were never so far away that an ally, however awkward, could be squandered.

'Indeed,' he said. 'But I was elected to be mayor of all the city, not just to represent the, forgive me, narrow interests of one section, however much I value the support and share the views of that section personally. As you know, there are many who think the Health Enforcement Act and its agents to be a gross infringement of civil liberties, a powerful force against pursuing happiness.' He shrugged. 'What can I say? This is New York. Everyone's a lawyer.'

Gotfelt rose. 'Narrow? An abuse of civil liberties? I doubt that is a description the good, decently proportioned folk who cast their ballots for you would recognize. Health is a human right, not to be bartered in the ebb and flow of politics. It is the absolute right of the majority not to endure the selfish, socially expensive indulgences of the minority.' Gotfelt paused, a preaching trick learned from his father. 'The founders of our great nation never had to address this terrible problem because food was once pure and unprocessed, a source of life, not a bringer of death.' He drew himself erect. 'May I remind you that the country now has a president committed to Control, to making this great land of ours –'

'– Fit for Christ, I know.'

'She will drive out the eateasys and those who supply them, mark my words.'

'Amen, Reverend,' Finch replied routinely. They sat in silence.

'Okay, Heston. Spell it out,' Finch said, closing his eyes wearily. He looked at his watch. 'On this day of such riches, I've a meeting with the Health Commissioner in thirty minutes.'

Gotfelt ignored the barb. 'Enforce the law. I want to see newscasts showing doors being broken down, burgers burning on magnificent pyres and brown smugglers in manacles.'

'Look. I'll talk to the chief, see what we can do.'

Gotfelt rose. 'Then I need take up no more of your time. God bless you and all who eat with you. Come and speak to my flock in West Virginia soon.' He clasped the mayor's outstretched hand, eyes ablaze. 'John, it is easier for a camel to pass through the eye of a needle if it is thin.'

'So I hear.'

'Blessed are you, O Lord, whose king is of nobility and whose princes eat at the appropriate time, for strength and not for drunkenness,' said Gotfelt, raising a hand and making the sign of the cross. 'Ecclesiastes.'

'On the street I hear Corinthians. You know, "if the dead are not raised, let us eat and drink, for tomorrow we die". But, hey, what do they know?'

But Gotfelt had already turned and swept out.

Self-righteous jackass, thought Finch, watching the oak doors close. He went to his desk, a position of authority he instinctively vacated whenever faith dropped by. 'Get in here,' he said sharply into the stern of a brass Venetian gondola.

A wiry, sandy-haired man eased through a side door, following the shadows into sight. Tom Lonergan had been with Finch since the early union days at Local 339, although they first met at community college. What Lonergan lacked in muscle he made up for in brains and they were soon a team. Finch had determination, force and charisma. Lonergan had ideas and a convertible, which was better for their double dates.

When they earned plumbing degrees (with honours), it was Lonergan who said, one drunken night at the lap-dancing club, that the only way to make real money was to get out of bidets and 'into the union game'.

It wasn't long, after a swift rise through a sluggish organization, before the rewards of office arrived: kickbacks from construction companies, tickets to the Knicks, seats for sold-out shows. They hired a manager with a business degree and modernized, encouraging payments by direct debit into offshore accounts. Soon, there wasn't a bowl or sink fitted in the state that they didn't have a piece of. But that was long ago. Now Finch could afford to be honest.

'How'd it go?' Lonergan asked breezily.

'Weren't you listening?' Finch replied, irritably tapping the desk with his fingers.

'Nah. I cannot abide that man. Kept getting messages from his assistant all morning. Couldn't face it. Caught a bit at the end, though. I'll read the transcript later.'

'Later? I don't know why I bothered installing that monitoring business,' said Finch, upset. 'Well, you got his big demand, anyway.'

'About the crackdown?' Lonergan spread himself across a chair, hooking his left leg over worn, aged leather and letting it swing as he chewed a mouthful of pistachio nuts. 'No harm in a few showy busts, I suppose. We'll get the cameras along.'

'But it won't end there, will it? We both know that. He means to break this city just to show everywhere and everyone else his strength. God, he's no political sense at all. Doesn't he understand how utterly impossible his demands are to enforce? Here of all places.'

Lonergan looked at the brooding face in front of him. 'And to think you used to be such firm friends,' he mocked.

'Of convenience. Tell me, how's the thing going? I won't take much more of him.'

'It's taken a while. He's connected and she's been busy with gorge parties, one-on-one feedings, so I hear.'

'Spare me,' Finch said, raising his hands. He wanted to know, but not so much that it could be threatening. Life was safer that way.

Lonergan smiled, although he was curious himself to discover why the timetable had slipped. Not that he was worried. There were always difficulties, but few of them challenged his pleasure from occupying the darker corners of political life. It was said he could pull strings without the victim knowing that they had even been attached. 'Well, I think we can still be sure that he didn't come all this way just to spend twenty minutes with you.'

Finch looked sharply at Lonergan and hoped he was right.

'Not that you're anything but excellent company, of course.'

5

They had been having a late lunch, Strong's idea, when she got the call. Devlin watched her let out a succession of 'uh-huhs' in response, picking at teeth absently with a toothpick. One always emerged at times of maximum concentration, he had noticed.

Devlin stared at her, almost for the first time, thinking how people often never observe the familiar or fully bother to detach and understand what they see every day: especially colleagues. He'd been thinking about relationships a lot anyway. It was the same with Sylvia.

Strong was pretty, but in a sensible way, more interesting than beautiful. He knew this in that nanosecond men take to make such assessments. There was dark hair, a gap between her upper front teeth and freckles across her nose which made her face lively, mischievous, like a cartoon. There were lovers, too, consumed voraciously and discarded, but never from within the unit.

'When did Homicide get there?' she asked, pausing to hear the reply. 'We're on our way.' She flipped the vid shut.

Enforcement was called to any killing 'related to or caused by proscribed or controlled eating substances' and Homicide usually found every reason not to designate a killing 'food-related' as a result. They considered Health easy-lifers, down there with the sanitary police. Health thought Homicide were arrogant hard-ons, up there with the sanitary police.

'Where?' Devlin found it hard to disguise excitement and expectation.

'Bedford, near Christopher. In an alley. And get this: she was wearing a customized chocolate bikini. Can you believe that? They're in season and nobody tells me.'

'A what?'

'They've probably been popping F in Dispatch again,' she said. 'Let's go see.'

Jane Ryan was one of the best, so they said. She had a quilt of citations and Devlin saw her watching him as he pushed through the excited crowds of craning necks, ten, maybe twenty deep. They shook hands and Devlin introduced himself, but was looking around.

'How'd they get here?' Devlin asked, jerking his thumb at the onlookers.

'Trauma counsellors. They listen to police radio bands.'

Devlin nodded sympathetically. 'So, what you got?'

'Female Caucasian, mid to late twenties. Brunette. No ID. Naked, more or less. This way.'

Devlin followed, ducking under the yellow and black police tape and into the narrow alley. The afternoon sun cast awkward shades and arc lights had been set up. It looked more like a film set than a crime scene.

He could smell it from yards away, the ochre of Ecuadorian arriba, cocoa bean of choice for those rich enough; fresh flowers and olives.

Ryan was looking at Devlin and he was looking at the body, Strong by his side. 'Some bikini,' he noted.

'There's no sign of a struggle, no clothes, personal stuff, and this is just off a busy street,' Ryan said, turning to face Devlin. 'If I had to guess, I'd say strangulation, but some place else because there's nothing disturbed around here,' she replied to his unasked question. 'Small pressure points on the neck. We nearly missed them.'

'You know, I shouldn't. But could I get a bit of her to go, a little whipped cream on the side?' Strong asked suddenly, stopping Devlin from saying what both of them knew in an instant.

'Don't I know you?' Ryan said, turning a measured gaze.

'Kate Strong. Hi.'

'Weren't you with the Eleventh Precinct?'

Strong had left the police long before being teamed up with

Devlin. There was talk of Internal Affairs, nothing proven and the Health Enforcement Unit, pressed to attract qualified recruits, didn't care much who volunteered. Devlin hadn't asked yet. It seemed too personal and he rather hoped she might just volunteer the information in a moment of trust, an offering of friendship.

'A missing DNA file before a hood's trial, some button man if I recall,' said Ryan. 'The guy walked. You screwed up.'

'But I try not to let failure go to my head,' Strong replied. 'Anyway, I left the department blemish-free, volunteering to join the just and noble fight against junk foods. Praise be. Anyway, that guy didn't walk far. He ended up in the Hudson. Justice done.' She raised her eyes and hands heavenward in a mock salutation.

The detective looked at her. 'Yeah? The way I heard it, nobody wanted a scandal.' Ryan had wavy brown hair reaching to her collar and steady, deep blue eyes. The two scars on her chin were raw and undisguised, small flashes of imperfection on clear, flawless skin.

Ryan turned to Devlin. 'I guess this must beat handing out tickets,' she said evenly. 'Any ideas?'

Strong was looking at Devlin, intensely, and he felt the gratification of a bond being forged, definitely proffered. 'I can tell you the chocolate smells high grade, probably Ecuador. We'll take a piece for sampling, see if we can get a precise fix, match it against seizures.'

Ryan nodded, handing him a card. 'The last one is home. If you call during the afternoon tomorrow, you'll be saving these knees from basketball.' She smiled. It was thin and distant. 'My two boys are at that awkward sporting age.'

Home. Devlin never gave out his own home number. But then Ryan was one of those driven cops everyone heard about; infiltrating the Mob in Jersey, helping to break a crime family when she was still in her twenties. It was exhausting even to think about.

Ryan went to the forensics team, returning with a piece of bagged brown. Devlin took it. The agents walked back to their car in silence.

'Well?' Devlin asked finally, although he knew the answer. 'Why didn't we ID Frish?'

'Who would imagine Cupid striking us twice,' Strong said.

'That wasn't the question.'

'Aside from the general attitude of Homicide and Captain Fantastic there, you mean? Well, I smell a little more excitement than usual entering our lives and don't tell me you don't, too. I saw your face in the diner.' She stopped in front of Devlin and sniffed the air, deep, exaggerated inhalations. 'Commendations, pay rises. It's a sweet scent.'

'What are you talking about?'

'Frish was a hooker with a habit and a rich clientele. It's obvious. That Porsche? Top of the range. Only rock stars and whores have them at her age. And we know where she lives. Who gets one of those palaces in their twenties?'

'Listen,' Devlin said. 'It's tempting. But we have to tell Ryan.'

'Oh yeah? And have her take the prize? No deal. Come on.'

Devlin stopped. 'I know you used to be a cop, none of which is my business. But that's over. I'm going back. It's regulations.'

She grabbed his arm with a surprising amount of power, enough to spin him to face her. 'Hear me out. Please. Forget about us, then. How good would it be for the agency if we got to solve a food murder?' Her eyes were wide, alive and pleading. 'The commissioner would be orgasmic. It'd help us. And you, new on the job. You'd be made. Promotions. Desk by the window. This kind of opportunity doesn't come around too often, trust me. Think of your kid. Maybe you could get her into that fancy private school in Albany you've been talking about.'

They were in the car, silent, watching late-afternoon shoppers walk past, slow, and crane their necks when they reached the alley.

'Maybe,' Devlin said. Ambition seemed a good, wholesome motive, and Strong was right about Sylvia. 'Okay, we'll check her place. But that's all. We tell Ryan soon as we're done.'

Strong smiled. 'Happiness is all about adding spice, my friend,' she said.

★

Montcalm was a street of steel and glass skyscrapers built on a landscaped park close to the Jersey shore. It was cheaper than Manhattan, a brief stop for young money before it grew up and went over to Greenwich Village, the Upper East Side or Tribeca.

Cupid Frish lived in a centre block designed with angles and sweeping slopes. The porter was nervous. He was from one of those countries that were hard to pronounce and sold bad biology to the highest bidder. 'Yes, we could come back with a warrant,' agreed Strong, whose professional charm iced water. 'We could come back with an immigration officer as well. Would you like that? Maybe they'd ask to see your Ethnicity Card,' she said.

Immigration. People disappeared in its system, packed to offshore camps on the say-so of a sniffer spaniel at the airport. 'You like greasy food? Maybe I'll check your weight licence, too, get you to run for me before sending an advisory to your health insurance provider. Truly, there's no end to the fun you and I could have.'

It was Devlin's turn, the Good Health Enforcer. He peered at the name badge.

'Listen. Ali, isn't it? We just want to look around. There's nothing to be concerned about. We're not going to steal anything. Promise. Hey, you see me walking by with a chair, call the cops. How's that for a deal?' Devlin smiled, showing off dental work done on the union tab after a humonster marched into the office back in Baltimore and got an angry, overweight fist in first, claiming some beat agent had lied about freezer contents during a parental access hearing.

Ali smiled back, relieved. He reached under the counter. 'These are spare keys. Top one for alarm.'

'Thanks.'

Strong was already by the elevators.

'Nearly second generation. I have documents,' Ali shouted, holding up his fingers as if boasting about a win at Atlantic City. 'Secondish.'

'Faisal was just about to relieve himself, right there,' Strong said with relish, clicking her knuckles. 'You know what I hate about this job most of all?'

'His name is Ali,' Devlin said.

'I hate the fact that even some gink from Nowheristanabia thinks he can treat us like shit.'

'Chill. Everyone treats us like shit. He was just doing his job. Anyway, we got the keys.' But Strong was right, he knew. Ryan, Ali. Nobody took them seriously. They were the joyless good-time busters. But as far as Devlin was concerned, they were helping people, that was all. Even if they didn't want to be helped.

'Hello, my name is Donny. What floor may I access for you?'

'Thirty,' Devlin said. The doors stayed open. 'Please.'

'That felt so much better, didn't it?'

'Dum, dum, dum,' came from somewhere above them. 'Would you like to ride in my beautiful balloon? Would you like to glide in my beautiful balloon . . . ?'

'Hey, do you have to?' said Strong.

'Oh, just ignore me. It's just my little way of getting through the day. Nice to see you –'

'– Just shut the fuck up, will you? Please. Thank you. We're busy, okay? Man, I hate the chit chatty machines.'

There was a soft, expensive ping.

'Well, here we are then. Da-da. Thirtieth floor,' said the voice, without rancour. 'Have a nice day. Eat safely.' They waited for the Donny to disappear. 'Up, up and away in my beautiful balloon' sank into the distance.

They looked around a long, featureless hallway lit by discreet uplights on the floor by its cream-coloured walls. 'What time zone for 510?' wondered Strong, whistling quietly.

'Right.'

'A buck says left.'

Devlin handed over the dollar a few minutes later. Not that they needed to bother with keys. The door was open, but almost imperceptibly. Devlin looked at Strong. Ryan? Not even with her reputation. It took time for retinals to be matched at Citizen Records, which was notoriously slow. Strong had her gun drawn and Devlin took the cue, unhooking his holster.

They stood on either side of the frame, Strong inching the door open with a foot. There was the sound of paper rustling, turning. They looked at each other and Devlin held up a clenched hand and started the countdown from five, mouthing each number synchronized to the thump of his heart.

Five. They eased in. It was a wide hall with closed doors on either side. The noise seemed to be coming from behind a sliding wooden partition ahead of them that was half-open. They moved slowly, Strong in the lead, gun arm outstretched and ready. Stress burned calories, Devlin thought to steady his nerves. How many was this worth. Five? Ten? Some consolation, and then he was thinking of Sylvia. He should have called her.

Not that she would mind. She had a date with Damon. Maybe it was just parental paranoia over the clearly bloomed romance that had begun at school. Damon had been for pasta à la Devlin, which was everything from the fridge hitting its sell-by with a pomodoro sauce that wasn't, and was never less than attentive and polite throughout. Perhaps he shouldn't be so suspicious, Devlin thought, wondering at that moment in the hallway of a dead person's apartment in New Jersey whether his child was a virgin. He felt the soft, cream carpet give underfoot. No, he answered himself. She'd discovered brown, hadn't she? They'd had the talk at least. She knew sex burned off about seventeen calories every five minutes while brown put on three hundred, give or take, all for just one minute of oral satisfaction. It made no sense, he reasoned. But she'd just looked at him blankly, giving nothing away.

Devlin forced his mind back. Strong was at the door to the living area. They must still have been undetected because the sound of pages turning, random but firm, was clear.

Something didn't feel right. Devlin was going to order them to back off, but it was too late. One, two, three, Strong mouthed quickly. 'FREEZE,' they both shouted, rushing in and waving their guns in search of anything to scare besides themselves. Nothing. No sign of the force it was apparent in an instant must have passed through, splintering side tables, slashing walls and gutting the furniture. 'In my own, humble opinion, the cleaner simply has to go,' said Strong.

Pages turned idly to the interest from an overhead air-conditioning duct. They had been spooked by *National Geographic*. Underground caves issue.

Devlin went to the desk. It was long, sleek and chrome. Strong did a cursory check of the apartment, kicking doors.

'Hey, anyone home?' she shouted. 'Better housework inspectors.'

There were two bedrooms, a standard exercise area and a large, marbled bathroom. It was some physical insanity, thought Devlin, looking at the battered tables, eviscerated cream furniture and smashed vases. The few pictures still on walls hung at drunken angles, others were on the floor, ripped and holed. Books lay scattered, their pages torn out. Devlin picked up one, or what was left of it: most of the back cover had been ripped off, a semicircular serrated wedge of about ten pages caught his eye. It looked bitten. Bitten? A decorative brass ceiling fan swung limp, twelve feet above, broken at its base; so was the one next to it.

They went out to the sun deck, picking a path through the wreckage, passing around the writing desk that looked bigger than Devlin's entire apartment and was probably more desirable. The breeze was warm, expensive and insistent. Even city air smelled good on certain budgets.

Devlin was glad of the warmth and the fragrance of tropical ozone off the Hudson. Manhattan was spread across the skyline and he could see up to the George Washington Bridge; small clouds of luminous violet chased each other between mid-town skyscrapers. Nobody paid attention to them any more. The World Peace Center and its defensive missile system caught the afternoon sun, and the yellow haze in Battery Park, resting a few feet above the ground, was barely visible. It was a peaceful, pleasing contrast.

'I don't believe you're doing that,' he said in disgust after turning back.

'Relax. It'll just go to waste. Want some?'

She handed him a small square. 'Of course not. That's evidence.'

'Homicide have got a kinky body. That's all the evidence they need. You know, this is good shit, man; brittle, crunchy, 75 per cent cocoa for sure. Wonder if she left any in the Porsche?'

Strong went back inside and quickly found the vid under the sofa. She called the operator.

'Kate Strong, HEA, ID three-zero-nine, six, seven, New York Bureau. I need access to records for this vid. Thank you.' Devlin watched her write down the security code and replace the handset.

'Do the honours?' she asked.

'Be my guest.'

Strong punched in the code and they both looked at the monitor to see who had called. The first image was a building supervisor promising to come by again tomorrow to fix the shower, the second was Ali about a grocery delivery in the lobby. The third was partially obscured. 'Call me. I'm in town,' said a voice, commanding, muffled and familiar. The message was timed yesterday morning. The fourth was what? A fleeting black shadow. 'Nada on that one,' said Strong as they looked at each other. 'Ghost in the machine,' she said. 'Hey, what about those?' Strong pointed at a pile of hologram discs strewn across a low table. Most were Christ the Fit products, fitness routines. Devlin flicked on the holomonitor. A compelling figure in black sweats stood in a health club, machines and weights scattered around him under brilliant lighting. The camera panned over expectant faces, supplicants in leotards, lean and wholesome. 'Heston Gotfelt,' Devlin said, recognizing the voice as the one on the vid.

'The Lord walked everywhere, up hills and along dirt roads,' answered the Bishop Instructor, his face sheened with sweat. 'He was, my friends, fit and whole. We can all share in that universal truth he showed to us through exercise and diet. A long life awaits those prepared to give themselves fit to the Lord. Are you ready?'

'We are ready to become fit for Christ,' intoned the crowd, their thin attended bodies beginning to sway. In the background, a musical soundtrack thumped out encouragement. Seventies disco. Chic. Clap Your Hands.

'Say after me: "Bend at the waist and touch your toes."'

'I bend at the waist and touch my toes,' came the response as they completed the prayer fluently. Strong grunted and struggled to reach her knees.

'Let us stretch at the waist to tighten our hamstrings.'

'We stretch at the waist for the Lord and not for ourselves.'

Devlin switched off the holo, worried his partner, flushed and wheezing, was about to seriously injure herself. 'Please. Much more of that and you'll be dying for Christ. You should take more care of your body, take the agency stretch classes.'

Devlin wanted to call Ryan, but Strong protested breathlessly. 'Gotfelt's in town tonight. Saw it on the news. We should question him. Know what? When a man says as few words as possible and disguises his face, I say that man's got a secret.' She winked.

Gotfelt. Friend of everyone who mattered, who had made a fortune off people who didn't. Devlin was one of them. This was his spiritual leader. 'We've had our fun. I'm calling Ryan.'

'Listen, Ryan's wonder squad will be here soon enough,' said Strong in a fast, pleading patter. 'We're just ahead and they'll just want to stop us getting a home run. Where's the harm, partner? Let them work it out. We'll leave everything just where we found it and tell them that some of the prints will be ours. Simple.'

'Ours? I've been wearing gloves. This is a crime scene, Kate. You used to work Homicide.'

She laughed and slapped a palm on her forehead. 'You're right. I forgot, what with the excitement and all.'

Strong was persuasive and Devlin was still smarting from Ryan's dismissal of their significance. The new closer relations with Strong seemed worth encouraging, too. She was grinning, staring at him, chewing a toothpick and cracking her knuckles, the royal flush of irritating habits. 'So? Game on?'

He looked at his watch and pursed his lips before expelling air, a moment of resignation and decision. 'Okay. Play ball. But let's move it. Ryan can't be far behind. I'd better check the bedroom.'

Devlin knew all about chaos theory, mainly from Sylvia's set texts, but had never seen it put into practice. Clothes were scattered everywhere; they were the silken sort hookers wore, with easy exit written all over them.

The bed was angled awkwardly against a far wall, as if somebody had been looking underneath. He picked up a slight red and blue cocktail dress torn down the back, ripped carelessly by an indiscriminate hand.

Devlin noticed another fan, also hanging loose and crippled from the high ceiling.

That image of a human, sex unclear, bathing in chocolate, hung above the bed. The original was in the Guggenheim. Devlin had seen it with Sylvia who, from somewhere, seemed to have a feel for art and would talk about it with confidence and enthusiasm. He encouraged her because, when she talked about paintings, Devlin assumed she was probably finding a proxy for talking about herself. This was a limited edition lithograph, signed by the artist. Sylvia had the unlimited edition print.

The dressing table was needless rococo, all twists and twirls, pale golds and whites. Everything once on the top seemed to have been swept off in one direction, if the scattering of bottles and brushes and jewels was any guide. Jewels. Devlin saw diamonds, gold, rubies. But he saw them. Not a burglary, then.

The bedside table lay undisturbed; tissues, condoms, alarm, a souvenir paperweight from Foodland, an old edition of Leanman, the one where he takes on those dark humonsters of the underworld.

'Hey, check this out,' Strong called. Devlin went back to the living room.

She held an antique Rolodex address keeper. 'Ever heard of *Who's Who?*' said Strong. 'Here's *Where*. Names, numbers, addresses.'

She passed it over. In no particular order were sports players, city council members, a television presenter and a daytime soap star.

'Hey, isn't that the guy who does the kids' puppet show?'

'Maybe I should get into prostitution,' said Strong. 'Good pay, plenty of time in bed and the chance to screw people without actually going into politics. Woman with my body should be sharing it around, don't you think?'

Devlin grunted. 'Let's leave this out for Ryan to find.' Then his eyes fell on two numbers. One was in West Virginia. The other was a mobile vid.

'Tempted?' asked Strong.

6

Heston Gotfelt tried to have sex before five most weekdays, pro-vided it could be arranged between rounds of television interviews, meetings and his other official duties. The Lord had pharisees, Gotfelt had inquisitive journalists. They were far more troublesome.

This physical routine rarely involved Mrs Gotfelt, who stayed home and concentrated on seducing young, ambitious Preparers, keeping hold of sanity in the hell of her perfect marriage more carefully since the embarrassing articles in the *Inquirer*. They had been embellished with photographs of her making exchanges with wasted youths who sold brown in the crusted, crumbling suburbs surrounding the church compound.

It could have been a public relations disaster. But the world loves a penitent, said Regard patiently at the crisis meeting that followed.

Anne Gotfelt was in rehabilitation, officially a non-user who earned unfettered access to her personal god, Visa, by touring Christ the Fit congregations and proclaiming the liberation of Control. 'If Jesus had recruited twelve public relations executives instead of apostles, he'd have avoided a lot of bad business,' Regard gravely informed a grateful Gotfelt.

This afternoon it was to be somebody from the Staten Island chapter, a blonde of thirty-four. He had seen her photograph after flipping through membership rolls and his office had called to offer a personal benediction, some dietary counselling. It never failed.

But he was still thinking about the one with emerald eyes. It was absurd, risible, her threat to ruin him and that demand for money. Who did she think she was? Nothing, he had told her, venom in his voice.

He had been naïve and weak, yet licked his lips involuntarily at the memory of that last encounter, the brown-soaked hours in Hoboken. She had unwrapped, luring him with chocolate sauce and a tart, arresting balsamic vinegar reduction. He ate to reassure himself of its vile, insinuating evil as she danced for him, naked. Not that he noticed her body too much. 'Get behind me, Satan,' he yelled, groaning with an awful, pained ecstasy as her brown-daubed lower stomach arched for his tongue. 'Soon.'

Aortic pulses thumped and he tried to ease them by concentrating on the sermon he would deliver at the Jewel. What would be its themes? Long life through Control was always popular.

The meeting with Finch still consumed him. There had been little deference. It was time to show him the power that Heston Gotfelt controlled. There was a light knock at the door. She was early.

'Wanda,' he said, clasping her outstretched hand in both of his, speaking softly as he led her into the suite. The eyes that looked back were adoring, dilated and bathed in faith. He hoped it would be easy. He needed to concentrate on the address without the blinkers of kindliness and concern or pity. They were fake emotions, anyway, contrivances to obscure the natural instinct for voyeurism and superiority.

He indicated the couch. She was wearing . . . what was it? Yes, too much.

'Apple juice?'

'Thank you, Bishop. This is such an honour,' she said, sipping delicately. 'I have all your holograms, the fasting doll set, and I love the print of the devil serving a cheeseburger. Got it hanging in the kitchen, next to –'

He stopped her nervous babble through the merchandise with a raised hand. 'The honour is mine. I read about your work with the sugar addiction clinic and wanted to meet with you, thank you personally, the next time I was in the city. It is people such as yourself who are the bedrock of our Church. The very foundations.'

She sat transfixed, following his every move. Straightforward, he thought.

'I was sorry to read about your husband,' he glanced at the writing on his palm, 'Wanda.' He put a hand on her shoulder, squinting in what she may have mistaken for depth and concern, but which was his effort to recall the briefing note.

Her face tightened at the memory. 'Raymond was a good man,' she said. 'Sincere, a true believer. He'd lost thirty-five pounds before he got taken with the trash. He was just sitting on the porch. They picked him up with the black bags, didn't pay no mind to his screaming.' She started sobbing despairingly. 'It was an accident, I know that. But, dear Lord it's hard, so very hard. But at least he died fit, fit for Christ. I take comfort from that fact.'

Gotfelt tried to feel her pain, pinching the flesh between his thumb and first finger sharply to induce tears. 'He will be in the kingdom of heaven, where a plan was already made for him to lose those extra pounds,' he said, moving to sit beside her. 'He will eat figs and grapes and the fish of the sea. He will live in eternity where nothing is adulterated and no carbohydrate too complex or too salted. But I know that these can be small consolations to those left behind still waiting for their own recycling.'

She looked at him, beseeching. 'If it wasn't for the Church, I'd surely have been eating myself in these bad times.'

'I understand. It must be so terribly lonely for you.' He patted her upper leg gently, edging himself closer and letting his hand linger, stroking. 'The Lord has shown you the way and is most merciful, bounteous to the chosen ones.' Platitudes worked well, one of the things watching politicians had taught him. Perhaps he should have his people at Belief discover a Book of Platitudes somewhere in the Sinai? He moved his face and saw her eyes close, the early stage of surrender.

He moved quickly, plunging, his jaws like a Great White shark, and in seconds they were tangled, thrashing and foaming, kissing deeply while he guided her towards the bedroom. She was agile. They consumed each other, hunger and longing and loneliness all fighting for the relief that regular yoga helped her contain, but never quite remove.

Maybe Proverbs, chapter twenty? 'Keep deception and lies far from me,' he recited under his breath. 'Give me neither poverty nor riches,' he gasped aloud as the bed heaved and roiled.

'Oh yes, yes, yes,' screamed the voice beneath him in jubilant response, but muffled by a pillow.

'Feed me with the food that is my portion,' he bellowed, climaxing with spasms and shudders as they collapsed into spent silence.

'That was rapture, Reverend.'

'Proverbs,' he corrected through rapid, shallow breaths.

Wanda limped to the bathroom leaving satisfaction and guilt on the bed.

At last he had a text. Sex liberated theological thought as well as burning calories. The ancient popes knew that, with their concubines and catamites. But it had rather gone out of fashion. He had thought about producing a free sex video to encourage its return.

'Won't play in the heartland, Bishop,' warned his marketing chief. 'Don't matter if it's ninety minutes of missionary positions. Stick with exercise and recipes. They go down real well, if you'll excuse the expression.'

Gotfelt stood, slapped his altar-stomach and began to dress. Wanda was singing in the shower, a tune he eventually recognized. He had always disliked 'All Things Bright and Beautiful', however many street sounds and gun noises it came accessorized with for modern ears. She would have to leave promptly, he thought, feeling a small pounding in his left temple.

She emerged wrapped in white towels from head to toe and smelling of floral hotel shampoos. 'My dear Wanda,' he said, deep and resonant. 'If only I could spend more time with you. How I want to hear more of your life on Staten Island, about the clinic.'

She looked at him and began to open her mouth as if to tell him; confusion was somewhere as she accepted his gift of her clothes.

'Sadly, I must compose myself for tonight. But you have helped me, incalculably, and I am most grateful. You can dress in here. Please, take your time, but quickly.'

Wanda took longer to dress than undress. Gotfelt stood, annoyed, as whole minutes passed before she emerged.

He reached into a box and produced his autobiography, *God Loves A Thinner*. 'I've inscribed it, "to a loyal friend of Control",' he said, handing it to her. 'And I've enclosed tickets for tonight's prayercise.'

'My. Thank you. I can't tell you how much this time has meant to me. Perhaps, perhaps we could –' the sentence hung, unfinished, unformed, but perfectly complete.

'Next time I'm in New York I shall be certain to call so that we can spend time together, talk properly. After bodily intimacy, the mind is free,' he said. 'We will break bread and fruits together.'

He entombed her hands in his own, which were freshly moisturized. 'May the Lord eat with you.'

'And also with you,' Wanda replied automatically, allowing herself to be guided out of the suite. A shaven-headed Sentinel showed her gently to the elevator as Gotfelt closed the door, barely hearing the ping of guilt descending.

'Hi, my name is Donny. Up, up and away in my –'

A focus arrived at the hotel writing desk, taking his mind to where it regularly rested: to North Dakota and the endless bitumen strips bounded by fast-food sellers, their corrupting products tormenting his adolescence, siren calls to excess, but all that they could afford from the pitiable offerings his father's calling returned.

How he had fought to contain his weight within acceptable limits. The fearful warning from Coach Kolbeck that if he got any slower, his place in the line-up would disappear. He shivered at the memory, the knowledge of how close he had come to leaving the Dickinson Devils ('D, D Dickinson, others come and then they run,' sang the cheerleaders) because of food and with it the chance of a full scholarship to state college, the start of a road to freedom he had charted for himself.

'The Lord tempted, but rescued me,' he wrote beneath The Five Seasons logo (a United Nations committee had still not agreed a name for the fifth season). Then it began to flow, the unity of thought and word that made his Church so successful, the fastest growing in the country according to *Forbes* magazine. Rich enough to own oil wells in Texas, a bank in Omaha and swathes of orchards in California.

'Better is a dish of vegetables where love is, than a f*ttened ox served with hatred,' he wrote, noting in the margin that this, too, was from Proverbs.

His audience would be the usual mix of professionals, indulged devotees of exercise and lonely souls struggling to worship their body in the hope that others would worship there, too.

When he had opened his Bible in despair that abandoned night in the motel off Interstate 94, thunder clapping and shaking the earth, Proverbs had been the first passage he read. The effect was immediate. It was a sign. As he listened to his father practising patiently his sins of the flesh schtick in the room next door, railing hopelessly against a chipped dressing-table mirror, Heston Gotfelt heard the Lord speak to him for the first time, quite separately.

Outside, he could see the McDonald's sign, garish, vulgar, inviting. It was beckoning him through driven rain, a leering, bedizened barmaid, bright red clouds dancing through its golden arches. 'Damn you,' he yelled out of the window as heaven howled and raged, shaking the tin roof of the motel. 'I shall damn you.'

He was shaken from his reverie by the vid and looked at the number, recognizing it instantly, feeling faint for a moment. It wasn't possible. He pressed receive. 'Cupid?' he whispered slowly, careful to modulate the surprise, the certainty of how impossible it was that she could be calling him.

'No, sir. Matt Devlin, Health Enforcement,' said an entirely different voice.

7

Strong was bent double. Ha, ha. Devlin was tongue-tied. It certainly embarrassed him to be talking about a murder with Heston Gotfelt of all people. 'Excuse me, Mr Dalai Lama, can you say where you were between the hours of such-and-such and so-and-so. Any witnesses, sir? Hey, Mr Pope, your alibi isn't stacking up. St Peter's basilica you say? Did anybody see you praying?'

Devlin stumbled, unclear, awkward and self-conscious. Gotfelt seemed shocked. His face dropped and the screen filled with black hair while he regained composure.

'May the Lord feed her soul,' he said finally.

She was a user, one who found her way to the Church, he said, a lost soul struggling to find dignity in life. They had met during one of his stadium tours. The voice drained away. He was too shocked to talk straight away, if they didn't mind.

Devlin didn't, relieved, and arranged to meet him at the Jewel Health Club later. The Jewel was where disciplined bodies worked up sweats in designer gear, or they sent their assistants to do it for them. The salad bar and its rawafarian chef were stars in their own right. His walnut burgers won awards and he was always on television being interviewed about issues of the day: global warming, race relations, what to do about the pollution clouds, how to hold down a stressful management job.

It was always hard to get tickets for appearances by Bishop Gotfelt. Devlin tried for a prayercise at Radio City Music Hall as a treat for Sylvia last Christmas, but it sold out in three hours. Sylvia wasn't religious herself, but she enjoyed aerobics, which was good enough. Whatever else caused him hell, at least she wasn't f*t. She would, he was certain, be attractive enough to win a place at college. She was already thinking of voluntary work overseas, helping countries struggling with weight and diet, possibly making salads in Scotland through a charity she found on the Discovery Channel. 'It's bad, Dad. You know they still deep fry?'

The Bishop invited them to stay for the communion salad, which was being put together by his best Preparers, the display team. Devlin looked forward to it. They arrived early. Strong had insisted on stopping at a favoured old-style diner because she wasn't a believer and wouldn't be communing herself at the Jewel. Devlin watched her make an inflammatory display of macaroni C followed by sweet C cake. She was doing it to bait him, a goyim insisting on bacon before the bar mitzvah, and he felt their unity of purpose disappear as mysteriously as it had arrived.

'Hey, they've got a humonster petting zoo in San Diego,' she said, reading a newspaper. 'How about that?'

'Really?'

'Yeah, says here it's to help kids understand that f*t people are human, too. Ah, ain't that sweet.'

'They should just lose weight and prove it, show some willpower,' Devlin snapped back. 'It's all that separates us from the zoo anyway.'

'Man, did you take your peace, love and understanding supplement this morning? You know how bad you get when you don't. Tense, aren't you?'

Devlin looked at her. 'Yes. I mean, I know he isn't anything to you. But Heston Gotfelt anchors a lot of lives. He talks sense. I'm not comfortable talking to him about –'

'– Go on, say it. You know you want to. Murder. A murder.' She laughed. 'I'm going to visit that zoo, next time I'm out west.'

The Jewel was full, its cavernous and glass-domed interior a low murmur of expectant voices. There must have been three hundred people squatting on padded blue exercise mats, or astride static bicycles. Some were stretching, lifting arms and legs in silent prayer, muscle toning for deliverance.

A raised stage was placed near the window, an exercise bicycle and weights were settled by the simple altar; a wooden table, two candles and a large metal cross in biker-chrome. Cable wires snaked along the floor and camera crews put the finishing touches to positions; public assassins, professional and detached, tuning in and training their lenses.

Preparers were mixing vegetables for the communion. Devlin saw beetroots, olives, capers, peppers, potatoes, basics from the Book of Indulgence, in huge glass bowls along trestle tables.

They wore white surplices and sliced and diced expertly, warming up the congregants. Each cut was covered live on overhead monitors, separate screens split and slowed the action and showed different angles of penetration, juices falling in slow-mo.

A female choir wearing gold-spangled bikinis sang, swaying gently, raising their arms to the glass ceiling that was dotted with tiny lights, a small heaven of energy-efficient bulbs.

Strong whispered in his ear: 'How come they ain't wearing brown? And look, the choir's got no soul, they're all whitebreads. Interesting, huh?' He brushed her away, annoyed. He should have come alone.

The warm-up Instructor appeared with perfectly bevelled teeth and a newscaster tan. He ran to the stage among whoops and hollers, clutching a microphone. 'Awesome, awesome,' he said, holding out his hands to the band and clapping at them in appreciation. From overhead, a sign began to fall: God Is Love. A strobe light worked to the rhythm of electro-gospel. The band fell silent, expertly and without a stray note, as quieter, pre-packaged music took over.

People in front rows roared as a single Preparer expertly juggled an apple and paring knife in a final flourish. They gasped as knife and apple fell perfectly into his hands.

'Ain't that joyous,' said the Instructor into a microphone that whistled sharply. 'Testing, testing. That's better. Hey, I am struck like a dope by this thing called hope, good people. We are here to atone. And what's that second syllable?' He cupped a hand theatrically to his ear.

'Tone,' roared back the audience.

51

'That's right. The Lord wants us to tone for our sins. It's there. In the good book. Always was. Now, sowing and reaping also sets us free. So, when you give your tithe tonight, don't forget we are sowing for the reward of healthy souls.' His voice escalated and he punched the air. 'Now, let's look at these images, remind ourselves why we're here.' He peered into the distance and drew a circle in the air. 'Roll it, Louis.'

Lights dimmed and a screen came to life. Coney Island. There was no mistaking that wistful shoreline and the tired, creaking attractions. An anonymous outstretched arm held a microphone.

'Sure, I'd like to be thinner, but I cain't control mahself,' said a big woman, looking awkward and embarrassed, shuffled and cowed. A man was surprised eating a slice of pie, but recovered with defiant confidence, his drooped breasts and bare belly a pregnant pop. 'Shoot. Life's too short, man. You gotta enjoy yourself,' he said. 'Hell, no. I don't believe in no Control. I think we should be left alone and government should get out of the food bidness.' And so it went on. There were jeers from the audience. They heard fifteen voices, angry, outraged, defeated, unsure, diffident, but all overweight. The health club lights came on again, spots illuminated the Preparers, who were still at their craft.

'All that salad shit's making me queasy. Can't that guy keep his apples still?' grumbled Strong. 'I'm allergic.'

'To apples?'

'Religion, too.'

Overhead lights dimmed except for seven brilliant tunnels of yellow illuminating the stage. There was a hush, like a small wave breaking on a comforted shore, and, slowly, applause spread from the back and far side of the room. Devlin craned his neck. Nothing. But Gotfelt was certainly making his way forward, a presence marked by the rippling of hands. Devlin followed the sound as white light shone on a tall figure walking purposefully, long strides, down the right-hand side; an eruption of claps soon filled the room as Beethoven's 'Ode to Joy' soared.

Devlin leapt spontaneously, clapping at the same time.

'I hope this means you're going to be totally impartial, you know, give this dude a hard time,' said Strong as Devlin sat back on the hard, plastic chair. 'Hey, he stole his act from the World Wrestling Federation,' she said. 'Look at those biceps. Put him up for five rounds against Mad Machine Mulligan. I'd watch.'

Devlin ignored her.

Gotfelt stood in light and lifted his arms for silence. 'Cheese, the big C.' He whispered the words.

'Cheese,' answered the worshippers in a soft mewl.

'Oh, man,' Devlin heard Strong mutter.

'Before we stretch and focus on abdominals this evening, I want to talk a little about dairy produce.' There was a low sigh from the auditorium, the exhalation of memory, loss and longing.

'Now, the Bible is not specific,' said Gotfelt, his voice deep and confident, a seasoned piece of timber carrying its load across an unsettled ocean. 'But what we do know is that the Lord chose to feed the multitude with fish and loaves, not fondue or cheese-burgers or chocolate.' There was a murmur of laughter. 'That is clearly a sign. But Satan, my friends, is not foolish. He understands that a healthy, radiant body is a glory to God, a temple to the Holy Spirit and one that he, the keeper of eternal damnation, shall not enter.'

The congregation clapped.

'Satan, from the very beginning, planned his assault on us. "But of the tree of knowledge of good and evil you shall not eat," Genesis, chapter two, verse seventeen. "For in the day that you eat of it you shall surely die."' Gotfelt raised his voice and spoke, slowly with deliberation. 'God alone is the author of our peace, of our welfare and of our harmony. Yet Satan succeeded in the Garden of Eden, friends. Is he ever likely to abandon a plan that worked so well for him? No. You must learn to keep him away so that your physical temple is worthy of receiving the Holy Spirit, which is wholesome and pure.'

There were whoops from the crowd.

'Let us flex,' said the Bishop, raising his arms towards the heavens, and, bending his right leg at the knee, he extended his left leg rigid. 'Now hold,' he ordered. The congregation swayed and struggled to stay in position, but he was a statue of resolution. Their rock. The control was perfect.

Devlin wanted to participate, but held off. He found his mind drifting to Montcalm Avenue, wondering at the uncertain turn of fate that had taken him from there to here.

Gotfelt led the congregation through bends and twists and turns of another kind. Those fortunate to have secured spin cycles were taken through a ten-minute routine; the rest held a sequence of yoga poses.

The temperature in the hall had risen noticeably by his closing homily; the air acrid and fetid with sweat and breath.

'You are now pure,' Gotfelt said, eyes ablaze, his face glowing with health and zeal. 'Bless you for purging out the impurities. Bad eating, consuming the junk of the abominants, leads to weight gain and numerous illnesses. We keep the memory of when the heads of all the corporations stood up before our own Senate, raised their right hands and swore, my friends, swore, that there was nothing addictive about their so-called food. But we knew. We knew that they deliberately polluted with syrups, sugars, cheese and choco-late because they were as opiates, my friends, hooking generations just as knowingly as the cocaine cartels of Colombia did all those years ago.'

There were boos from the congregation as an image of the twelve corporate heads was shown in that infamous moment. Devlin had them on disc, those hearings after the Great Crash.

'God wants our bodily temples secure, not crumbling and cor-rupted with additives and f*tness,' said Gotfelt, his voice rising. Outside, a turquoise cloud hovered, unnoticed, by the stained glass windows.

Gotfelt strode the small stage speaking softly, as if intimately to himself. 'There is no Book of Fast Foods in the Bible. The good Lord, a walker, fed the multitude on the Mount with healthy, organic produce. And as for drink, he turned water into wine, not calorie-f*ttened cocktails and sodas with ten spoons of sugar in each can.' He clapped his hands together and held them there.

'Moses, brothers and sisters, lived to one hundred and twenty years. We have it within us to expect the same. All it takes is power to resist the call of the abominants.' His voice rose.

'Repeat after me: "My body belongs to me."'

'My body belongs to me,' they returned.

'I live for God. Today I eat with him.'

The words echoed back from the faithful.

'You may now have sex.' The 'Ode to Joy' began again, rising in a crescendo as the crowd roared its applause. The stage was suddenly black. After moments in total darkness, the hall lights came on with strobes and pulses and disco sounds.

Devlin and Strong were escorted through couples binding and copulating to a room at the back of the club. Gotfelt was drinking from a large water bottle and indicated chairs. 'Forgive me. They make me wear this detestable foundation cream for the cameras,' he said, applying make-up remover and staring intently into the glass, contorting his face.

'Me too. I have to do that every night. Real drag,' said Strong.

'Thank you for seeing us,' Devlin said politely. 'I'll get straight to it, sir. We were surprised to find your personal vidphone number in the address book that Cupid – Ms Frish that is – kept.'

'Hidden,' added Strong, sucking on a toothpick.

'Well, certainly not easily visible,' Devlin amended diplomatically, wishing he'd left his colleague in the diner. 'Do you mind telling us why you called her?'

Gotfelt sighed heavily as he finished wiping off the make-up.

'Cupid Frish came to a prayercise last year in Brooklyn. Worshippers are chosen by my staff for me to see personally when I visit. I like to understand anxieties, you see, to offer personal advice. It keeps me in touch with the grass roots.' He was staring at the mirror, wiping adeptly with tissues, elongating and squeezing his face and drawing expertly along its contours. 'So much time these days is spent in meetings, on corporate matters. I need to remind myself that I am a servant of the Lord above all else. It is my calling to reach out.'

His voice was low and mellifluent. What Devlin would have given for just five minutes with him, a chance to unburden about

Sylvia, his own desiccated love life, the weight worries that never seemed to disappear.

'Noble. But the thing of it is this,' said Strong, a grin lighting her face. 'Cupid Frish knew a lot of men, a lot of rich, powerful men. She seemed to be their punch on the other side of the river. Now, it could be she was just getting advice from a load of important folk interested in her wellbeing. I know the Lord loves that sinner; I just didn't realize so many other people were in on it. The loving part, leastways.'

Gotfelt stiffened.

'As I was explaining,' he said tightly, 'I met Ms Frish once and gave her a number to call should she need further guidance. I was in town this weekend and wanted to see how she was coping.' He paused and sipped from a glass of water, clinking ice from side to side as he appeared lost in melancholy.

'Why were you so freaked on the vid?' asked Strong. 'Shifty.'

'Shifty?' Gotfelt said gently. 'What an intemperate, charged word. I had nothing to hide, whatever it is you're implying. It would be a breach of trust to say more, but I suppose it doesn't matter now. Ms Frish was a troubled woman.' He looked at Strong. 'I know what she did for a living, understood her compulsions and, yes, her connections. I won't deny she tried to tempt me. But I'm a pastor, bound by a set of standards that requires me to minister to, to help, whoever they are. There was scepticism in your voice, Agent –?'

'Strong.'

'There are many like you out there, Agent Strong, who hate my ministry and feel threatened by it. I assume you are not a member of the Church?'

'I was raised Catholic, a full-f*t faith with cream and guilt still in the main course. I'm more confident now, believe in myself.'

'Ah yes,' said Gotfelt, 'one of those who hold that the noble soul has reverence for itself. Nietzsche, Agent Strong.'

'Never eaten there. But my colleague here, now he sweats buckets for you every Saturday and eats oh so wisely.'

Gotfelt seemed pleased. 'Well, Agent Devlin. I must commend you to the Health Commissioner. He's a friend.'

'Thank you, sir. Listen, maybe we should wrap this up. We've taken a lot of your time.'

'I'm always happy to help the forces of Control. But I don't know what more I can tell you. I was most upset to hear of her death, naturally. Guilty, too. If only I had managed to get to her before she –'

'– was murdered and dumped in an alley,' Strong tossed in.

'Is that how it was?' He looked into the distance, a private place, and his eyes seemed to moisten as he spoke of intending to tell Cupid that he was too busy with meetings, interviews and preparations to see her.

Devlin wanted to speak, but felt disarmed by Strong, embarrassed by her blunt disbelief and barely disguised disrespect for Bishop Gotfelt. All he wanted to do, Devlin realized, was leave, and he rose quickly. They never should have come in the first place.

Gotfelt shook his hand. There were tears. Devlin thought of all the people who had looked into those eyes for sustenance in this ruined world of appetites. The power he wielded, the envy he inspired. Yet, here was this man, worrying about the fate of just one person. The tears weren't fake, either. He'd wept enough of his own to know that. Of course Gotfelt ministered to Cupid Frish; a lot of women were scarred by weight issues. So she was sexual? So what? So was he and it wasn't illegal. It didn't make him a killer because he knew a hooker. People had sex all the time, even just to burn off calories. Devlin just wished he was one of them.

'What horseshit,' said Strong as they walked back to the car, through the health club, where supplicants, spent and sated, were bent over reviving bowls of salad.

'What is wrong with you?' Devlin shot back, stopping in front of her. 'Not every person of principle is a crook, you know. You should have some faith in human nature, in goodness.'

Strong looked quizzically, as if confronted by a weird psychiatric case study. 'Trust is a dangerous thing, you'll see.' They walked on in silence. 'Well, we did get something,' she said cheerfully.

'What?' Devlin exploded.

'We know Goodness was lying.'

8

Finch was at his desk, feet resting on its surface, reading the monthly crime digests. Eateasys were being raided at the rate of not too many a week, he noted with satisfaction. The memory of being insulted by Gotfelt was still raw, and any notion of his city trying to function without the rush of junk food unimaginable. If only Gotfelt could be reasonable and prepared to compromise. The eateasys were a pressure valve, release for pent-up energies, an illicit thrill and relatively straightforward to manage. But he just didn't get it. Finch recalled when smokers were rounded up, herded off to cold turkey camps. What a waste of resources, that had been. Beat cops poking around back alleys, sniffer dogs stalking office complexes. Terrible. Expensive.

The digests told him that clouds of intolerance still settled over the city, along with all those mad coloured ones. Vigilante groups were hurling bricks and stones through the windows of shops they suspected of selling Class A foods, burgers and brown in particular. Shamans from France with chocolate cures were regularly beaten up, as if anybody ever believed happiness was a mocha or some rippled whirl of brown packed with marzipan.

At least they were easy to monitor, the Control crazies. It was the usual group of do-gooders and zealots, Church of Christ the Fit fanatics doing their bit.

Then a paragraph caught his eye. Mitchell's delicatessen off Tompkins Square had called the cops when a masked gang, armed with clubs, burst in and destroyed low f*t mozzarellas, the sort still permitted under a trade agreement with Europe. Low f*t? And the graffiti they left behind: 'Food Fascist Finch' and 'Munch The Mayor'.

'Hysteria,' said Finch under his breath. 'Crazies. All of them. They deserve each other. But they won't tear this city apart while

I'm in Gracie Mansion.' His political career was founded on roping together competing power bases. Bash heads, twist arms, raise glasses, share a meal. That was the Fourth Way, said *Time* magazine, and who was he to argue with their struggle to codify the gut instincts of an ambitious plumber.

Lonergan sauntered in, shelled nuts in hand, without knocking.

'You read about this Mitchell's business?' asked Finch, waving a sheet without looking up. 'Benny Mitchell's a campaign donor. What do you think? He called me at home this morning.'

'Well? Who are they? Does he know? I've never heard of anywhere being attacked because their food was too damned wholesome. That's a new one.'

'Neither had he.'

Lonergan was also intrigued. The Church of Christ the Fit was at least disciplined, in the open, although he wondered, briefly, if this was part of a Gotfelt plan to undermine the mayor. No. Too sophisticated and cunning. These people, masked and shadowy, were a blunter constituency altogether and he had no idea where they were based or who was leading them.

Organized opposition to food laws was generally muted, cowed and built around the Republican Party. They never got a look into New York politics, so Lonergan had ignored their undercurrents and was regretting the omission. Groundswells could be dangerous.

'I'm getting close. We've been getting hints of an underground of sorts, militant eaters if you will. Health Enforcement are on –'

Finch flung the report on his desk. 'Find out who these bastards are. Get me a report by the end of the week. This could escalate.'

Lonergan adroitly changed the subject. 'Remember our turbulent bishop?'

Finch raised his head to acknowledge the limit of what he was prepared to know. 'Of course, the thing. What of it?'

He paused to fill his mouth with nuts. 'She's dead. They found her in an alley off Christopher. Strangled. Gotfelt left a message at her home.'

'And?'

'They've assigned Jane Ryan. She's good. Reputation for straight shooting. Not a woman to prop up Rafferty's, if you know what I mean. Still, I'd say it's all pointing towards Gotfelt.'

Lonergan paused and both men looked around the room, deep in private contemplation. In fact, it was shared.

'Intriguing,' said Finch softly. 'Isn't it, Tommy? Life. Just bloody intriguing.'

9

Devlin was taking advantage of a bathroom empty of teenager: a free run at the salts, bubbles, lotions and candles scented with jasmine. It was a man thing. If he closed his eyes, life was rustling palm fronds, a light ocean breeze and the rhythm of waves on a shore; not a noisy, damp, rat-hassled shoe box on the Lower East Side. It was soothing and he lay, eyes closed, trying to ease the day by reminding himself of Susan, passionate and alight with electric energy. She worked for a charity that helped humonsters find work. He had been giving evidence at a weight tribunal and saw her staring from the back of the court. It was disconcerting, but he worked patiently through the evidence. Then she was called to the stand and spoke, without notes, pleading persuasively for the arbuckle to get a weight adjustment extension so that he could continue to work. She kept sweeping a hand through her thick, tangled dark hair. Devlin caught up with her on the courthouse steps afterwards.

'Good presentation. He was lucky to have you.'

'Thanks. Agent Devlin, isn't it?'

'Matt. Call me Matt. The agent thing is only for special occasions.'

'Really?' she laughed. 'You mean it actually impresses people?'

'No, not really. Listen, can I buy you coffee?' He was an impulse shopper.

She looked at him, then at her watch. 'Sure, why not? You can never know too many Enforcement agents.'

She had a full smile, sudden and bright and startling. Susan Daschle was from Iowa and it didn't take long before they fused, two strangers to the city. It was still an unlikely union: the Health Enforcement agent and the f*t advocate. The fault lines soon appeared, shaken into visibility by disagreements and her nervous self-doubt. He felt ashamed and awkward at the way it ended, blaming his search for a kind of certainty; for wanting rocks and absolutes in a world that seemed to offer him neither. He had enough doubt already.

He closed his eyes with regret. Paradise, such as it was, lay at the back of the apartment, a place where traffic was dulled to a hum and the neighbour's atonic, tuneless electric sitar practice failed to penetrate. It was where he felt at peace and the demons of loneliness left him alone.

Sylvia was doing homework with a friend down the block. Devlin had asked about her date with Damon. 'Fine,' she blocked.

'Hey, come on. Where did you go? What did you do?'

She crossed her arms. Time out.

'You definitely need to find your own life, Dad,' she sighed.

'Hey, you are my life.' But he knew she was right and kept trying not to begrudge her the pleasures of awkward adolescence. At least Sylvia had no body image issues. Sex and drugs he could handle; she was old enough. But the brown worried him. Her generation was lucky to be spared junk and the advertising that went with it. He just wished they talked more, but the good parent/bad parent show flopped when you had to play both roles.

The last time she was doing homework elsewhere turned out to be neither at a home nor work. He'd caught her smoking a joint with Alice Philips at the Turkish coffee bar at Eighty and Twenty-Third.

Alice's parents worked nights at the hospital, so she was often alone. Still, Devlin liked her. She had a sensible body shape and was clearly a young woman in control.

The vid sounded. He didn't recognize the number and hit connect. Staring back was Jane Ryan. Staring at her was a man wearing bath bubbles. He turned the vid away.

'Detective Ryan. Let me slip into something less embarrassing.'

He put on a bathrobe, one Sylvia had stolen from a hotel in South Carolina and presented to him last birthday. It was quite touching and it hadn't taken long to unstitch the H. I. L. T. O. N.

'You caught me by surprise. How'd you get my number?'

'Just returning the compliment, Agent Devlin, and I'm a detective, if you recall. Now, care to tell me why you didn't identify

Frish at the scene for me?' She spoke evenly, rolling the sentences together without a pause. Straight to it. Her voice was measured, but measuring anger.

'We were going to tell you, but –' He braced for impact. How could he explain that moment of personal weakness when, for the first time, his partner seemed to be just that, a partner? So, he said something else. 'I was going to tell you. But Strong convinced me you'd make her easily and she used to be in Homicide.' It was a lousy, court-appointed kind of defence. 'You did make her easily, right?'

There was a silence. Devlin stared at the digital image for clues. 'Look, it was unprofessional.' He sounded weak. 'We just saw a chance to contribute.'

'Unprofessional doesn't begin to cover it. Do you have any idea how much time we wasted finding out who she was, dealing with those morons in retinal records? Time is everything in murder cases, but maybe they don't teach you that in Health Enforcement classes.'

'Look, I'm sorry. I wasn't thinking and, yes, they do teach that, as a matter of fact.'

'This is a disciplinary matter. I'm willing to bet you found the message from Heston Gotfelt.'

Devlin nodded.

'Just don't tell me you've contacted him. Tell me then was the moment you thought about your job, about – what's the word we in Homicide like to use?' She clicked her fingers. 'Ah yes, that one again: professionalism.'

He told her they'd contacted him.

'That was one dumb move and I'm willing to bet your smart-mouthed sidekick put you up to it.'

It was tempting. But loyalty was thicker than water, the clear and flavourless kind, and Strong had earned some back, despite her behaviour at the Jewel. 'No. It was my call. I'm the boss.'

'Have it your way. But that woman has attitude issues, Devlin. And they're all bad. Don't be fooled by the party-girl act.'

Devlin felt himself stiffen. Strong might be a problem, but she was his problem. 'I've known her only a short while, it's true, but she has good judgement,' he said. 'At least in my opinion. There are second acts in life.'

'I know. You just moved from Baltimore for yours. Not that I blame you for getting out. That is one single-act town.'

Devlin felt the water cooling on his back. 'We wanted to check out her place, find a food connection. It's what we do . . .' He let his voice trail off and heard a grunt. It could have been pleasure, recognition or a blow to the solar plexus.

'Some temptations are best resisted, Devlin. Anyway, we need to meet,' she said. 'There's a problem I want to talk about, but not over the vid.'

There was so much secret vid tapping going on these days that he understood. 'Where and when?'

'Gringos.'

'On Delancey?'

'See you in an hour.'

There was extravagant detour, because of road works, past the Union Square weight clock as it counted down the number of obese in America. The cab eventually found a route in the right direction, through the Bowery, with its luxury apartment buildings and boutiques. The statue of the bum caught the late sun. Its fountain was turned off to conserve what passed for pure water these days, but it was unsettling still to see that outstretched palm with nothing spurting out.

The Anti-F*t League had a new hoarding on Houston, a site they seemed to monopolize. 'Vote As You Eat.' The image was a glowing chiquita and her man. She was holding his arm at the elbow and looked designed, with tight abdominals, but also fresh and androgynous. They were nearly identical. There was a bowl of green salad between them, dominant, lusty and pure.

Devlin felt a twinge. He had almost forgotten how it felt to have a woman hold him. Susan was the last. A small circle of city workers outside the vehicle licensing office walked in a tight ring. 'Fix It For

Us Finch' read a politer placard. Piles of trash on the sidewalks spilled on to the street.

The cab driver swerved to avoid an oven; a rat swerved to avoid the cab. Devlin realized how much he wanted to be one of the people eating healthily together on the hoarding, a couple. He stared at them and thought about his own efforts to find love, the awkward internet dating where everyone was a sincere animal lover with a good sense of humour. They all adored walking in the country and gave money to charities that helped overeaters. Devlin often wondered if the entire single female population of Manhattan was out hiking and laughing, sincerely, with their pets, just without him. Was there some kind of agreement? Had they all met and decided not to date him? How? By a simple majority? A show of hands? But optimism helped, the expectation that it was still possible for people to spark spontaneously without the tap, tap, tap of a keyboard sending out its Morse code: panic, life adrift. Devlin was so used to the company of loneliness, he feared being lonely without it. He had considered rented electronic company to ease some of the needs and the longer nights. But that story in the *Post* had put him off. Faulty hydraulics. Poor guy.

Gringos become famous for a while about every fifteen years, or whenever some ascendant writer or actor recalled their favourite hangout during the Struggle Years, only to slump back into its true identity, a neighbourhood bar where people with hopes and no money waited for life to offer either.

There was nothing inviting about the small, low windows, greyed by grime and apparently designed to scare off passing trade. The neon signs for Budweiser and Coors had long gone with the ban on alcohol advertising; their memory was left traced on the glass, a mystery for future generations, like the face on the Turin Shroud.

Devlin opened the door and adjusted to a primordial light that barely bothered to illuminate any surfaces, but kept drinkers in the comfort of shade. The mismatched wooden tables and chairs were empty, except for a few students and an old man with the sports section. A football game danced on a big screen above the bar, its volume turned down. Devlin assumed Ryan would be on one of the faded, red banquettes that clung to cracked wooden walls.

He passed signed photographs of old Yankees greats in those sporting postures that probably seem absurd to passing aliens: 'Hey, look at me with one leg and both arms in the air and a stick.' But Devlin had never liked sports, especially baseball, which was just hanging around and statistics. He couldn't see the point of adding rules to exercise. Besides, he'd got the Church.

Ryan pointed to the space opposite. She was sipping a shot of wine. A fifth of beer was on the other side.

'I figured you for a Brooklyn lager guy.'

'Damned if you haven't found the key to my soul. I'd better hide it better,' Devlin replied.

'Cheers.' She raised her glass and nodded, watching him through eyes that were steady and even.

Devlin had already decided she was the distant, silent type, not given to verbal foreplay.

'Heston Gotfelt doesn't have an alibi, you know,' she said. Devlin didn't and wished instantly that he'd pushed the interview harder.

'He was in the city all weekend, from Thursday night until this afternoon. But he didn't seem to do much. For a guy whose waking hours have practically got a stock exchange listing, there are gaps. His assistant says she saw him at breakfast and that was it; has no idea where he spent the rest of the time. She spent the weekend with a sister in Queens.' Ryan took another sip. 'Lost hours are always worth trying to find, don't you think?'

'Not necessarily. He takes time out once in a while,' Devlin said. 'It doesn't make him a killer. Time of death?'

'Not yet. Still waiting on the autopsy, which is why I'm asking questions in reverse, ones such as what leaves him out of it? He preaches against brown, she's found covered in it; almost symbolic, don't you think? And they knew each other.'

Devlin sipped and shrugged. 'No evidence, no motive, a presumption of innocence. He must know a lot of lives clinging to the edge in this screwed-up world.'

Ryan looked intently at the face opposite, at eyebrows tight in concentration. 'People are murdered by somebody they know. Usually. And it's always about sex, money or concealment. You're a member of his Church, aren't you?'

'It isn't a secret,' Devlin replied.

'Your judgement might be clouded, that's all. Frish was a hooker, a successful one. We found recording equipment behind the bed. There's no evidence of her attending any church services, by the way. She didn't donate. Yet he says she was on their rolls. No disc in the recording equipment either. He's a man with a reputation to protect, more stock than blood. Blackmail can sometimes bring out the worst in people.'

A thick dark rain was falling outside. F*t drops of poison-filled water.

'I'm no detective, but don't you need evidence?' said Devlin. 'And if you think I can't separate the private and professional, then you haven't looked at my file too closely.'

'Oh, I have, believe me. Impressive, turning in your cousin. What was it for? Remind me.' A small, distant smile played.

'Distributing Class A: brown mixed with sugars and milk solids,' Devlin answered, drawing on a memory not meant for display purposes. 'It was for his own good, although you may find that hard to understand.'

'Let's hope he didn't,' Ryan replied.

'The man was dealing to kids. I have one and wanted him off the streets, cleaned up. He got two years and an anti-addiction course. If he'd gone on much longer someone else would've caught him and he'd have ended up serving five to ten or beaten up by some rival. I did him a favour. He's married now, got children of his own and a good job. I could tell you more, Detective. Only it's none of your business.'

Devlin felt angry. So did she.

'You're right, it isn't. But withholding evidence is. I went to the central computer. Guess what? There was your name next to a weight stop on the Long Island Expressway less than three days earlier. Did you think I wouldn't find it?'

There was a silence and they looked away from each other. Devlin breathed slowly. 'You're right. I'm still sorry.'

'Well, it isn't all bad. Gotfelt probably assumes he's off the hook. I take it you asked him how he knew the deceased, where they met and all that, then requested his autograph,' she paused. 'For your kid, of course.'

Strong was right; Homicide were assholes. Ryan wasn't even looking at Devlin, but taking notes in a tiny, unlined black pad. Her handwriting was neat, precise and small. Each row of text sat evenly and obediently below the one preceding it.

'Bet you won all the writing classes at school,' Devlin said, watching her. 'All joined up, too.'

She looked up, careful, expressionless. 'I got given a set of these special pens by my grandfather once. He was a printer, taught me to appreciate calligraphy, the order and symmetry of it, the way letters lead into each other, logically attached. There's a real craft to it. I never won anything at school, though.'

'Me neither. We should've gone to the prom together.'

Devlin found himself offering up a childhood in Missouri, joining Health Enforcement, and a marriage that withered through mutual indifference. He talked about parents, the wrong kind of Generation Y dropouts who viewed the Anti-F*t League as horseshit. Both of them worked, too, because in those days people without degrees could get jobs. He used to eat anything because his mother barely bothered cooking. She was always busy. He and his little sister would hang out at the malls and take in all kinds of bad things. It was cheap and made them happy. 'We both struggle to keep our weight down to this day. I guess that's how I got into Enforcement, where the interest came from. The Church came later, but, if I'm honest, joining was probably a rebellion against upbringing. Control seemed to offer structure, I guess.' He shrugged.

Ryan signalled the barman for another round.

'Yeah? Ryans have been cops or firefighters for five generations.

That was my structure, my religion. Never was much doubt I'd be one or the other. I chose the one without ladders.'

'Sensible.'

Someone put money in the jukebox for Miles Davis to soar, an angel rising through crescendos and cornet dips.

'There's another thing,' she said.

'Shoot.'

'I got a call from the mayor's office, a contact, but not somebody I know well. This guy made it clear they were clicking worry beads about us linking Gotfelt and Cupid Frish.' She paused and turned her head from side to side as if to relieve a strain. 'Finch thinks one of his biggest supporters is about to be dragged down, I suppose. What's odd is we haven't marked Gotfelt for anything. Nobody at Homicide was making any link with City Hall. I just don't know where that's all coming from. As far as I'm concerned, your saint just has to explain himself,' she said, adding pointedly, 'to me. The postcard from the mayor's people seemed to be telling me to back off.'

Devlin frowned. 'Curious that they'd draw attention to themselves.'

'Yes, it is.' She sipped her wine.

There were no signs of assault on Frish, Ryan told Devlin, apart from the barely distinct bruises around the neck. 'But the autopsy should reveal more.'

Devlin promised analysis of the brown early in the week from tests that might indicate where it came from. This wasn't always possible, he warned her, because cocoa beans were often mingled before refining.

It pleased him that Ryan was still waiting for her own pathologist to report. The strike was hitting state workers, not federal ones like him. People were walking out all over. The local news was filled with stories about ambulances not turning up, people driving themselves to hospital to get bullet wounds treated, births in the park.

Gringos was far away from such things, spent of the students and uptowners who filled it on Fridays and Saturdays. Neither of them rushed to leave.

Frish seemed to specialize in chocolate kinks and mild role playing, Ryan said. She worked alone. There was no criminal record.

'Handcuffs, chefs and waiters, aid worker and victim, that kind of thing. But her specialty was brown. We found pestles and mortars, moulds, all the tools of her trade. She was a feeder. Not much stashed in the apartment, though, so I doubt she was dealing.'

Former clients were being interviewed. 'They're the usual mix: bankers, lawyers, golf professionals. Lots were casual contacts, johns to develop, so to speak. Investments surprised to find themselves in her portfolio. She kept a low profile. Been at that apartment about two years. Doorman said he believed she was in marketing. She'd given him some line about working for a cosmetics company, travelling a lot, bringing people back to see the merchandise, which was kind of true, I suppose. He said she was always very friendly, a big tipper. He's either a good liar or had no idea what she really got up to. I'm inclined to the former. Good tips buy a lot of blindness.'

She paused and glanced over at the game. 'Notre Dame are shit this season. He says she left the apartment on Thursday afternoon, around three, came back early evening, alone. We don't know where she was in the Hamptons, or if she was there at all, whatever she told you. We're checking hotel registers but, if she wasn't lying, it's more likely she was staying with friends or a john. Her clients were the sort to have places out there. We're cross-referencing names and addresses. It's slow. A lot of the property out there is registered to corporations, not individuals.'

Marijuana cigarettes were mild, because of the other herbs mixed in to reduce the bad effect on appetite, but Devlin could only handle two a day without feeling hungry. Ryan must have smoked two in the time they were together.

'How do you manage so many of those?'

'Practice and stress,' she replied. 'Like they say in the ads, helps me see through the fog of life.'

'The destruction was so frenzied in that apartment,' Devlin said after a few moments. 'More than you'd need to make a point. Why didn't the noise draw any attention?'

It was disconcerting how deeply blue her eyes were, like some striking watery jewel.

'And it's weird that no china was broken.'

'Would have made a noise,' he said.

'Exactly. We're hoping neighbours may help. Nothing yet, though. But it's that kind of place, insulated and private. We're still doing the interviews. There's another thing you should know. It's your boss, the commissioner. Fenwick and Gotfelt seem to be the only clients without alibis and Fenwick definitely saw her some time between when she left the apartment and when she turned up chocolate-dipped.'

'Health Commissioner Fenwick?'

'I read your report. When you stopped Frish on the expressway she was heading from the Hamptons, but I don't think she was ever going to the Keys. There's weird weather shit predicted for down there, ice storms and worse. Why would she?' Ryan sipped her drink. 'She was due to meet "F" at a mid-town hotel early on Saturday evening, at least according to the diary. We checked the letters against that Rolodex. There was only one "F" and the number matched a private vid registered to Fenwick. Only she never made it. I'm interviewing him tomorrow. He'll know you're working the case with us, obviously. I need you not to mention that we've talked tonight.'

'F' for user. Fenwick. Devlin was surprised.

'Well,' he started to say, hearing the doubt in his voice.

'Don't mention anything to Fenwick.' She stopped for a second and looked, unflinching. 'And I won't mention your career-throwing breach of regulations. Deal?'

Devlin nodded.

She looked at her watch. 'Good. Are you up for a Sunday evening mystery, no commercial breaks?'

There was no sign of Ali when Devlin and Ryan reached Montcalm Avenue. Donny welcomed them into the elevator by name this time, and then complained of sore connectors, saying he'd rather not chat.

The apartment was transformed. Men in white protective jumpsuits dusted for prints, and were stooped or stretched. Others carefully collected torn books and ravaged paintings.

Ryan beckoned a jumpsuit. 'This is Fritz Hanson, best forensics guy we got. Fritz, meet Health Enforcement Agent Matt Devlin.' She introduced a short man with the sort of puppyish, open face that wins awards at dog shows. On the dog, usually. He wore round, metal-framed glasses.

'Hey,' he said, reaching out a gloved hand. Devlin took it. Hanson looked at Ryan, who nodded. 'Tell him.'

'Okay. We're picking up a lot of prints. But some of them, a great many, are very peculiar. In fact, the best ones, apart from the deceased, are from your colleague Agent Strong,' he smiled weakly.

'Following procedure is not her best quality. I'm sorry,' Devlin replied quickly. 'Peculiar?'

'Prints come in all shapes and sizes, depending on whether the object being lifted was heavy or light, or whether it's been thrown. There are lots of different ways you normally find them. Why? Because we hold things differently all the time, a rose more delicately than a stick, and in all sorts of irrational ways when we're angry or riled or hurried. If something's been thrown, say, the print shows that. It's blurred. But here, there's no side detail to any of the ones we're getting. None. Normally, when something has been held, like a glass, prints are going to come up showing most of the finger, especially in a messy scene like this one,' he said, waving his arm around Hell's panorama. 'But what we've got, consistently, is the central to top area of a digit. I've lifted more than eighty prints so far, they're all the same. Not a single one shows any side detail.'

Ryan looked at Devlin and waited for a reaction. He shrugged. What was there to say? She guided him to the balcony.

'Puzzling, huh?' She looked out over the river; egrets and herons migrated from the cold south perched at its edges. The sky was a palette of mauve and pinks, a streaked fire on the far horizon. 'But that's not the strangest thing. Everywhere was torn apart, except the kitchen. Undamaged. The skin of an apple had been sliced away, delicately; the pulp was untouched. There's a food angle I'm missing. Cupid Frish, hooker and gorger, turns up dressed in chocolate, dead in a back alley. Some kind of vengeful hell passes through her home, nothing is touched in the food preparation area except the fruit bowl, which is emptied, but carefully. Plates are untouched. I'm drowning here.'

Devlin was struggling to tread water himself. 'We deal with brown and burger smugglers, sugar violations and eateasys all the time. Apples are on the side of the angels and get a pass. But I'll check tomorrow, see if we got anybody out there with priors connected to fruit.'

'Good. Frish must've come up against some dangerous people in her line of work,' said the detective.

Ryan watched Devlin leave and looked at her watch. It was late and she wanted an alert team. 'Fritz? Wrap it for tonight and seal up. The shots are on me.' There was a laconic, weary cheer from around the room.

Soon they were all sitting in Joe's, a dive bar on Claremont, slumped and weary. She'd left a police guard on the apartment door, just in case. Of what, Ryan could only speculate. Outside, sulphur-stinking sheet rain was storming the building in a maddened rage. They sipped beers to unwind. Hanson was in the corner, on his own, puzzling over sketches and photographs of fingerprints. He caught her eye.

'Don't ask. I've run them against records. The pattern's too bizarre, Ryan, especially the long index. I mean, it's longer than long.'

'I hear you.'

'The prints are crazy enough, but put them with the mayhem, the way things were just, well, destroyed for no reason. But not everything. Nothing stolen. It's like some huge, howling fury just blew into town. The noise alone –'

'Neighbours say they didn't hear a thing –'

'How can that be? Come on. It's trashed. Books were thrown

around, ceiling fans half-ripped away. Every single one, I might add.'

Ryan shook her head. 'But no plates or glasses were broken.' The investigation was surrounded by fog, nothing to signal a direction as their flashlights darted this way and that. No route at all.

Nathan Molloy joined them with his glass and swagger. This was his first case since transferring from Vice. He laughed.

'What's so funny?' said a voice, grudging.

'I was just thinking,' Molloy said, heaving with pleasure, 'about her place.'

'What about it?' asked Ryan.

'It's like a wild animal was loose in there, man. I mean, who else would empty a fridge, even want to, yet leave a box of jewels?'

'Hey, it's your f*t wife, Tony,' somebody shouted.

Ryan allowed herself half a smile. 'So, tell me, why would a wild animal kill a hooker?'

'She overcharged?' said Molloy.

'Perfect murder weapon, an animal,' said another voice.

Laughter trickled away like rainwater down a storm pipe.

'Not much you can't train a creature to do. They got killer dolphins in the military. Dogs are man's best friend, right? They'll gut you soon as lick your face. Hannibal had elephants.'

Ryan sighed. 'Thanks, Molloy. I get the picture.'

'Don't mention it.'

'It's been a long day. I'm turning in. We should have a decent autopsy report tomorrow at least. Meantime, I want everyone to work their contacts, anyone who might know about a contract killing. We're working on the assumption that Cupid Frish was killed in a way that was supposed to leave a message. It was organized. Maybe in her own place, maybe not.'

Ryan looked evenly at Molloy. 'Either way, this was a methodical hit, I'm certain. Sorry, buddy. But this woman was carefully dressed by somebody she might have spent time with, personally or professionally, somebody who had time to spend with her.' He turned to leave. 'I guess that rules out zoo life, Molloy, especially as we're definitely not investigating your love affairs.'

IO

Only a handful of smugglers in the city brought in high-grade brown. One way or another, a slice of the action went to just three of them: Mickey Furillo, Charlie Wiseman, who they called 'The Lick', and Tibor Gunduc, the most powerful of all.

Devlin came across him soon after arriving from Baltimore. He discovered that Gunduc and Strong had a private war going, one that seemed to go back to childhood. They both grew up on the same street, Strong said one day, as if that explained everything. She just dropped it into the conversation after they'd stopped him for what Devlin assumed was a random fergie, but was evidently a regular event on his partner's pick-a-fight-a-day calendar.

'He's a douche bag,' said Strong.

'And he's a criminal,' Devlin added.

'Yeah, but mainly he's a douche bag.' Yet the two of them did manage to rub along and, without it ever being stated, Gunduc had turned into one of their contacts. They gave him a sort of protection in return. But they couldn't save him from himself. Gunduc weighed four hundred and twelve pounds, the price of habitual use. He was practically in residence at the Weight Correctional Facility near Buffalo. They'd even given him a suite and choice of wall colour and he still ran his empire, watched the moves like a lizard; immobile, but only on the surface.

Devlin took the train from Grand Central. 'For security reasons, do not leave food unattended. Food left unattended may be removed and destroyed' warned the electronic message voice sternly. People huddled furtively in the public-eating zone as he walked across the echoing marble hall to platform twelve. The carriages were full, except 'Sized Only', which was furthest away from the buffet car, its seats large and reinforced. Devlin decided to abuse his badge and occupy one.

'They make me drink this shit all day,' Gunduc said, sounding outraged. 'Vegetables.' He was still in shadow, a hulked humonster with shaved head and a shirt that billowed in the breeze from an open window, like a schooner's sail.

'It's good for you, Tibor. Make you live longer.'

Devlin glanced outside where the sized were being put through their paces, chased and prodded with sticks that gave them a small shock. Most tribunal sentences were reduction related. Lose the pounds and lose the time. It worked. The children's camp was next door and Devlin could hear them playing.

'You brought me anything?'

Devlin passed over the bag. 'Twelve. Count them.'

'That all?'

'All I could get authorized, pal. You got strawberry, chocolate, three caramel at least.' Devlin watched him poke around and pull out a single, partially deflated doughnut.

He winced. 'You should've put them in a box. I hate it when this happens.'

'Sorry.'

He ate delicately, nodding at some hidden contentment as pow-dered white sugar flaked the balconies and esplanades of his chin and throat. 'Nice.'

'They should be.'

'Jimmy's?'

'No, he left town three months back. We heard he's running an eateasy in Fort Lauderdale. A new guy. Bakes up in Washington Heights.'

Gunduc nodded. 'I think I heard of this man. He pays The Lick.' Devlin watched patiently as the last section was eased between two plush red lips. Gunduc sat, impassive, sated, and stared at the ceiling, drawing the back of a hand across his mouth.

'Your broad worked out of Jersey. Very private work.'

'And?'

'She bought brown from me, decent customer, always paid on time. I had no complaints, if that's what you're wondering. I prefer my buyers alive.'

'Who might want her dead?'

'She was murdered? You surprise me.'

'I saw the body. It was dumped and dressed in brown. Somebody was sending out a sign, a warning.'

He shrugged. 'I never got involved in her clientele.'

'You're involved in everything. Is there some kind of turf war going on? I mean, you're out here, things fall apart.'

He smiled. 'No, it's all under control,' he heaved into laughter at the unexpected pun. 'I heard she worked an eateasy. Maybe she was keeping too much.'

'Which one?'

'There's a limit to my cooperation for,' he shook the bag, 'twelve sweet ones. This I'll give you: she was screwing that food fundamentalist guy, Heston Gotfelt.'

'He says it was platonic.'

'He's lying.'

There was a pause as Gunduc worked over one of the caramels. 'The camera doesn't lie.'

Devlin felt his heartbeat quicken. 'There's film?'

Gunduc shrugged. 'Could be only gossip. You know, while we're watching our surrogate eaters work a chocoburger, talking helps pass the time. Aversion therapy is dumb shit.'

They sat in silence.

'You didn't bring you partner along,' Gunduc said finally.

'No.'

'You like her? She's pretty. Wild as a prairie mustang. You should let a little wild into your life, you know. Enjoy the city. Corrupt your sanity a little.'

'It's got enough challenges and I don't go there with her. We're getting along.'

Gunduc looked around and rubbed his scalp, fast and harsh. Devlin heard bristles grate. 'You think so?' He laughed. Mind games. Poison in the well. Devlin couldn't blame him for trying.

II

'And the exciting thing, Bishop, is that every ingredient is in Deuteronomy.' Olaf Grabiner, Director of Food Ethics and Product Development, sounded triumphant as he wiped sweat from his brow.

Gotfelt sat behind a dark oak desk, seemingly rapt as flow charts sailed by on a sea of costs and profit, broken down by state and socio-economic group. Above him a sign carried the new campaign slogan: 'The Treat You Can Trust'.

Grabiner turned his round, untroubled face to the assembled executives. 'Brothers and sisters, Bible burger will revolutionize snack eating in this country and pull the rug from under additive-filled brands. And all at only ninety calories a portion.'

He had once worked for a food multinational, before joining the church, bringing a wife, three children under twelve and all the zeal of the convert when the bottom fell out of e-numbers.

'Yes, sir,' Grabiner said, voice rising. 'This pleasure is packed with protein, carbohydrates, vitamins, minerals and fibre authorized by the Lord himself, which means there'll be no copyright issues, by the way. This is the treat people can trust, the one to give the kids,' he concluded firmly.

Gotfelt sipped apple juice and tried to focus. This was the first move by the Church into food production and there were many risks. 'Barley and wheat are proteins, fine ones, and olive oil is the greatest source of mono-unsaturated f*ts bar none,' continued Grabiner with intensity and energy. 'Honey? A source of strength and a brilliant antibiotic. And as we all know from the good book, grapes are just the perfect anti-oxidant.'

As he went on, listing the merits of figs – 'God's mineral machines' – Gotfelt was thinking about Cupid and about the Health Enforcement agents.

They had barely asked him a question. He could have told them she did chocolate better than any woman he knew and that occasionally they had sex, too. Cupid the Temptress, the goddess of molten cocoa, sucking through a straw on fine brown bubbling in the chalice; liquid and mysterious, carnal and silken. She would stare into his eyes as her body absorbed without flinching the burning pain when he poured. 'It's liquid sex, Heston,' she'd purr through short, sharp breaths of ecstatic pain. 'And you can use your tongue.' He would stare, transfixed, dazed and hungry from marijuana and the penetrating Eastern music that played in the background, rhythmic and soft. She would draw him down with her hands, feeling the greed of his lust, on to the brown.

Perhaps they were interviewing everyone who knew her? The male agent had seemed awed in his presence. His insolent colleague was attractive. Fine body. Firm thighs. He smiled slightly as he wondered how she would look bathing naked in bubbling brown.

'You are so right to be happy, Bishop,' said Grabiner. 'For the Lord has blessed our enterprise, truly. We've got a billion-dollar winner here.' He sat down dramatically, nodding appreciatively at applause from around the table.

Gotfelt forced his mind to the present. 'Thank you, Mr Grabiner. And the sample you left me was good enough to make me wonder why Satan hadn't tempted Eve with it. An apple seems so very ordinary by comparison.'

There was a murmur of appreciative laughter at the joke, one Regard had slipped him on a piece of paper.

'Marketing?'

Reverend Mathias Garland rose. He was a former advertising executive on Madison Avenue brought in at a million a year, excluding bonuses and stock options. His title was honorary, but useful for tax purposes, and he smiled with an easy confidence.

'Looks good, Bishop,' he said. 'I think we can get into Burger King and, obviously, we'll push it through Church groups. We're projecting a five million dollar upside in year one, rising to seven in year three. Of course, the figures could change if we need to advertise heavily.' He sipped from a glass of juice. 'Looking further ahead, I think we should get a shot at sponsoring the next presidential election, top billing at least.'

Gotfelt nodded. What a prospect. He looked through the windows at his campus, which was being erected around a square to suggest ageless academia: a Harvard or Yale. Things were moving fast. Artificial ivy from Chile lay in stacks beside pre-aged bricks from Korea, all ready for adhesion to the cinder-block walls.

This was the memorial that would survive beyond his own mortal life. He thought again of those early years, the crucial decisions and the pressure to build in other places. He admired the Mormons but resisted setting himself up in Utah. Multiple wives was a good twist, but its day had passed. The Mormons needed to be where the power wasn't because of their particular marketing device. He needed to be where it was, close to Washington.

His wife had fought hard for Salt Lake anyway, arguing that the skiing was excellent and real estate prices were low.

'We could have a pool and a tennis court, Hestie.'

'Did the Lord do laps and play tennis? No. Apart from any other consideration, the competition's too well established. We've been through all this.'

She sighed.

'I must face Washington and have a toe in the South,' he explained wearily. 'It's business. You understand, surely? West Virginia is where all the important Churches are these days, not to mention near the Pentagon.'

'There'll be mosquitoes,' she replied, too weakened by a double shift at the Taco Bell, Baton Rouge, to argue; the struggle to pay the rent on their hot, small two-bedroom house left her drained of fight.

He had laboured for weeks, months, to find his angle into God, working out his frustrations in a city gym where the hologram screens were always filled with weeping clerics urging viewers to donate. One humid afternoon, the Revd Kay Z. Mole strode across a stage in a white, tasselled Elvis costume, yelling at his congregation. Elvis! A hackneyed choice, Gotfelt had said to himself.

'Good people, you have got to supersize the Lord Jesus in your lives. He is your thirty-two ounces of refreshment.'

And so it arrived at Level 3, 8 mph, 50 minutes, 860 calories, just as the camera panned across an audience of enraptured worshippers. Gotfelt knew, in a moment of clarity, that the future wasn't loose morals but loose guts.

He hit emergency stop, barely showering before hurrying home and contacting the manager at First Mutual Bank; all before the end credits and donor numbers had begun rolling on *Kay Z. Mole's Rockin' Morning Absolution Show*.

'The Church has concentrated on the soul at the expense of the body,' he said in a tumbling sales pitch, pacing purposefully around the bank's conference table.

'They take references in the Bible denouncing the flesh literally and shrug, saying the body is evil and mortal. Move on. They've been concentrating on what's supposed to be good and immortal, the soul, and that's where I can fit in: get it back to the body, which is all people care about these days.' He thumped the table exultantly.

The more he reasoned, the more he saw. All around him churches spread love and tolerance, treating gluttony as some acceptable, little sin.

'People don't give a hang about eternity, ladies and gentlemen. Not these days. It's the here and now they worry about. And that's where I intend to pitch my tent.' F*t is the fifth horseman.

First Mutual did the numbers and soon gave Heston Gotfelt a rolling line of credit to build his spiritual corporation.

Then the real work began, and in the small kitchen of his rented home he devised a back story. A Bible code was important and came first. It revealed messages against overeating hidden in the first five books of the Old Testament if he took every fourth letter, or whatever worked, and then read either along a line, down one, at diagonals, or with the occasional step. There were dire warnings, at least with practice, within this liturgical line dance. 'Burgers Kill', was one, 'Chocolate is Hell' another. Eventually, scholars would pore over the Torah, finding guidance, especially when he started giving grants to encourage them. There were persistent irritants, messages warning that the world would end through asphyxia (spelled several different ways) and under a monstrous fog of gases. These were cast aside.

There were other difficulties, especially with chocolate, which had no origins in the land of the prophets, travelling to Spain from South America and then only in the sixteenth century. They had sat around for a whole weekend, day and night, trying to incorporate this awkward historical truth. Joe Regard, who made a living writing local advertising copy, produced his master stroke at three in the morning. 'Well, therein is the genius of prophecy,' he said, looking around, clicking his fingers and taking a swig of foaming cold Jax beer. *The Eating Code* was Gotfelt's first best-seller.

Budgets for the burger were approved after little discussion. Gotfelt was relieved. President Bryant was making the commencement address to undergraduates in two days and he needed time to compose himself. There would be publicity and the last thing he wanted was scandal to absorb the media. Anything linking the head of the Church of Christ the Fit to a murdered, brown-addled hooker was bad news. He knew a lost soul. What did that prove? Most of the country was fallen into sin, fighting food impulses. If only Cupid had listened, she might have been saved.

He was looking forward to private moments with the President. Twenty minutes was all they would give him. But it would be enough. Health Enforcement needed more money, extra resources to fight smugglers and eateasys. The director, Brett Sumner, had called on a secure line and briefed him.

He would press for more raids and federal burnings in public parks, especially those of New York where the regulations were being flouted so openly. Finch. Gotfelt rubbed his temples, feeling a headache beginning, and he wondered about Regard's assessment that this mayor was the sort of politician who responded only to pressure, the absolute and unrelenting kind, because that was how he himself had achieved power. But was it going to work?

'No calls, Sadie,' Gotfelt told his secretary after the last council member had left. He lay on the green futon in a dark, windowless private sanctuary, unsettled and wary, and listened to the animals outside: the lowing cattle and howling simians, restless and roaring with futile anger.

It was comforting to hear God's creatures over which he had such complete control appearing to acknowledge his power. They were being trained for the tableau he had long planned, a spectacular recreation of the Ark being filled. An early attempt with animals loaned from a zoo in Dearborn proved a disaster. Few of them would be led or cajoled up a ramp into the huge wooden ship. The tigers killed a gazelle within moments of arriving on set and the wolves, somehow, seized both peacocks. The elephants panicked, retreating in a bellow down the ramp, squashing the small, obedient parade of marsupials, rodents and tortoises, all arranged neatly in order of size, turning the imposed order into a mess of crushed bones, feathers and bloodied jaws as God's creatures devoured each other in a berserk carnival of death. The director had stormed out. 'This is not going to work,' he had screamed, tossing a script at Gotfelt. 'I cannot be creative in these conditions. I don't know how Noah did it, but I can tell you, those two-by-two animals must have been on something, that's all I can say. These are just brutes. *Brutes.*'

There was also a lot of shit and it stank too much for a family show. No wonder Disney stuck with cartoons. Gotfelt decided that only trained animals should be used, preferably those with theatrical experience, the sort that could be relied on not to kill or eat other cast members. It had been a learning experience. The animal sanctuarium, as he preferred to call the caged zoo, was a place where the natural world, so crazed these days, was at least under proper control.

'You're practically a regular on *Saturday Night Live*,' Regard noted at their regular meeting earlier in the day. 'Racy James has a whole routine going. Ten minutes.'

'Haven't you said anything?' he had replied, enraged.

'A complaint to comedians is oil on their fire. They live for it. Best just to pretend it doesn't matter. Makes you look like you can take a joke.'

'Well maybe I can't. There are no jokes in the good book. Besides, they make me seem like some killjoy, a hypocrite.'

'Sure. But what better way to prove that you're both than to complain? Look, it's late-night comedy for kids, arrested development nobodies, for Chri—' he stopped himself. 'For goodness sake. They're not our demographic. Never have been, never will be. None of our donors watch that bull.'

It was still wounding. Insulting. Disrespectful. Gotfelt waited with closed eyes for the headache pills to work. He would sleep for a while and tried to unwind, turning the air conditioning to M, smelling the marijuana as wisps of scented smoke seduced the room. Soon the rhythm in his temple retreated to soft brush strokes and he made himself think of a river of brown as he drifted away. Cupid was swimming. She winked at him while the water turned dark.

12

Strong was on a subcutaneous identification course in the Bronx, so Monday was going to be a desk day for her partner. The sun shone on the f*t beggar in Ray-Bans crouched with his handwritten sign: 'Jobless. Money for Slimming Pills.' Devlin threw a handful of quarters. It was padding, otherwise Ray-Bans would have been off the street. 'Thanks, friend, you're looking thin today.' He said that to everyone, but it seemed fair exchange for a Monday morning.

People were down on climate change, thought Devlin, breathing deeply. But when he caught the scent of tropical mimosa trees on Fifth Avenue, it was hard not to feel more positive.

He hadn't been at work twenty minutes before the brusque call from Ravenski to 'kindly step' into his office. Ravenski used to be a schoolteacher and it showed as he stalked his cubicle, deep in office matters or an algebra problem.

'Ah, Devlin.' He pointed to a hard wooden chair and folded himself neatly into a softer one on the other side, moving a pen across the tidy surface. His small, rimless glasses caught the sunlight. Devlin felt uneasy. Men with tidy organized surfaces and no nasal hair unsettled him.

'And where is Strong this morning?' Ravenski asked in a voice tinged with strain, condescension and suspicion. Strong was right, he did sound like a school principal.

'Sub-L course, sir. It's been scheduled for some time.'

Ravenski sighed. 'Such a pity they don't do insolence removal. Still, at least you're here.'

There was a silence. It was always this way, as if every spoken sentence was an unwelcome savings withdrawal. He turned his grey face to Devlin. Its skin, a size too small for the surrounding bone, was pulled tightly and shone with poor, pale health.

'Tell me, how is the Frish investigation progressing?'

'There's not too much so far. We're working with Homicide; they've hit a few walls,' Devlin answered cautiously.

Ravenski nodded, staring out of the window, across the sea of skyscrapers to the Manhattan Bridge, under reconstruction since food terrorists destroyed the central section. 'Leads?'

Devlin paused. Ravenski and Commissioner Fenwick were friends. Who was really interviewing him? He remembered the agreement with Ryan.

'She was a hooker, high-end. We should get forensics back on the brown this afternoon. Homicide are working through an address book we – that is they – found. They're still waiting for an autopsy.'

'Is that all?'

'Yes, sir.'

'Quite sure?' He inspected perfectly clipped fingernails for signs of rebellion among the cuticles. 'Only I heard you interviewed Bishop Heston Gotfelt.'

Devlin felt pieces move across the board, unbidden and alarming.

'Yes, we did. I wouldn't call it an interview. He left a message for Frish, so we decided to check him out as he was in town. Seems she was a Church member.'

'Like yourself.'

'Right.'

'And?'

'He knew her. She went to him for counselling. But so do a lot of people. Personally, I don't think it means anything. I would, too, if I got the chance. As a Church member, that is. Homicide are going to interview him again.'

'There's interest upstairs in all this,' Ravenski said, raising his head in emphasis. 'I don't like storms, Devlin; let's leave that to Mother Nature and whatever mid-life crisis is going on there. Do we understand each other?'

Devlin nodded. Ravenski picked up a pen and began writing. 'Keep me informed. Let Homicide deal with Gotfelt.' Finally he looked up. 'That's all.'

Interest upstairs. Gotfelt and Fenwick, partners in lust. Devlin remembered what Ryan had said.

There were two messages on his vid. One was the traditional one from Sylvia's school. Yin. Where was she and could he call as a matter of urgency? The second was from Sylvia herself, saying she was sick and staying home. Yang. Lovesick probably. Ms Stevens had sounded testier than usual. The vid rang. It was Ryan.

'Good morning,' she said. 'Anything I should know before seeing Fenwick?'

Devlin felt complicit and looked around instinctively to check that he was alone. 'I was called in to Captain Ravenski. He wanted to know what we'd got. I kept it vague. I didn't mention the mayor, but he told me to keep him in the loop, said there was interest upstairs, meaning Fenwick, I assume. He knew we'd interviewed Gotfelt, by the way. Told me to back off, leave him to you.'

'I like your boss already.'

Devlin told her he was expecting forensics on the brown.

'Great. Every little helps.'

There was a long pause when he asked about her own lab reports, so long that he thought the audio was lost. 'Hello?'

'I'm still here.' And then she said words that Devlin never expected to hear, except as a punchline to a Racy James gag. 'They've lost the body.'

'What?' he laughed incredulously.

'They can't find her at the morgue. It's chaos everywhere these days with the strikes and walkouts and the electric storms screwing up communications. Seems the city's getting as disorganized as the weather.'

Wait until he told Strong. It was good when information made your day before lunch. The warm mood soon disappeared when he called Sylvia. Her vid was switched off. The trace said she was at home. Like hell. Probably eating brown in an alley. He called the school and felt his nerve ends exposed by concern and anger.

'Sylvia is missing very important parts of the syllabus,' admonished the principal. 'I must insist on doctor's certificates. She's skipped chemistry, porn-ed and food coordination today. She still has to pass theory in all of them, however boring. One day she might want to go to university.'

Why not call me a liar to my face, he almost said, but promised to speak with Sylvia again. 'She's been under a lot of stress.' He rubbed his eyes.

'We have counsellors, Mr Devlin. Is it food?'

'I don't think so. We've had the talk. It could be she's just having trouble settling down and misses Baltimore.' He was floundering around the edges of what little he knew about his daughter.

He decided to mention the chocolate. 'One thing, Ms Stevens. I think my daughter is using brown.'

There was a pause. He watched the face at the other end take on a defensive expression.

'I hope you're not suggesting we tolerate food abuse,' she said coolly.

'No, I'm saying there are users and suppliers who get to the kids.'

'Do you have any evidence, Mr Devlin? I have surveillance in every room, including the chapel. There are security patrols. We haven't seen anything, I can assure you. Look, I know how hard things can get. But your daughter's a bright kid, great potential and her body fat grades are excellent. I just don't want to see her blow it all. I expect to see her at rollcall tomorrow.'

'She'll be there,' he promised her. Even if he had to use dragging chains, he promised himself.

13

Strong returned to the precinct late afternoon and stared at her desk, rigid and frowning, as if the meaning of life was lurking somewhere, waiting to be interpreted in its scattered papers.

Devlin watched, curious. He'd not done much since meeting Ravenski and was still trying to process their conversation, search out the risks.

She began to move files, cautiously, as if they were some odd life form, and then with gathering intensity, rifling her in-tray, pulling out the metal drawers. 'Damn,' she said.

'Lost anything?'

'Bowling tonight and I can't find the fixture sheet. It's either the Second Precinct or St Patrick's.'

'Forget about bowling for a minute.'

She stopped, sat down and looked at him. It was no good. 'Here from the well of wisdom that is Matt Devlin is my advice: call your beer buddy Colman.'

Strong brightened. The sun was back. 'Your insights, indeed, know no limits.'

'But not now. Cupid Frish.'

She leaned back hard in the chair, balancing it perilously at forty-five degrees, feet on the desk. 'Go.'

Devlin told her about Ravenski and the vanished body. Strong whistled; a grin played over her face. Out came the toothpick. Then he told her about Fenwick being caught in the investigation and her eyes seemed ready to pop.

'All that tofu and lettuce putting lead in old Fenwick's pencil. I am truly in awe. You know, from the well of wisdom that is Kate Strong, people are not what they seem. Fenwick, your holy guy. And the body. Man, this is the most righteous of days.'

'It's probably just tagged wrong. They'll find it. Listen,' he said, lowering his voice. 'I've promised Ryan our full cooperation in return for a pass on our earlier solo outing.' He looked hard at Strong. 'The emphasis here is on the "our". Ryan is pissed we didn't tell her about Cupid. We need to be more helpful, especially on the brown.'

'Ryan? She'll recover, trust me. We'll turn up a bone to get her tail wagging again. Besides, you think she doesn't ever work alone? Come on. That's how you win prizes.'

'We were out of line and I don't know how I let you talk me into that shit.'

'Sure you do. For the glory, child.'

Devlin told Strong about the trip back to Montcalm Avenue. She listened intently and without interruptions. When he finished, he said: 'I'm heading to the lab, see if I can get anything from Leung.'

There was a moment early on in their relationship when Devlin understood that Strong was embedded in New York City life, with connections rooted firmly in the safety and invisibility of City Hall or the crevices of minor crime. There seemed a limitless supply of contacts in useful places, often relations; people she was careful never to identify by their real names in his hearing. She didn't trust him and he felt it. Just like Sylvia.

Devlin worked through channels; Strong knew the uncharted tributaries. She seemed to enjoy seeing him trapped in the maze of procedures and then picking up the vid herself, covering the screen, to ring 'Party Girl' or 'Beer Boy'. He was supposed to be the boss, but she was in charge.

One tense morning, after a futile attempt to reach the com-missioner's office for a warrant to raid the home of Wayne Fetzler, the Yankee outfielder, his frustration had spilled over. It was a big tip. He was buying brown by the crate, said their informant, mid-grade from England. 'Nuts, raisins, the whole deal,' promised Billy in return for fifty bucks and a big, barely legal, greased breakfast.

But senior agents were unavailable to sign warrants, a trick they pulled if it looked like bad publicity in next day's *New York Post*.

'I think "budget meeting" is code for "fuck off",' Devlin shouted, furious and frustrated, slamming the vid closed for the fifth time.

'Relax. Minx is a Mets fan. She'll work it.' And she did. The raid was perfect – perfectly late. By the time they reached the home, any brown had long gone. Fetzler was waiting by the door with his attorney and personal photographer. Strong asked for his autograph.

'I need you to work your contacts,' Devlin said. 'We need to think hard about who might dump Cupid Frish in an alley dressed in brown; who might spread that kind of money around and why.'

'You don't ask for much now, do you?' Then she let the chair fall to the ground, picking up her vid at the same time, shielding the image from Devlin and turning her back. Their meeting was over.

Ronnie Leung had rooms up flights of wooden stairs that architectural geography said shouldn't be there. They connected to part of an old tenement block taken over by the department during expansion.

He was tall for an Asian, mocking and twinkling. He and Devlin got on fine. They were both outsiders. Leung had transferred from the FBI in Seattle and didn't get invited to Strong's bonding nights either. Devlin felt this particular exclusion at least bonded them. He peered through the glass door before knocking firmly. Leung beckoned, then bent over a polished metal table and whatever he was picking at with a spatula. It looked like pepperoni.

'Agent Devlin. You early.'

'Heat from the seventh floor's burning my ass, I'm here to cool off. Fenwick's taken a personal interest in this one.'

'Really?' Leung's face brightened.

Devlin decided to give him a morsel, but not too much. 'Seems he knew the deceased.'

Leung raised an eyebrow.

'But we don't know in what capacity,' Devlin added diplomatically.

'Wonder why fifty-five-year-old man know twenty-four-year-old. Maybe they discuss world peace and angry clouds, Agent Devlin?'

'A lot of people do. What you got?'

Leung held a diploma in chocolate tasting, which meant he could blind-taste his way around most of the world's varieties, and could also guess, within 5 percentage points, the purity of the cocoa. He hated the mass-produced matter from Europe that called itself chocolate, but which were adulterated with sugars, milks and vegetable f*ts to reduce the amount of cocoa needed and, instead of snapping crisply when broken, came apart without a sound.

'Brown is unusual pure, probably Venezuela. Definitely not Ecuador, although quite similar. Some of best I seen. Very expensive, well refined. Porcelana. You know it? Cost lot of money. No corruption with dairy or vegetable f*ts. Very little flaking, so not old. Would say probably made in last three months max. Travelled well. Kept in good conditions.' He folded his arms, pleased with himself.

'Thanks, Ronnie. Good job.' Porcelana. It was for the rich and feckless. Small fifty-gramme bars had a street value of $1,500. Less than 5 per cent of global chocolate production came from Criollo cocoa beans, a South American variety, and less than 5 per cent of that from the Porcelana strain. They grew it exclusively north-west of Caracas. Devlin had tasted some at the academy. It had a distinctive, naturally sweet taste tinged with hazelnut that users craved.

'This dangerous good, Agent Devlin,' Leung said, suddenly serious. 'More than 80 per cent cocoa butter very rare shit. Twice normal amount. This 100 per cent. Someone spend a lot dressing this broad. Be careful.' Then he cackled. 'Cheaper go Barneys buy Chanel dress. Hey, you going Strong Night tonight?'

'No. You?'

'Sure. She invite me.'

'She did?' Devlin barely hid his surprise. 'Well, that's great. I guess she gets enough of me during the day. But have a good one. I'm kind of busy anyway, doing the Dad thing.'

'Ah yes. Children. Love them, but not eat whole one.' He turned back to his desk shaking with pleasure and cackling over his exhumation from the joke crypt.

'I could,' Devlin said under his breath. He had been trying to call her intermittently, pathologically, since the morning. Eventually, he found she was with Alice at Raoul's, the dope and coffee shop at the end of their street. Alice never left home without her vidphone. Devlin called her instead and put a trace on it. Now that was one good kid.

He went back to the office, but thinking more about Sylvia than what Leung had told him.

Strong was leaning back on her ever-forgiving chair, feet resting on the desk. 'Any news from Mr Magoo?'

'Some. Reckons he's got a fix. Just what we thought: high grade. Porcelana from Venezuela, which rules out the street dealers. He reckons it's fresh, probably came into town in the last three months. We should hit the boutique shippers.'

Strong was rolling a pencil stub between the fingers of her left hand. Devlin had never known anybody who needed to keep their hands moving so constantly.

'You?' he said.

'Killing Joke over in Vice says our angel worked an eateasy on Bleaker. Some place called Atom's.'

'The vegetarian joint that gets all the awards?' Devlin was puzzled.

'No, another Atom's,' Strong winked, sly with pleasure. 'This one is buried and you never get to read about it, so KJ says. It's just a block from where they found Cupid doll.' She leaned forward. 'And get this. Big shots go there for rare brown, the purest of the pure. It's all word of mouth, smart mouths that keep shut, which is why we ain't even heard of it. Bet they got Porcelana.' She paused and smiled. 'I feel a bust coming on. I can see the headlines now. What I wouldn't give to arrest the chief.'

'What chief?' Devlin asked.

'Any chief.'

'No. A bust would scare everyone out of the undergrowth. We should be more subtle; go in, talk with the owner, see if we can trade a blind eye for information, don't you think? Ravenski doesn't want waves and we should cut Ryan in.' He picked up his vid.

93

'Whoa,' said Strong. 'Let's just consider that, shall we? "Cut Ryan in." Why? So she can grab another commendation?'

'I'm not going for medals any more.'

'Gotfelt wasn't a lead, man. We were just cruising around, finding our feet, getting in a little practice. This is the entrée and we got it during our normal inquiries, food inquiries. Imagine how grateful Ryan is going to be when we hand over a suspect. You can forget about being reported. New guy like yourself, that would be good news.'

She was needling and persuasive. Devlin couldn't put his finger on it, but it was a tick Strong had about trouble. Most people stepped across the street to avoid it; she seemed to honk her horn and drive right in just as fast as she could ratchet through the gears. Generally trouble got out of the way, but not always.

'Come on. This is what we do, bust eateasys. We got every right to go there, more than Ryan. We know the score, what to look for, got the tip. If Homicide go in, you just know that eateasy will shut down and be out of state before they even find the grease trays.' She raised her hands and clicked the thumbs and fingers of both for emphasis. 'Gone. This guy's our bust. I'm handing over my best lead to them? No way.' She angled her head at the window towards Police Plaza. 'This is our smoke-out, partner. We got a right to pursue inquiries. I ain't being rolled over by Homicide and you shouldn't be either.'

Devlin let his hand hover over the disconnect button. Ryan would be on her way to interview Commissioner Fenwick, so they needed to make a decision. Strong was giving an obedient look, but he could tell she was prepared to uncoil. 'Shit,' Devlin said as his contribution to rational argument. 'Let's do it.'

14

Strong had a predilection for Hawaiian shirts and wore a lurid example of the genre to celebrate their trip to Atom's. Dusky maidens garlanded with leis of purple flowers were somehow joined in a tableau of surfboards, barbecues, missiles, volcanic eruptions and pineapples.

Devlin knew all this because when Strong took the wheel it was generally best not to keep an eye on the road. Driving was an extension of pinball to her. You had to bump a few things to make the game worth playing. She already had three endorsements for hitting humonsters. Another two and she could be banned for six months.

'Have you ever tried driving slowly?' Devlin asked. 'Just to get the contrast.'

Strong peered quizzically at him. 'Where *is* your sense of adventure?' She turned sharply up Twenty-Seventh Street, tutting to herself. 'Man, I bet your memoires would make a dull read on a wet Sunday.'

They arrived intact.

A waitress came over as soon as they walked through the glass door into the modern, steel and glass interior. 'Table for two?'

Devlin flashed his badge. 'Health Enforcement. Luther Atom around?'

'Certainly. Please wait here.'

Devlin watched as the small frame of a fragile man, his face kubaki pale, weaved between the tables a few minutes later.

'Luther Atom,' he announced in a rueful monotone, a hand outstretched several yards before reaching them. Devlin automatically took the limp proboscis and made formal introductions, although Strong had moved outside shaking distance and was looking around the restaurant, studying its contours with alert eyes.

'It's been a while since I had the pleasure of Health Enforcement agents visit my place,' said Atom, looking at Devlin as if the word pleasure was, in this instance, a regrettable medical condition. 'Now I get two. How can I help?' Devlin asked for somewhere private and they were led through a side door to a sitting room. There were armchairs, three-seat divans and coffee tables piled with the latest magazines.

'Like a doctor's,' said Strong, looking intently at the wood-panelled wall. 'Only cheaper.' She walked to a far wall and began searching for stresses and inconsistencies, hairline fractures in the wood, the clues to hidden entrances, recessed hinges and handles. She tapped the walls gently. 'Don't mind me. You two go right ahead,' she said.

'Mr Atom, we're investigating the death of a woman named Cupid Frish, a hooker,' said Devlin politely. 'She was found in an alley near here over the weekend.'

'I heard. Bad business.' Atom screwed his face into sincerity. 'Still, at least her modesty was, well, looked after. I mean, it could have been worse.'

'Not much, Mr Atom. We think she was murdered. Did you know her?' Devlin asked.

Atom sighed. 'No. But to anticipate your next question, I couldn't say for sure that she hasn't been into my restaurant. It's very popu—' he never finished the word, because at that moment Strong let out a triumphant 'Got you'. A huge grin spread across her face.

'What might be behind here, Mr Atom?' she asked.

'It's a cavity. Old brick, I'd guess. Let your imagination run hog-wild.'

'Really?' said Strong, sucking on a toothpick. 'A cavity, you say? And it's so hard to get closet space in this city. Ain't you lucky to have so much you can block it up.'

'I put the panels in a year ago. More classy than bare brick, at least according to *Good Housekeeping* magazine.'

'Tell you what, Mr Atom. You want to open this, or shall I break it down?'

'Or shall I ask for a warrant?'

'Oh, we don't need a warrant,' Devlin said, because he knew the manual. 'Not if we suspect an eateasy is being run back there.'

Luther Atom laughed and looked shocked. 'An eateasy? Here? Please. This is the top-rated vegetarian restaurant in the city. You think I'd risk an illegal eating den, given the traffic I get?' He shook his head from side to side. 'You're nuts. I got Zagat stars.'

Strong was running her hands firmly over the panels and making 'uh huh' noises, the doctor tapping a chest for signs of sickness.

'It's good, very accomplished,' she said finally. 'In fact, this is maybe the best I've ever seen. My compliments to your carpenter, Mr Atom. In fact, this is so darn good I need the big S. Uno momento.'

Devlin looked at Atom, who in turn looked puzzled.

'Sledgehammer,' Devlin explained. 'It's what she calls it, the Big S.'

'You're making a mistake,' Atom said quietly, almost regretfully. 'I hate to say this, but I am a personal friend of the Health Commissioner. He eats here. Ratatouille, made with olive oil and slow-cooked for twenty-four hours.' He looked at Devlin. 'That's the secret to good ratatouille, by the way.'

'Thanks for the tip. What's behind the panel? It could save a lot of noise and mess.'

'Like I said, bricks, mortar. Excuse me, please.'

He pulled out his vid and pressed speed dial. 'Bo? I got Health Enforcement here, a Devlin and Strong, and they're about to bust down a wall to look for an eateasy . . . Yeah, you can imagine my outrage. I'll pass you over.' He handed the vid to Devlin. 'Bo Watz, my attorney. He does my outrage.'

A round, pocked streetfighter face stared at Devlin, who identified himself. 'I represent Mr Atom,' said Watz. 'Do you have a warrant?'

'No, and I don't need one. We believe an illegal eating den is operating here.'

'Probable cause, Agent Devlin? Luther Atom is a legal and successful businessman, a highly respected member of the community, a supporter of the mayor,' and so it went on, a full three minutes of bluster before Watz must have reckoned he had earned his five hundred dollars.

Strong was back. She looked at Devlin. He looked at Watz, who promised to sue if they went near that wall without a warrant. 'Sue ahead, counsellor,' Devlin said firmly. Strong was sure; that was good enough for him. She was better at this than judging weight abusers.

He handed the vid back to Atom and nodded at Strong, who smiled and took a fairground swing at the panel, then another and a third before it splintered apart in a high-pitched, screaming crack. Devlin took out his torch. Atom was holding the vid so that Watz stared at the same wrenched hole, at the promised bricks and mortar. Devlin felt his stomach sink and looked at Strong. Her lips were taut. Some waiters were at the doorway, drawn by the noise.

Atom broke the silence, sounding conversational. 'That was piranha pine, by the way. It comes up from South America, the rainforest. Very expensive on account of its rarity. You got good savings?' He shrugged. 'I do hope so. Well, I guess that concludes our business for now. Bo Watz will be in touch, won't you, Bo?' He turned off the vid before Watz could earn any more.

Ryan would be furious. Fenwick would be apoplectic. Ravenski. It was too terrible to imagine. But there was no turning back. Somebody once said attack was the best form of defence. They were wrong, Devlin knew. He'd gone through a divorce. 'It seems we made a mistake, Mr Atom, based on bad information, and we'll take the heat. But we still need to talk to you about Cupid Frish.'

'You do? Because she turns up a block away from my front door? I mean, what are you guys? F*t cops, for chrissake? Since when did you people get involved with crime anyway, real crime, I mean? Next time get me a detective. They do the courtesy of asking questions before they start demolishing property; at least they did in my day. There used to be,' he paused and looked up, scrunching his rheumy eyes as if to recall a distant memory, 'yes that's it. Evidence. Look it up in the handbook, son.'

'We're not related and you might just want to ponder the

consequences of not cooperating,' Devlin said stiffly, part of what he hoped was a managed retreat.

'Not cooperating,' Atom repeated slowly, looking at the shattered wall. 'Agent Devlin, we've never met until today. You turn up, no call or nothing, and next thing a hammer is swinging and you're suggesting I may have information about some dead broad just because she turns up in the neighbourhood. This is not friendly.'

'We made a mistake, Mr Atom, a bad one and there will, I'm sure, be some kind of hell to pay that will include a shipment of piranha pine,' said Devlin. 'But that's no reason for you to make a mistake.'

Atom looked at Devlin, a poker player studying his opponent before making the next move. He raised.

'A mistake? If I were you, I'd be leaving now, quietly, barely putting a dent in the air, praying it was all just a bad dream.'

He gently led them to the door into the restaurant and raised one finger theatrically to his lips as the sea of staff parted. Customers craned their necks to watch. No more words were spoken and Devlin looked straight ahead as they walked out. Strong followed, but turned at the front door and pointed a thumb and two fingers like a cocked pistol.

'Hey, Luther Atom. We'll be seeing you. Count on it.'

Devlin drove slowly and politely through the traffic, in no rush to reach Downtown and Consequences. Strong was uncharacteristically quiet. Even her hands were stilled, subdued by failure.

'Damn,' she said, punching the dashboard angrily.

'Damned might be more accurate.' Devlin impatiently signalled an old lady to cross, illegally, in front of them, her electronic dog moving arthritically slowly, an early Sony, before seizing up entirely in the middle of the lane.

'Rust,' said Devlin.

'Probably, yeah.'

'We should have got a warrant, some authorization.' Devlin watched the dog move forward again after a kick from its owner.

Strong shook her head. 'I don't understand. KJ knows this shit. It can't be wrong. Makes no sense.'

'What are we going to tell Ryan? Ravenski?' Devlin wondered aloud, feeling what few fingers they had holding on to the case slipping from the ledge and sending them into freefall. Two leads. Two screw-ups. He wouldn't trust them any more, either. He looked at Strong. She looked back.

'Let's eat,' she said firmly. 'And make it dangerous. Joey's.'

For once Devlin agreed and made a noisy U-turn, turned on the siren and drove back uptown, nearly hitting the dog he'd just waved across, watching it in the rear-view tip over, as he roared along Ninth Avenue.

'What exactly was Classic Coke?' Sylvia had asked.

'Well, it was a very sweet drink that just about everyone used, and several times a day.'

'No way. I mean, was it legal and everything?' She sounded deliciously scandalized.

Devlin smiled. 'Sure. It was like a virus. You could get it at gas stations, delis, health clubs, churches, schools, movie theatres. It was everywhere. By the end, they'd even got it in sponsored water fountains and coolers. In fact, some folk had a tap fitted to sinks in the kitchen. Hot, Cold, Coke.'

'Wow. Like amphetamines?'

'Exactly. Way back, it was even sold as medicine.'

Sylvia laughed before asking whether he'd ever used. Sure. It was fine. Everybody did. It was cool.

Devlin was about eleven when traditional colas were banned, one of the first to go and a big victory for the Anti-F*t League. Of course, they still made diet versions, but not The Real Thing. Well, they still made it, but only for Third World countries, bits of United Europe, certainly Scotland and – where was it – Litvia? Latvia? Some place on the retirement cruises, anyway.

He was telling Strong about Sylvia's surprise and that conversation, just to give them both a distraction. But his mind was thinking about Frish and how the day they pulled her over had been good, a quota buster. They even got some arbuckle in a Merc who said he was an engineer and knew the fergie was fixed.

'Yeah, yeah,' Devlin had replied, handing him a ticket and slapping a biological hazard sticker on his overcoat, for good measure and the lip. He was eighteen pounds over and turned out to be a serial violator.

The smart, tailored suit wasn't smart enough; Devlin made the call as soon as he saw him coming out of the park, pleased at his recognition skills. Adapted clothing makers advertised all the time, but Strong was usually best at spotting them. 'Look legal and stylish,' boasted one in the *New York Times*. It was there every week, bold as brass. And it was hard to pick one out on the sidewalks. Even Strong was impressed.

The man was bound to appeal, giving Devlin a long, slow morning in a court waiting room. Arbuckles always did; anything to avoid the criminal records that meant health insurance premiums nearly doubling, if they could get cover at all. Either way it was trouble, involving proof of exercise and liver function and there were big co-payments on any future claims. Some insurers sent food adjustors on random inspections to homes. But it was worth the paperwork, Devlin thought, not least because, for a fleeting moment on that day, he felt approval from Strong. Respect, even; a kind of acceptance.

Joey's was not on Devlin's approved list, but they had a deal, Strong's idea. Half the shifts they went to her diner and he picked a salad, the other half they went to Devlin's favourite, usually Cell-U-Lite on Madison, and she grumbled.

Joe Papadouris welcomed them with thick, open arms. But he was Greek. His apron looked as if it was cleaned sometime when mammoths stopped being served in the last Ice Age. 'My friend. It's been too long,' he said to Strong, embracing her. This was probably code for more than three days. He shook Devlin's hand more formally.

'Yeah, Joey, always,' said Strong, poking him teasingly in the stomach. 'You're lucky we ain't on duty, man. You'd fail my fergie for sure.' They both laughed and Strong asked how he was doing.

Joey shrugged his shoulders and did a million small things which seemed to say not good, not bad, fine.

After Joey left with their orders, they raked over the raid. It should have been straightforward and the tip-off seemed flawless, even if they did miss the warning signs. Luther Atom's rap sheet stank of smart lawyers and pulled-in favours.

'Former cops, always the worst,' Strong said. And you should know, Devlin thought to himself. He couldn't fault the connection: a dead prostitute covered in brown dumped yards from an eateasy where they probably served it was too much of a coincidence. Strong was right. But only if there was an eateasy.

Atom had been arrested a dozen times by Enforcement agents or the FBI, usually for running illegal eat-ins near Woodstock, raves and food orgies deep in the tree-covered hills. For a while he was Mr Food Impresario when the new laws came in. But there was no mention of an eateasy in the file.

Strong had ordered a vanilla milkshake and a creamy, spiced goulash that arrived bubbling at the table. Pieces of chorizo, smoked bacon, ham hocks and black pudding floated, jostling with peas and some other, indeterminate, vegetables. Joey said it was Cuban fabada, a slow-cooked casserole of white beans, and that the secret was in the garlic, smoked paprika and olive oil.

Devlin had pitta bread, fat-free humus and salad.

'You dating?' Strong asked through a full mouth.

'Not competitively,' Devlin replied, shutting her down. Not that the interest seemed more than passing. She knew little about him and the ignorance was mutual. Strong ate spice, he preferred plain; they knew that much about each other, and to ask about her love life was to invite a question back and it wasn't worth the intrusion. He knew enough. She was a discarder, not an acquirer, mating the same way as a black widow spider. Maybe she didn't eat her sexual conquests, but he was pretty certain she didn't cook them breakfast either.

They sat in a cautious silence. Strong ate noisily, relishing the feast.

'You're going to have to watch yourself,' Devlin scolded. 'When's your next assessment?'

'Man, you did study the manual. November.' She smiled. 'I'll pass and get the full 4 per cent pay rise next year, don't worry.'

'I'm not. Another conveniently employed cousin to guarantee that low index?'

She looked pained. 'Thermo-powered metabolism. Although, as it happens, a nephew has just transferred to Intestinal Affairs.' A look of rapture spread across her face. 'Coca-Cola.' She lowered her fork, determined to give the word full attention, puckering that small, sharp nose at the memory, as if recollecting a shared miracle they had both witnessed at some long-abandoned grotto.

'I used to drink Coke all the time. Imagine that? In school, can you believe?' She laughed.

Devlin smiled. It did seem outlandish.

'Then those religious creeps gotta hold of it,' she said, scowling the way storytellers do when they get to the wicked witch or the ogre.

'If you mean the Anti-F*t League, we owe them. It was the right thing to do and they weren't all religious, for your information,' Devlin insisted sharply. 'Come on; if it wasn't for their courage, we'd all be humonsters, eating ourselves to diabetes and death, paying even more taxes. I mean, look what they were up against; all that corporate power. It took a lot of nerve to take on Big Junk. Control is people power. Democracy in action.'

She snorted. 'Democracy my ass. Self-righteous killjoys, is all. Thin and mad, or f*t and looking for someone to blame; like life is this big bad thing you got to squeeze dry. God forbid we have a good time. How come there's always somebody wants to put up a big stop sign? Life is about greed, Devlin. Din is a calculation, not an impulse. Always has been, always will be. Don't you get it? Ain't natural otherwise. Greed's what gives us a reason to work every day.' She leaned towards him, jabbing her fork. 'There'll still be greed and need long after you and I are recycled.'

'Hey,' he said.

'No, hear me out. Why do we go to work every day? I'll tell you: for money, which is greed, right? Because it gives us pleasure, buys us life's diversions. Remember when pleasure was the thing, the shining star on the horizon? Then we screwed it all up and let health become the thing, like eternal life is hidden in a mushroom or a pill or a stretch.' She snorted. 'But, hey, that's just me.'

Strong and Devlin disagreed volubly about the food laws and the Founding Eaters within hours of being posted together. If they made it compulsory to eat cheeseburgers, he'd bet Strong would be first to refuse. Ding-ding. They went eight rounds in that one shift.

They'd been in Yonkers, patrolling the turnpike and trying to shake off a green, purple cloud that hung over the car. There were a couple of dozen in the city that day. Theirs eventually picked up an old truck and headed back into town.

Devlin felt Strong was only arguing because she resented him, the outsider with promotion, and, somehow, he had ended up telling her to take the tests. The advice went down badly.

'I do enforcement, not ingredients, okay?' she replied. 'All this? It's a job with good benefits. I don't give a fly's fart for the food freaks, okay? I'd hate you to confuse me with somebody who actually gives a damn. Just so we're clear.'

'Fine. I hear you. All I'm saying is go to calorie-induction, lick a little butt in the office and you may be surprised where it leads you.'

'I'm everywhere I need to be,' she replied and they had spent the rest of that shift in an awkward, spent silence.

It was a paradox Devlin often wrestled to understand, that a woman who hated being told what to do, who relished needling bosses, should end up in Health Enforcement at all. But he soon gave up trying to work it out. There was some kind of anger hidden behind the teasing, distant laughter. He knew she liked the perks, which if you found them in Enforcement were certainly illegal. Maybe that was her rush? Beating the system. Devlin turned a blind eye. If they arrested an arbuckle with a kilo of brown, half disappeared before it got bagged, tagged and back to headquarters.

There was still enough left to make convictions. 'So? I like consuming,' she'd say, bugging out her eyes. 'You should see my credit cards, maxed out. Live to the limit. You should try.'

'I've got responsibilities.'

'I forgot.' She laughed.

He knew. They often scammed, the career cops who made the switch, usually burned out or stalled, and it wasn't a wholesome relationship between Homicide and Health, but one of solid and mutual disrespect. The departments rarely worked together. They did conventional crime, Health stuck to food abuse, pulling up arbuckles and breaking smuggling operations.

Health knew Police Plaza was a sieve, leaking tips and protecting eateasys. Half the force visited them, stoking up on imported burgers, the unregulated kind oozing f*t, additives and forbidden preservatives.

'What you up to this weekend?' Devlin asked as Strong wiped bread around the smear of fabada left on her plate.

'I'll watch the game. Some of the guys are coming over. You? No, wait. Let me guess. Prayercise. A salad orgy, tossing back the old sparkly apple-lite like there was no tomorrow. Am I close?' Her face stared rapt with mock interest.

'Sylvia's got hip-hop in the morning and we're going to the Body Images exhibition at the Guggenheim.' Devlin wasn't going to tell her about his plans to visit an eating therapist. 'You should check it out. It shows what happens to people who abuse themselves, the illnesses, the unhappiness.'

Strong was enjoying herself. 'Yeah? I might have a powered-up burger on the way, at a little eateasy on Canal; chow down on all that unhappiness and remember what it was like to die after a life of pleasure instead of without one.'

'When you have a kid you'll understand,' Devlin threw back. 'You want them to have all the eternity you can pull together, believe me.'

Strong levelled her gaze. 'Want my honest opinion?'

'I'll take it over any dishonest ones you're selling.'

'I think people should make their own choices, do what they

want. What are we living for? Just to notch up another year? Of what?' She prodded the air with her fork. 'Food don't kill you, it's natural.'

'It was,' Devlin fired into the gap, before she could start talking about 'fruits of the earth' and 'Thanksgivings piled high with pies and meats', 'harvest suppers'. That part always irked him. He knew Strong never went to church.

But Devlin did, and he had memorized a *Time* magazine story, ammunition for just this sort of skirmish.

'Before Control, 75 per cent of children were obese. Little League baseball couldn't find enough players fit enough to last eleven innings. Baseball, for pity's sake, a game where nobody moves anyway unless it's to scratch an itch.'

Normally they stayed off the subject; it was easier that way.

Then Devlin's vid went off and he looked at the number. Headquarters. Not yet. He was too pumped up and ignored it, staring out of the restaurant window, at lives rushing past, at children on the corner lighting joints. He wanted suddenly to call Sylvia, see if she was home.

'Ravenski will go nuts,' Strong said with evident relish. 'He hates not knowing about high-profile busts.'

'Thanks. Keep throwing out those encouraging thoughts.'

'I bet that ball-busting lawyer has filed a complaint already and our very own Captain Cautious will have the blood-red carpet waiting for us when we get back. You'll see.' She chuckled.

Strong was like those ancient Greeks, thought Devlin: eager to laugh in the face of catastrophe. Devlin wondered why she even started breaking down that wall, turning a routine inquiry into a major rumble. Perhaps she got a kick out of discomfort, never happier than when winking back at the eye of the storm.

'Don't you ever worry about losing your job?' he asked curiously. Everybody had responsibilities. Fears. Even Strong.

'Nope. My guy never makes mistakes, trust me. I'll call him now. There'll be an explanation for this unexpected turn of events.' Strong never got the chance to call. Both their vids went off. Ravenski's name flashed. There was no ignoring it this time.

'Back here now.' The tone and curt message made it clear that the now in question was five minutes ago. 'Both of you.'

It was a bright-sky afternoon. The sun poured into Health Plaza and it was nearly a natural yellow; stunted, half-grown maples cast dappled shadows on the wide paved concourse and its borders of blooming myrtle trees. Devlin parked across the street from the main entrance. He didn't want to use the underground car park. They flicked badges at the security kiosk and walked across the square, passing friezes of heroic eaters, their mouths poised over vegetables as hands held axes and computers; young and whole-some, eater and eaten. The men had solid farm faces and broad arms; the women featured perky French Revolution breasts, like the ones in paintings at the Met.

Ravenski was waiting.

'Sit.'

Strong slouched in a chair, legs splayed, challenging.

'I've had Bo Watz, the attorney, on the vid. He tells me you raided the restaurant run by his client, and the commissioner's golfing partner, Mr Luther Atom.'

Strong and Devlin looked at each other. Devlin opened his mouth to speak, just in case Strong decided to open hers.

'Sure, we got a tip Atom was operating an eateasy,' Devlin said. 'It came from a good source. We decided to act immediately because his place is a spit from where Cupid Frish was found.'

'And what did you discover?' Ravenski had arched his hands together and looked blankly at the far wall.

'Nothing exactly.'

He repeated each word as if they were rare curiosities. 'Nothing. Exactly. I would say that was an understatement, wouldn't you?' He rose from his chair. 'Let me help. You found waves, large drowning ones, those ones I warned you about.'

'Well, I –'

'Now I wouldn't mind if judgement was at work here,' he interrupted. 'Any judgement, a twelve-year-old's. Let me spell it out for you. We enforce health standards. We ensure that the bad guys don't smuggle food and make the citizens unhealthy.

We protect the people from themselves and see them served good, wholesome produce. That's why the motto says "Protect and Serve Lite". It's on the side of your patrol car, in case you'd forgotten.'

Devlin opened his mouth, but Ravenski raised a hand to silence him.

'Occasionally, very occasionally, we might be asked to assist Homicide while they, and I mean they, work out with diligence and expertise who did the foul deed.'

He paused and looked at Devlin. 'We don't seek thunderstorms through our own incompetence, especially by wandering into areas where we have no remit or skills. We can't afford the sort of misjudgement you and your partner made today, harassing a donor to the mayoral campaign and, Lord, taking a hammer to his walls.'

Strong was sitting motionless, hands clenched and Devlin was grateful for that at least.

'They are angry at Homicide,' Ravenski went on. 'No, let me rephrase that. They are furious. And me? I am beyond rage and in another place entirely. I should take your badges and make you eat them.'

'Sir, I would have told Detective Ryan what we were doing, I just wanted to check it out –' Devlin could hear the desperation in his voice, '– before wasting her time. We've got the contacts and figured it was our tip-off, that we could go in there, shake the owner up and report back.'

Ravenski loosened his collar.

'No, Agent Devlin, you went for yourself, for a piece of the action, because that is why you transferred here in the first place. And you failed miserably, badly and incompetently. Tell me, what is this compulsion to prove that you're not still in Baltimore?'

Devlin felt himself redden.

'Detective Ryan is here at the moment, in fact,' Ravenski continued. 'With the commissioner. She's already filed a complaint. I don't have any choice.'

'Sir?'

'You're off the case. I'm assigning Dolby and Mailer to liaise. They're experienced and reliable. I want you back on the expressway tomorrow.'

'But –'

'You're all out of buts, Devlin.'

Ravenski's voice returned to an almost human wrath.

'What have you got to say for yourself?' he asked, turning to face Strong. Devlin prayed the answer was nothing.

'Always hated that game, Captain.'

'What?' said Ravenski, confused.

'Golf.'

Devlin rose and hustled Strong ahead of him.

'That man truly is a world-beating asshole with a poor disposition,' she tutted as they walked back to their desks, barely out of earshot.

'Well, he's right about one thing. We did screw up.' It had been stupid not to call Ryan, especially after Gringos and all his promises. Devlin knew this. But Strong was right, too. Ryan never would have let them shake down Atom. Shake down? That was a joke. He'd shown them the door and they had nothing to show for it.

His vid rang. It was Sylvia.

'Where have you been?' he said in a tone that mixed anger and relief, mostly anger because at that moment a target was useful.

'Hey, calm down, Dad. I've been with Alice. She's sick and couldn't go into school today. I'm working with her at home. We've logged into classes all day. Check the downloads.'

'I might just do that, young lady. I've been trying to get you for hours.'

'I went with her to the doctor's, okay, and we've been at her place ever since. She's got a stomach bug.'

'Then how come your vid was off?' he asked, suspicious. 'I had no idea where you were. I hate vanishing acts.'

'Hey, smoke a joint. We had to turn it off in the waiting room and I must have forgotten. Listen, I gotta go. Porn-ed in two minutes. Love you.'

'Kids,' Strong said. 'You don't trust her too much, do you?'

'I worry. There's a difference.'

'Not always. You can never have enough problems in life, I say.'

'Think so?'

'I called my contact and he swears there is an eateasy at Atom's.' Devlin wasn't convinced. Not that it mattered. They were off the case, he reminded her.

'Now that pisses me off?' said Strong.

'Low-cal cheese? F*t education classes?'

'That Atom guy knows more than he's giving up. Dead woman turns up near an eateasy –'

'Alleged eateasy,' Devlin interrupted.

'– big shot with connections and he only reads about it in the newspaper? I don't think so.'

'No? You don't think, period. We're in a fucking swamp because you can't resist doing the exact, precise opposite of what you're told.'

She looked at Devlin, unshaken, a small smile playing across her face. 'Trust me, partner. It's the secret to all the best relationships. You need to get yourself one of those, incidentally. You are definitely uptight.'

15

It was easy for Strong. She could crash on her Lay-z-Boy, switch the game on and tune people out. Not Devlin. He worried, about Sylvia especially, the only precious relationship he could claim; his singular responsibility and achievement. But their lives were becoming choreographed separation. Sylvia was out. He was out. She was in. He was in the other room. They were turning into exiles, but not the kind who talked at breakfast, more those bound by fraying ropes over a chasm. Everything was wrong and worth fighting over: food, him, politics. She never said 'let's go to the movies' or 'thanks' and he felt sad.

His work shifts were getting longer and that didn't help. Sylvia had a mother, too, but only biologically. Devlin drove over when she forgot that last birthday and strode in without calling first. The new husband stood gaping. Jennifer gave him a hundred dollars to give their child, but he bought the card. A week later, one cold autumn day, he decided to leave Baltimore and the memory of a marriage, to pursue his career in a bigger city agency and give Sylvia distraction and opportunity. He applied through internal channels and New York came up within the week. He still wondered what kind of parent leaves a colonial-style house, with four acres and friendly neighbours, for a cramped two-bedroom walk-up on the Lower East Side of Insanity. The traffic was constant, echoing from streets filled with lives indifferent to his own. Neither of them slept properly. Maybe that was why they argued, though you couldn't blame insomnia for everything.

He liked to think of her as bright and stubborn, not undisciplined and lacking motivation. Sylvia had been a straight A student in Baltimore, but was now a borderline B. She scornfully described her teachers as 'forty-thirds' when he raised the poor reports. Devlin considered it disrespectful and rude, a slur on the old President, so they argued about that, too.

Sylvia skipped classes and wandered the streets. He tracked her mobile vidphone all the time, obsessively, which is why she left it turned off or wore vintage clothes, those ones without chip implants.

His child was on the cusp of knowledge and that was part of the frustration. He might say: 'If you don't get yourself an education you'll end up with some crap job, you'll have no choices in life, young lady.'

And she would now reply with whip-crack speed: 'Like you.' But he had made choices, all of them, since his bad one, giving up education. He'd met Jennifer when they were both twenty. Sylvia was conceived their second year in college and fifth night together. Devlin believed he was giving up his studies for love, only it turned out he was just giving them up. Jennifer continued with her degree and sent him out to work.

'It makes sense, babe,' she'd said, stroking his hair in a tender way. 'I'll qualify, get a good hospital consultancy, and then you can go back to study.'

The words sounded good, only they didn't stay together and she walked out on him for a plastic surgeon with prospects, leaving him the baby with diapers. Instead of a degree, he joined Health Enforcement, hoping to trade a few years tracking arbuckles into a real city police job.

None of his hopes had been realized. But that was life; the gradual shedding of ambition. You start wanting to save the planet and end up writing letters about dog shit to the local newspaper.

Sylvia somehow sensed it all, slamming his hurts together into one critical mass wherever she could find them. 'It's not my fault you're single, Dad. That's you, not me.'

She'd storm out, slamming the door, and he would drop his head.

Devlin had started going to Christ the Fit for meaning, and for help with the brown cravings that came with stress and the job of resisting temptation every single day. He wasn't religious and one thing he liked about the new Christianity was the small part faith seemed to play. The Saturday communion was a perfect purging. The church had social evenings, too. Reverend Instructor Fisher was liberal and it had a mixed congregation; several guilty of size trying to comply with exemption orders were made to feel quite welcome. Devlin liked that, not living in one of those weight-segregated communities where humonsters were excluded, left to live and shop together.

Confession came after the spin class at midday. 'Forgive me, Father, for I have eaten,' Devlin said quickly, making the sign of the cross.

'The Lord is bountiful and it is ours to choose wisely,' Instructor Fisher replied as required.

'I'm having trouble with Sylvia, my daughter. She's missing classes at school and I'm worried about not being there for her, putting in the time.'

'Why do you feel that?'

'I'm with Health Enforcement. The hours are crazy and I guess I've been concentrating on the job. It's new, tougher than I expected.'

'Yours is fine work, a calling even.'

'Sylvia doesn't think so.'

'She's young, rebellious. That's the sign of a healthy mind. It's a stage they go through. Believe me, mine are there. They think I exist solely to deny them pleasure. We're not on the cool side of Control.'

'You can say that again, Instructor.'

'Give it time. Give her time. She'll come around. You're still her father. How is your love life, by the way?'

'Non-existent.'

'Are you taking exercise outside of services?'

'Yes.'

'Good.'

Devlin wished Strong had children; it would have been good to talk about Sylvia with her, to get a female perspective on his parenting anxieties. He tried once, during those optimistic early weeks, only to be rebuffed with a joke about how they should be the next thing Congress banned.

Ryan was standing beside a car outside the apartment block, under a lamp near the moss-hung oak. The air was damp, fecund and filled with the sound of cicadas. Devlin didn't want to see her and said nothing. He juggled his keys. She stood impassive.

'It's okay. Don't move,' he said as a bag slipped and fell, spilling on to the steps, bowling groceries down the concrete stoop. She picked up a cantaloupe that rolled to her shoe.

'What can I do for you, Detective?' he asked.

'A lot less than you have been,' Ryan replied smartly, throwing back the fruit.

'Don't worry, we're off the case. You've got Mailer and Dolby now. They do what they're told.' He was feeling sorry for himself and knew it probably wasn't pretty. 'So?'

Thunder rolled across the skies and rain smashed and dimpled the sidewalk. She turned up a coat collar but Devlin wasn't going to invite her up. Out of the corner of his eye he saw a rat scuttle, hunched, for the cover of a trash pile. Rain was an equal opportunity annoyance.

'I'm busy, Detective, and it's raining.'

She looked at him. 'Just tell me this: why in the name of Jesus and Mary didn't you say you were heading over to see Luther Atom? We had a deal.'

'You were interviewing Fenwick and I thought . . .'

'That you and Strong would go bust the case wide open, solve the crime, beat the dumb cops. Luther Atom? Have you any idea how connected that man is? Did you even bother to check?'

'It was Strong's tip. She's kind of possessive. We do have eateasy experience, in case you'd forgotten. We thought finding it would be leverage to find out what he knew about Frish.'

Ryan snorted. 'Strong again. She's got you wrapped tight. And you didn't bust it, did you? We've got about as much leverage with Luther Atom now as a mouse snapped in a trap. He's been calling just about everyone from the mayor down complaining about harassment.'

'I don't need permission to bust eateasys.'

'No? But don't you just wish you'd got it anyway?'

'We're off the case. Savour the pleasure.'

'You and your partner have kicked up a lot of sand over the last couple of days, but I don't see no castle. That's all I'm saying.' She lit a joint.

'Castles? We're waves. Ask Ravenski.'

Ryan looked puzzled.

'Forget it. Private joke. We were trying, that's all.' Devlin turned, staring into the heavy, paint-peeled front door. In case of emergency, break ego. There didn't seem anything left to say. 'Goodnight, Detective.' He didn't bother turning around.

'You might be interested in something,' she said, so quietly that he almost didn't hear. 'Cupid Frish; she really has gone missing.'

He stopped and turned. 'What?'

'She isn't in the system.'

It was starting to rain hard and Devlin didn't feel like staying outside. He invited her in. She followed up the two flights silently as the skies rumbled and clamoured, rude and insistent. The hanging light outside his apartment flickered to the groaning of winds outside.

'Wiring looks like a lawsuit waiting to happen,' she said, picking at a line of black cable hanging in the chaotic, packed hallway, navigating around the bicycle, discarded Rollerblades, the general detritus of teenage life. She seemed oblivious. Then he recalled that she had two of her own.

She trailed him into the kitchen. 'The morgue people say they've been into every storage unit. No sign. Docket says she was delivered and we've interviewed the drivers. We even talked to the guy who signed her in. He swears she was left in a holding room for full autopsy.'

Devlin found himself laughing.

'It's funny?'

'Yes. No. I'm sorry, it's not funny. I was only wondering how

115

a body goes missing. It's not as if it gets up and goes home after the show.'

She rubbed a hand along the sink while he made herbal tea.

'You're right, which is why nobody watches them too closely. There was a shutdown that night, too; most of the attendants went out on picket duty. But they didn't close the place, said they kept somebody at reception. There were cops about, always are, and your people were bringing in saps overdosed on insulin. Nobody could have walked out with a corpse without a lot of paperwork or a lot of balls.'

They took their tea into the living room. Sylvia was out. He checked the monitor.

'Tough gig, aren't they?' said the detective. 'Teenagers.'

Rain was beating against the old, peeling windows, trying for forced entry and succeeding. Devlin watched a line of water trail down the frame. It meant another letter to his landlord, the Happy Corporation, a mail box number in Tampa. Must be crowded in that box. They'd say climate change damage wasn't covered by the insurance, read the small print, tenant's responsibility.

He still wasn't clear why she had come. To gloat? Guilt? There was caution behind those dark, steady eyes; a warmth, but measured out in calibrated units, not much heat or light.

'What else is bothering you?' Devlin asked, emboldened by camomile. 'There is something, right?'

She sipped gingerly. 'What isn't bothering me? I got no autopsy, so I don't know what time she died, let alone how or where.' She looked at him. 'This is my first walking corpse, by the way. So, all I've got is a crime scene guess that she died sometime on Friday night between the hours of when nobody was looking and when they still weren't paying attention.'

This was better than feeling bitter and wounded. 'So, let's get this straight.' Devlin ticked them off on his hand. 'You haven't got a victim. You haven't got a cause of death, a time of death or a place of death.'

'Life couldn't get much better,' she agreed, rubbing to ease tension in her neck.

'Challenging,' Devlin said.

'Tougher. Fritz Hanson has run tests on the fingerprints and he can't match them with anybody.' Outside, a sheet of lightning illuminated the sky. 'The prints seem to belong to an ape, a gorilla in all likelihood.'

Devlin stared at her. Words were clearly called for. But it was hard to know which ones. 'You get many homicidal primates in this city? I'm new here.'

'Not before now. We were shooting the breeze in a bar and somebody mentioned animals. It was just a joke, a guy on the squad riffing. Hanson suddenly rushed off. Called me at five in the morning all excited. He'd been on to a zoo in San Diego and they sent him over some ape prints, a full range, nine different species. It's not what I wanted to hear, believe me. I told him to run more tests, look at the prints again. It had to be wrong, or a scam, a prank.' She sipped the tea. 'And on top of all that, your commissioner was nervous, tight.'

'There's a wife and kids. I met her once. No primates in the family, far as I'm aware.'

Ryan rubbed her chin. 'This gorilla thing's a complication I need to sort out first. I'm not about to put out a press release saying we're looking for an animal, answers to the name King Kong. Here boy.' She whistled and patted her legs as if calling a dog to heel.

'Fenwick's in government. He'd figure it would get out, cause him embarrassment. Bad headlines at least. I don't see him taking that kind of risk, let alone getting someone else to kill her.'

She talked about the meeting. Fenwick had insisted that Frish was a casual acquaintance. They'd met at a city function; she had asked about working for Health Enforcement.

'But you found her with brown on the expressway. She was a pro, we know that much. So he started on a lie and I doubt he ever left it. If she was blackmailing him, which is possible, then that's somebody else with a motive and, perhaps, not enough time to think through an alibi.'

The commissioner claimed he met Frish for coffee at the Soul

Stop hotel on Fifty-Eighth. Devlin knew it; cocktails and pickups. In his case, usually just the cocktails.

'He was probably interviewing her cleavage. Of course, I asked whether it was usual for a man in his position to carry out recruitment interviews in low-lit hotels. He said he met a lot of people in quiet places to avoid tongues wagging in just the way that mine was doing.' Ryan sipped her tea. 'Well, there wasn't much I could say. A bowl of baloney tastes the same whoever dishes it up. I didn't tell him about the call from City Hall.'

'– That the commissioner was one of Cupid's johns? Good to keep an ace hidden.'

She nodded. 'Could be a joker. But he was in her diary and didn't deny they were due to see each other. Anyway, that's how we left it. He's not going anywhere.'

Devlin saved her from asking. 'You want inside track from the department, don't you?'

'The way I see it, she was killed by someone with access to brown and lots of it. That means they either store it, sell it or are rich enough to use it. This was planned. It was meant to communicate. Someone was making a point with a great deal of confidence. I need to find out what, to read it somehow, find out who the message was for. Brown is key to this, I'm certain. God, I hope so, because none of the other forensics make sense at all.'

'Mailer and Dolby are good, more experienced than me and less crazy than Strong; Boy Scouts with all the badges.'

'I don't doubt it. But the way I see it, only Matt Devlin has no incentive to protect his department. Ravenski? He's the commissioner's man. I don't see him stretching himself to help on this one. He'll get your replacements to go through the motions, but no more, especially if his boss is drawing heat. I think I can trust you, and I'll need to, especially if the track keeps heading back to your place of work,' she said.

Rain thrashed the glass and they sat without speaking. 'Someone went to a lot of trouble, didn't they,' Devlin finally said aloud. 'They wanted to draw attention to what they'd done, like poking a stick into a beehive to rile it all up. Homicide. Health. City Hall. This wasn't exactly a low-profile death.'

She got up and walked to the window, drawing a finger along the glass. 'You got condensation, too.'

'If there's a problem in the northern hemisphere, it's represented in this apartment. They pick on low salary grades, at least in my experience.'

She paced, circling the table. 'In mine, murder is a moment of white heat, followed by panic or calculation, and hasty disposal. Or it's planned and discreet. This doesn't fit. You're right. It's too show-and-tell. Except for a serial killer and there's no sign of that; not yet, at least.'

They talked in circles. Ryan had interviewed the list of Cupid's clients. They had alibis, or obviously weren't in the killing business. There was no pimp either. The only ones with a big enough motive were Gotfelt and Fenwick. Both had to be checked and neither wanted to be.

'I'm getting media interest in this,' she said. 'Information's leaking from somewhere. City Hall most likely. It's a good distraction from the strikes and shutdowns. The ape thing.'

'Dark,' Devlin said.

She drew a hand through her hair. 'Can't say I blame them. "Naked hooker with links to Health Commissioner dead. Gorilla suspected."' She looked at him. 'I'd read it.'

'They'll be doubling the guard at the Empire State and wheeling out those old biplanes. Did you tell them about the brown bikini?'

'No. That's all we have. More so now we don't have a body. But wait until that reaches the wires.' She leaned over. 'Funny thing is, you've now got the only forensics from her in that small bag from the scene. Ironic, isn't it? I gave away my only evidence to people who gave me none of theirs.'

Brown, source of all trouble. Pleasure nearly always was, thought Devlin.

'Look, snooping around Fenwick would be tough, dangerous for me. I've only lost face and a case so far. I could do without losing my job.'

She nodded. 'But you've got the brown. I don't even have a body.' It was as if that certainty outweighed everything. Perhaps that was how you ended up being a top detective at thirty-three, by putting it all on the line, thought Devlin.

Ryan said she would interview Gotfelt on his own territory, in West Virginia, and try to find the lost weekend. Gotfelt. Church leader. Pillar of the community. Friend of the powerful. Scourge of food abuse. The more Devlin contemplated helping Ryan, the more of a bad idea it seemed. Then there was Strong.

Ryan seemed to read his mind. 'I have reservations. Shit, I got a ten-thousand acre Indian-sized reservation about her. But it's your call. Personally, I think she makes bad decisions, did before and does now. I don't think she does you any favours.'

'I know her better than I know you,' Devlin replied quietly. He still didn't want Ryan judging his partner, especially as Strong seemed, at last, to be building connections to him in her skewed way. Ryan had no such hold, just good blue eyes.

'Hey, you don't wear make-up,' she said suddenly.

'No.'

'Odd. For a man, I mean.'

'I'm old-fashioned that way.' It had been a long day and he felt weariness embrace. He yawned and promised to consider helping. Ryan nodded and rose to leave.

'By the way,' Devlin said on impulse, 'You've drunk my tea, got me busted and tripped over Rollerblades. That's enough points to call me Matt.'

'Nathalie, or Detective, whatever works for you. I'm not big on abbreviations, though.' She turned and smiled. It was an illumination, a Fourth of July flash. 'Bet you're glad curiosity got the better of you, Matthew – Matt – back in that alleyway, when Strong dangled the eighth deadly sin,' she said, walking down the echoing stairs.

'What's that?' Devlin shouted.

'The sin of silence.'

'Most days are callipers and fergies; getting to hook up with a murder investigation affects your judgement.'

Devlin heard her laughing all the way to the front door and outside into the rain.

When he awoke in the collapsed seat of an armchair, it was to the sound of some techno thump. His mouth was dry and he looked at his watch. He'd been sleeping for nearly an hour. Sylvia was home.

'Hey. Come on out,' he shouted woozily. 'How's Alice?'

'Fine. Hey, don't give me that look. I know what you're thinking.'

'No you don't, sweetheart.'

'You're thinking I've been goofing off all day. Well, it's not true, Daddy. I can prove it.' She paused. 'I've got an alibi and witnesses.'

'You and half the city. I haven't said anything and I'm not thinking it. I'm just beat. It's been a hard, bad day.'

Sylvia was standing in the darkened doorway, hard to see. Devlin could hear the music playing, adult-alienating harmonies, repeated endlessly, tuneless and annoying; to him anyway. F*t rebels were cool and Big Pun was on her bedroom wall, all 650 pounds of him. Barry White, too. Devlin hoped it was just a phase.

He wanted to talk about job worries, the visit from Ryan, but did Sylvia need to hear? Then her vid rang. 'I need to get that,' she said, turning away to lock into a private world. Together but alone. For a moment they nearly talked.

Company. Why not? 'Strong,' he ordered into the receiver. She disliked Ryan, but craved real police work, knew how it functioned, about the city's dark places. Maybe that would balance into rational advice, he reasoned, as a distant connection was made, then a metallic voice said that the vidphone respondent was unavailable. He could leave a message or try again later. Of course she was unavailable, probably sinking beer shots in some Williamsburg dive, telling tales about the stuck-up jerk she worked with every day. Devlin looked at his watch and sighed. Time to feed the incubus.

'Microwave on,' he shouted.

'Microwave on to you, too,' came the even reply.

'Please, I haven't got time for this. Level three.'

'All right then. Level three. Intense. Can I interest you in a song? I've learned "It's A Beautiful World".'

'It isn't and no you can't,' he answered. Strong was right. Smart technology was better when it was still stupid. He moved around the kitchen, throwing together meat-free chilli like an automaton: carrots, tofu, celery, a spicy sauce and a can of tomatoes, oregano and tabasco for seasoning. He was brooding, his mind concentrating somewhere else; in a cheerless place, sensing cracks. Everything was unexpectedly treacherous. On the radio, President Bryant was being interviewed about rumours of cuts to Health Enforcement. Was she worried about militant eaters attacking food stores across the country? It was a police matter, she replied. Everyone understood bad food was killing the nation, that before anybody had done anything about the epidemic in the early years of the century, two-thirds of Americans were obese or overweight. What about the deaths in Wyoming from adulterated meat products? It was being monitored. The important thing was to focus on the big picture. The nation was healthier and people could look forward to longer lives. What about the climate? People said it was Armageddon. That was a matter for the United Nations; the focus for the nation should remain on staying fit and thin.

'You tell 'em, sister,' he said, hardly paying attention. She only had a country to run. He had a career running on empty, its fuel line nearly severed, the marker in the red zone. All that and a teenaged daughter.

Devlin was half-asleep when the vid sounded. It was dark outside and quiet. The rain had stopped. He looked at the clock. Five-thirty. Who'd call that early? He looked at the receiver. Strong. Who else.

'Yeah?' he said through a fug of irritation and disorientation.

'You asleep?'

'No, I'm playing the fucking violin.'

'Guess where I am?'

'Should I care?'

'Hey, if you need a clue just ask: piranha wall, smartass guy.'

Devlin shot up. 'Tell me you aren't in Luther Atom's.'

'Not the one we were at this afternoon, that's for sure,' she replied. 'I'm in the other Atom's, the secret Atom's that somehow we weren't shown. You should see this place.'

'What do you mean?'

'It's a galaxy-beating eateasy, partner. This guy's running a full-blown, illegal den. I've never seen so many burgers, full f*t ice cream and there's hotdogs. Wrappers everywhere. Even Krispy Kreme doughnuts. Needles on the floor.'

'Hold it. You've broken into Atom's without a warrant?'

'Sure,' she answered casually. 'Don't sweat it. What's he going to do? Sue? Come on. We can ask him anything now. Besides, I haven't told you the best bit.'

He sipped from the glass of water beside the bed.

'I found a cache of brown in a storage area. Guess what?'

'You ate it.'

'It matches the brown they found dressing Cupid Frish.'

'You certain?'

'I did the field test. I'm willing to bet Mr Magoo says it's a straight match. Consistency, flaking, bloom, crack.'

He couldn't see Strong, who seemed to be in a semi-dark storage area. She panned her vid to give him an eye on a subterranean world, one they had failed to find earlier, a place of bright-coloured walls similar to photographs of old fast-food places. The tables were moulded plastic. Devlin could almost smell the money, hear the tinkling voices and see the high-rollers, models, rock stars, celebrity Christians; all gorging on glutinous burgers guaranteed to be from at least one hundred different cattle, some adding molten C and a sachet of fries and washing it all down with illegal Classic Coke chasers for the sugar rush.

'If this isn't enough to pull in Atom, I don't know what is,' said Strong, sounding pleased.

'We're off the case.'

'Right.' She sounded offhand, as if he'd raised some tedious point of protocol. Devlin wondered, fleetingly, how she had got in.

'Who gives a shit?' Strong said. There was moisture on her brow.

'His attorney for one. We need to be sure about that brown

123

before we hit Atom again. He's too powerful and connected. I mean it. I intend to pay for that piranha pine with cash, not my badge.'

Reason. He'd give that a try. Atom wasn't going anywhere. The worst they could do was shoot their bolt too early, get flung off the unit altogether. They had evidence; why not see where it led? There was no point in getting Atom spooked. Strong eventually agreed, promising to replace the brown and take just a fraction for further analysis, before wishing him a night of sweet dreams.

But Devlin was too awake and alert and stood by the window. Ryan was right: his partner did have a problem with authority. There was another problem: he had difficulty imposing it. Ravenski was not going to be happy at Devlin's failure to keep his deputy on a leash, whatever story the brown had to tell.

But at least she had them back in the game and with a good hand to play. Now they could link Cupid Frish directly to an eateasy, if the brown matched. And not just any eateasy. There was already a connection with the Health Commissioner. He ate regularly at the above-ground Atom's and saw Frish hours before she died. Chance? Devlin felt the information rush by like a fluorescent hydrocarbon cloud, if only he could snatch it. Did Fenwick know what was being eaten beneath his feet? Did that explain why they didn't?

Outside, the storm had begun again. Sheets of rain beat down and the heavens grumbled, an ominous percussion tearing at the city's fabric and its architectural vanities. But to Devlin it was an orchestra playing in harmony for the first time. The moon briefly appeared, illuminating a cluster of clouds, long elliptical tadpoles hurling themselves mutely against apartment blocks or dancing above the sidewalks. They looked quite glorious.

He eventually slept, restless and fitful. Ryan was in his head. Alarm bells were ringing on the edge of her encampment; an unseen power was stalking the investigation and beating its chest, and she could sense it.

16

The sun was making an effort to be normal, throwing light but a strengthless heat. Gotfelt shaved, savouring long views from his bathroom over the campus, which remained a stage set of scaffolding only hinting at the grandeur to come; pre-moulded turrets and flying buttresses lay scattered on the ground.

There were no weather threats; smoke from the latest Amazon fires had congregated in Georgia. Nobody knew what they planned next, but the National Guard was mobilized.

On the radio, a reporter said Himalayan glaciers were going to disappear within five years because of climate change. It was a catastrophe, she said. They sustained the Ganges, Bramaputra, Mekong, Yangtze and other Asian rivers. Rice-growing regions that fed one-third of humanity were about to vanish. Gotfelt turned it off. The groundstaff were making a final sweep outside for horrors that might offend the President, such as slogans, inappropriate wrappings.

A cigarette had been found recently by an observant lecturer. Tobacco! Fortunately, it hadn't made the news. The last thing they needed was a scandal. More surveillance cameras were in place to catch the dealer or user.

There were to be no demonstrations anywhere within sight, he told Security. Months had been spent anticipating this day, when every network television station would be at the centre of his world. It was not to be jeopardized by free speech. This was a chance to spread the word to millions of abusers who yearned for the past and lives of unfettered eating. Oh yes, he knew their bleating pleas about civil rights, made despite the Founding Fathers never mentioning a 'freedom to eat' in the Constitution. The Supreme Court ruling on that matter had been an early victory for supporters of Control.

The Pursuit of Happiness clause was next. Church lawyers were working up a Pursuit of whose Happiness counter suit, one flavoured with legal canapés to attract the court: what are 'Happiness' and 'Pursuit'? He would raise it with Bryant. But before the private moments, the public ones. The President would be by his side and so would the cameras. There would be a meal for the world's media to witness.

The Preparers had promised an enriching salad of zest and glory. It was to include imported Kobe lettuce of exquisite crispness, each leaf massaged daily throughout its growth to the highest standard required by Japanese laws. The tomatoes were tiny and sweet, designed by Natural Corp scientists to pop in the mouth and unleash a concerto of complex flavours, some to replicate the carbohydrates found in candy, others to mimic tryptophan, an amino acid found in serotonin, the mood regulator. They had been bred in his own greenhouse laboratory, hand-reared on site. The new Bible burgers would be revealed. The President would perform an inaugural flip at the grill.

The only problem was arriving earlier, from New York. Her name was Ryan. She had been blunt: an interview or a subpoena delivered, in full view of the President, ordering Gotfelt to New York. She was due at nine.

Gotfelt, uneasy, scanned the newspapers over breakfast for diversion. The presidential visit was highlighted, at least by his publicity department, with red markers. There was talk that she might use the occasion to announce an extension to the index of banned products. His people had been lobbying hard. But soya oil farmers were organized and fighting back. They still had a powerful voice in Congress and it had been hard enough to get sugar rationing passed. He would probably have to settle for the usual: products here and there with no real purpose. It was a source of continuing frustration.

While individual elements could not be consumed alone, many were still permitted as ingredients. It was the usual politician's loathsome compromise. Nobody was willing yet to take on apple pie, to his chagrin. The limits on cinnamon use were ridiculous and made no difference. He would raise these matters with the President.

The detective was attractive, Gotfelt noted, as she walked through the door to his study. 'Good morning, Detective. I must apologize for seeming abrupt on the vid. As I said, this is a rather important day for the university.' He reached out his hand and smiled, signalling Ryan to a pocked, red-leather armchair. It faced his desk and the more impressive, winged chair in which he carefully arranged himself. There was no point in being obstructive, Regard had advised. Not today. 'I hope you won't be offended if I ask you to be brief. I have already been through this,' he paused, 'matter.'

Oddly deep blue eyes stared at him.

'I understand, sir. Speed works for me, too.' Ryan replied. 'Although I'm sure the President would understand, seeing as how big she is on law and order.'

A Preparer brought in fresh apple juice. They sat silently, looking at each other, until he left. Ryan had a notebook, which she made a show of reading. 'I need to eliminate people from my investigation, talk to those who knew Cupid Frish. It's just routine.'

'As I explained to Health Enforcement in New York, I make a point of keeping connections with troubled souls and, whenever I visit somewhere, try to find time for a private, pastoral moment. You can check with my office, Detective. There are men and women, young and old, whom I see all over the country.'

'I have no interest in your relationship with Cupid Frish.' She raised a hand to stop Gotfelt interrupting. 'But you are going to have to account for where you were on Friday, the day she probably died, because you did try to establish contact.'

Gotfelt leaned forward. 'My life is utterly public, Detective. Can you understand that, even imagine it? I'm stopped wherever I go. People seek me out, cross streets to ask for help. Because I come into their homes on holocasts and they read my work, they think I care for them personally. Once in a while I need to be on my own, to be anonymous. I am only human.'

'So, where were you? One human to another.' Ryan looked steadily at Gotfelt.

'I stayed in my hotel room between meetings, read, watched a movie. Oh yes. I exercised at the health club; a secular routine, naturally. I went for a walk. Central Park, north around the reservoir and across to Riverside Drive. No witnesses. Although now, for once, I rather wish I had been recognized.' He let a distant smile form. 'I wear a baseball cap and scarf, you see. It's a perfect disguise. I doubt even the hotel doorman saw me leave. But, without wishing to be dramatic, it is hard for somebody in my position to escape attention. Privacy is a treasure more than gold or brown, Detective, because once lost it's impossible to recover. Jesus didn't have to worry about autograph hunters.' Or tabloids.

'You're saying nobody can vouch for your movements?'

'I'm afraid not.'

Ryan tapped her pad. 'But you left a message for Cupid Frish?'

'Yes, I did. But, as I said, she never got back to me. I never saw her.'

'You looked uncomfortable.'

'Facial expressions are not a crime yet, surely?' He looked at his watch and paused as Ryan wrote. 'Unless there are any more questions?' He let his sentence hover unfinished.

Ryan rose, folding her notebook closed. 'I don't think so, no. Thank you for your cooperation. Until next time, Bishop.'

'Next time?' said Gotfelt, arching his eyebrows.

'It's just a figure of speech. Often.'

Ryan walked unescorted along quiet, carpeted corridors back to a reception area. Secret Service agents stopped her three times and asked for identification, checked retinals. Outside, the sun was drenching a grassed quadrangle in an intense wash of colours. An FBI helicopter hovered overhead. There was a fairground air that did little to lift her mood. Strings of bright pennants hung from a white canopy, fluttering wildly above the raised dais where President Bryant was to sit. Rows of gold-painted chairs were laid out, bordered with small tubs of flowering plants. Ryan watched sniffer dogs work the area in frantic zigzags, noses inches off the ground, tails beating mad semaphores of pleasure and purpose. There had already been one attempt to harm the President. A food zealot was shot after hurling himself at her motorcade in New Hampshire, armed, as it turned out, with bags of sweetened cream strapped to his waist. He was a forty-nine-year-old baker and left a note in the small, harbour-town duplex where he lived surrounded by the paraphernalia of consumption.

Police removed stacks of cookery books, many of them from the 1990s. 'He was driven by food perversion, a tragic waste,' said the mayor of New Fenton, secretly thrilled by the notoriety. The protest brought his town its own grassy knoll and the sort of fame money could never buy through a million jazz concerts, movies-of-the-week locations and book readings. Tourists soon followed, especially to the waxworks of infamous chefs from before Control; a place where explicit recipes were mounted behind protective glass. School trips would sit, gasping, as dangerous ingredients were mixed up, live, in front of studio audiences from the old broadcasts. There was squeezing, pummelling, pulling, massaging and stroking, almost everything imaginable. Food was manipulated. Every position. On camera. They would sit giggling with nervous embarrassment at the display, as if watching jungle animals coupling.

Ryan walked through cloisters to the car park, under a stone arch engraved with its stern stricture, 'Abuse of Food is UnGodly and UnAmerican'. She stopped and stared into a distance with no end.

There was too much turbulence around the death of Cupid Frish, the awkward need to work with Health Enforcement agents. There was also the City Hall interest in Gotfelt, a man with no alibi, yet nothing to put him where the body was found.

Ryan called the city morgue and had to shout above the noise of blades whop-whopping above her head. 'Bill Kenton, please,' she said, turning from the downdraft to see Preparers laying out their tables, carrying containers of leaves and colourful salad ingredients. They wore green cassocks.

'It's Ryan.' There was a pause. 'Where is she, Bill?'

Kenton sweated on the other end of the connection. He had

worked for the city all his life and this had not happened before. The worst of it was that Ryan had the transfer documents, so there was no question of trying to claim she'd got the wrong morgue, or that the corpse never arrived. Fucking protesters, making his department seem like amateurs.

'Look, bodies don't just walk, do they?' he reasoned nervously. 'They don't just get up and say, "it's too darn cold in here".' Seriously, no they don't. We had seventeen stiffs over the weekend. You know what it's like, with the strikes and everything. Maybe she was reassigned someplace else. For all I know she was sent out to a recycling home already. We're tracking it back. We'll find her.' He wiped his forehead and hoped for at least the rest of the day. Ryan – of all people to draw seven years from retirement and that condo in Miami, the condo with an eating den at the end of the street where hookers fed eclairs through food holes.

'I'll be back in the city tonight,' said Ryan. 'You will have some sensible news for me, Bill.' It wasn't a question. Kenton felt queasy, the same as when he was caught coming back home late, stomach full of prohibited pleasures.

'Sure, I mean how far can a cadaver get under its own steam. No taxis with the strikes.' He laughed weakly. But the connection was already dead.

Gotfelt watched through the stained glass window, staring at Ryan beneath the Gate of Eternal Vigilance pacing up and down, talking into her vid. Who was she calling? He felt a rush of anxiety. But nothing was going to be allowed to spoil the day. His speech was ready. There were to be a few words of welcome, graceful and generous praise of the administration, a modest acclamation for the new university, sweetness before the bitterness of his demand for action against more foods, French fries at the very least.

He would hand the President the gift, a Christ the Fit running altar for the White House; the latest model with a course styled on the Mount of Olives. Marketing said the machines weren't hitting sales targets and the publicity would be good. She already had a boxed set of prayercise holograms.

★

'F*t is a universal evil, Madame President, ladies and gentlemen, an evil threatening the woven beauty of our society, condemning us to short, miserable lives,' Gotfelt railed, reaching for the glass of water by his side and trying to ignore the sun, pure yellow for once, beating on to his forehead. Sweat needled his skin mercilessly.

'We are victims of terrible excess. We polluted our stores and homes and schools for so long. Gluttony is a sin. But we forgot and allowed the processors and packagers and their friends in high fructose and added salt to poison us with stealth and cunning.'

The audience was rapt, taking in the fire and passion and indignation as the eateasys across town were readying for the routines of another day: brushing floors, heating f*ts in hidden places, opening silver foil for the secret sod-coloured pleasure they kept fresh.

'The whole universe of God, down to the smallest particle, feels and responds to the all-pervading, dominating and electrifying beatitudes of his Controlling powers.

'It is Control that makes it all possible, that trains all our impulses to ensure that they contribute to our progress and mental and material comfort.' On the platform bathed by a glowing heaven, Hèston Gotfelt felt the intimate presence of God; a small froth of spittle formed on his lower lip and each word was delivered with emphatic, slow precision.

'It is Control that regulates and modifies our passions and impulses; those of pride, ambition, anger, love and courage. Our personal comfort and relations to the world, all the qualifications of our senses, are made to contribute to our happiness by the restraining influence and dominating restraints of Control.'

He lowered his voice and turned to a dais plumed with politicians, civic and business leaders. Most seemed well fed to him, perhaps confident that their status would protect them from fergies.

'Control expresses the dominating influence of God's will and sovereign power and it is through Control that God manifests his love to the world, ladies and gentlemen.' He raised and lowered his voice in a cadence of soft waves seducing a lonely beach. 'The towering mountains, the trackless oceans, the wavering forests, all rejoice in the grand, all-pervading and bounteous protection they receive through Control. May the Lord bless your sustenance.'

He sat down to a rapture of applause from his own students in front, polite clapping from those about him. The President reached to shake his hand and to mouth 'thank you' slowly enough for the cameras to pick up.

She had been thinking about Irving. Dear, conniving, dedicated Irving. Her closest adviser was dead now, playing air guitar with the Lord and probably trying to interest him in an image make-over. 'Ditch the white, Father. And the beard has to go', she could hear him saying. 'It'll take years off you.' The divorce had been a problem. Irving had earned his fee and her gratitude. 'Men will think you're available and women will feel superior, or sympathize with you for dumping a philanderer.'

'I was the philanderer,' she pointed out. Irving Dunworth barely missed a beat. 'But Fenimore would have been, if he'd been man enough. He probably was. Better yet, he drove you to it, through abandonment or failure. After all, you haven't got children.' She hoped Irving had found something useful to do in eternity.

'We have made great advances,' she said, standing erect at the lectern. 'Some people say Control is restrictive. I say it has liberated us.' She raised her voice to encourage a cheer and it came. 'We are no longer dying on the feet we stopped using, nor supersizing ourselves to an early grave for corporate profit.' The cheers were soon loud and ecstatic and Bryant responded. 'We are free. We have command of our bodies once more. Control is freedom, freedom from the desires that destroy, freedom from those whose disregard was killing us. That's what our ancestors fought for all those centuries ago, the right to be free.' The air filled with more noise. Gotfelt raised himself to clap.

'These people in Wichita must not have died in vain,' she thundered. 'We owe it to their memory to purge our biggest killer, to properly outlaw junk substances and punish those who distribute, contributing to the physical decay of our great nation, the evil riddling us with diabetes and heart disease.'

There were cheers, wheezes from the asthmatics in the front.

'Ours was a nation built on plain, simple values of honesty and integrity, my friends, by people who ate plain, simple foods. We have lost sight of those values, what it is to be true Americans,' she bellowed, thrusting out the jaw created by Eugene of Beverly Hills.

Ryan watched from the back of the quadrangle. She could have gone back to Charlotte airport, caught the shuttle, but the chance to see the President in the flesh didn't come along often. Yet she found herself staring at Gotfelt instead. Manipulator? Zealot? Liar? Huckster? All of them, Ryan decided. But murderer?

The sun was passing over the university, dancing shadows over young oaks planted around its perimeter. Ryan was aware of a figure by her side.

'Joe Regard,' said the shape, who seemed to be a cast shadow himself, hard to distinguish. Ryan shielded her eyes and squinted. It didn't help. 'Director of Public Affairs for the Church. You spoke to my office yesterday.'

'Of course. Nathalie Ryan, NYPD.' They shook hands.

'Get what you wanted?' Regard was looking straight ahead, as if transfixed by the spectacle. He made the question sound almost incidental.

'Some,' Ryan replied evenly.

'He can be awkward,' said Regard. 'Let's say he has problems with people. It's no secret. He's like a lot of visionaries, Detective: flawed, difficult and self-absorbed. Don't read too much into it. If I can help at all.' He handed over a small card. 'Call me any time. I'm a light sleeper.'

'Me too,' said Ryan as Regard walked away, keeping close to the dark, cloistered walls, turning in the half-light.

'He's got a lot of enemies and ministers to people I'd not put in a campaign pitch. But it goes with the territory. From time to time he strays, gets tempted. Another thing you might want to keep in mind is that powerful people have lost money because of Christ the Fit.' Regard smiled, thin and unrevealing. 'I'll leave you with those thoughts.'

'And I'll keep them up there,' Ryan replied, tapping the side of her head. Time to leave. The President was in full flow, promising an extension of Control, even fewer tax breaks for food processors, tougher sentences for brown smugglers, more armed units on the borders, health insurance reductions for regular exercisers, curfews for the chronically obese if she got a second term. The usual rabble-rousing bullshit, Ryan thought, turning to the car park. A pink cloud had settled over the hired Ford. She drove out of it, pulled over and looked through her mirror, watching it find another car to squat over. She called a name into her vid on impulse. At least she'd feel better if a gorilla was off the list. Hanson answered immediately.

'Boss, I'm afraid you're not going to like this.'

17

Strong pushed over the small evidence bag. 'Proof positive, wouldn't you say?'

She wiped coffee from her upper lip. Devlin considered the options, whether to go to Ravenski with what they'd found.

'What about security cameras? If Atom –'

'Cameras? You think he needs records? I doubt his customers do. It was four in the morning. I didn't even have to break a lock.' She looked exasperated and sounded withering, surprised that Devlin could be questioning this decision to flout a direct order and put both their careers on the line.

'Let's see what Mr Magoo says before we leap to conclusions,' Devlin said, sounding firmer than he felt. 'I don't want to rush this. We absolutely need to be sure the brown matches before we tell Ravenski.'

'Sure, sure. But it will.' She was impatient, pleading and persuasive.

He wanted to believe.

'You really think Ravenski isn't going to ask how we came to have this? We can hardly say Atom called us back. "Hey guys, look what I got. The evidence linking my illegal eating den to your dead hooker. Must have quite slipped my mind."'

'It'll be fine. This is going to be our lucky day,' she said.

Atom did have a camera and Ravenski was waiting. Fortunately, they had passed Leung's office and dropped off the brown. He said to call him early in the afternoon.

'Get in here,' Ravenski ordered, face tight and under the sort of immense discipline that eventually leads to something nuclear.

He spoke as if to especially backward adolescents. 'Imagine my surprise when the commissioner calls me at home wanting to know who authorized a raid on Luther Atom. He mentions your name, Strong.' An expression of tired surprise tried to form on Ravenski's face. '"No commissioner," say I. "It must be a mistake. I've already warned Agent Strong over the first unauthorized raid. No sir, she couldn't be that stupid, that brainless, to disobey an order in the certain knowledge of suspension. What, sir? There's film?"'

It was awful to Devlin, like hearing sandpaper drawn over a soul, and it wasn't even his turn. Strong sat motionless. There was a silence. Ravenski looked at her. 'Is there, can there be, an explanation?' he asked in a tone that made his own opinion plain.

'You're bawling me out for breaking into an eateasy?'

'Don't be naïve. We knew about Atom.'

Strong looked puzzled. 'What?'

'The reason you're there and I'm here, Agent Strong, can be summed up in one word: judgement. I have it, you don't. You'll be ticketing humonsters until the day you retire, if you ever get that far. Did it ever occur to you to wonder why a place with Atom's profile had never been busted? Did you seriously imagine that you were the first ambitious Enforcement agents to make their way to his other door?'

Strong and Devlin looked at each other.

'In return for his cooperation, Luther Atom is allowed to run his illegal eating establishment,' Ravenski went on. 'We get information from him. Only a handful of people know.' He caught their stares. 'If we shook him down every two weeks, where would that leave us? I'll tell you. With a lot of influential people breaking the law all over the five boroughs and some very expensive surveillance. This way we hear about shipments, turf wars, hits, users, and stay within budget. We also keep an eye on Luther Atom. It's cost-efficient. If you'd asked, followed procedure before blundering in, you might even have been told that information, or at least to back off. Sometimes, there is a bigger picture.'

Devlin was stunned: I'm new in town, I had an excuse. Why didn't she see this coming?

'Okay. So, it was stupid to go in there without clearance,' Strong said, grudging, almost an apology leaving her lips. 'I don't know how much protection Atom gets, but I found a stash of brown in there which looked mighty like the brown found dressing Cupid Frish, same bloom and tone.'

Devlin was watching Ravenski, saw his eyes narrow.

'Where is it now?'

'With the lab. Mr Mag . . . Leung . . . said he'd have a result by this afternoon,' Devlin interrupted encouragingly. 'Captain, if we can tie the brown in the eateasy to the victim, we've got to question Atom. Obviously, we'll keep Homicide in the loop.' He tried to sound reasonable, conciliatory, as if it was all making sense.

Ravenski was surprised. Devlin could see his mind making instant calculations as he rubbed his chin with two fingers and frowned. 'You're making leaps, don't you think? All it proves is that the brown came from the same consignment. I don't see how it makes a connection between Atom and Frish, as I'm sure his attorney will point out.'

'It gives us probable cause, at least an excuse for a search warrant,' said Devlin. 'We can go in, turn the place upside down properly.'

'A warrant? So that you and Strong can do legally what you've been doing illegally? Give me a break. I'll never get a warrant past the commissioner. Not after this mess. You've blown that option and left a pile of shit for someone else to clear up.'

'You're saying a positive match isn't worth anything? I wonder if Homicide will see it that way,' Strong said angrily, adding with cunning: 'We have to tell them what we've found, to liaise, as you reminded us last time we had the pleasure of being here.'

Ravenski stared at her. 'Don't be smart, Strong. It clashes with your idiocy. You work for this department, for me. Ryan gets what I say we give her, what the commissioner and I deem is pertinent, nothing more.'

'Let's just see what Leung makes of it, shall we?' She was barely bothering to disguise contempt. Devlin had to admire her. If she was going down, it was with everything firing.

'No,' Ravenski replied, soft and tense. 'I will. You're suspended. I'll need your badge and gun, Strong. And as for you,' he turned to Devlin. 'You're on militant eaters. Find out more about them, before they pull off any more stunts for the seven o'clock news. This has come from City Hall, the top.' He called in his assistant. 'Marian, call Leung. Tell him to bring the results of the brown he's analysing for Devlin and Strong directly to me.' He looked at them. 'That's all.'

It was crushing and even Strong was silent when they left.

'Listen, I'm –' Devlin started to say.

'I'll deal with it.' She walked over to her desk. Heads turned. Bad news travels fast along invisible currents. Maybe they'd known all along.

'What an asshole,' said Jack Shamus, his red, ravaged face flushed with rage. Others murmured their support. But not too loudly. Ravenski pulled down his blinds. He didn't want to see or didn't care. They ignored Devlin, who sat and watched them congregate around Strong, workers with their queen, as she pulled personal items from drawers, bagging them in a carrier. 'Well, compadres. Looks like I've got some home time,' she said, all swagger. 'I'll be at Leary's, if anyone wants to join me in toasting our esteemed leader.'

Devlin noticed that she didn't look at him. He caught Shamus's eye. What was he thinking, Devlin wondered. That I should have thrown in my own badge and made some big gesture in support of a partner, the reckless partner who ignored every order I gave her, the one who got us into this mess? He returned the stare, unwavering.

Then his vid interrupted. Ryan. It was a relief to hear her voice at that moment, an ally of sorts. She wanted to meet. Although he was eager to escape the rank, threatening atmosphere, Devlin wanted to speak to Strong, but the timing seemed wrong. Later. He left the back way and knocked on Leung's door.

'Well?'

Leung looked at him and put a finger to his lips. 'I no supposed talk to you,' he said, slowly. Then a big grin opened his face like a split melon. 'So, I no say you got match. Same bloom, discoloration patterns. Made in last three month. But I no tell you, yes? Definitely no tell.'

'Thanks, Ronnie. I don't know that it's going to make any difference. Ravenski's suspended Strong and got me reassigned.'

Leung looked grave. 'Strong say when we bowling that Homicide gonna screw this up big time. She hate them real bad. Maybe better you off case, no? I got bad feeling about this one.'

18

Devlin met Ryan near Tompkins Square. A light fog hung over the avenues.

'Hanson got a second opinion from the new Environment Behaviour lab in DC, the folk trying to understand cloud activity. Turns out they've got a division that specializes in animals. No doubt about it, he says. The mayhem was caused by a gorilla. I know, I know. Don't say it. I've got a meeting with the chief tomorrow morning.'

'Well, it's a novelty,' Devlin said. 'But a gorilla would need a human accomplice, don't you think? Somebody to move Frish, coat her in brown? That needs a brain, a calculating human brain.'

Ryan sighed. 'This is some kind of situation, isn't it? We've done bad by the animal kingdom over the last few thousand years, but I don't think that provides motive or opportunity.'

'Me neither.'

Ryan sounded tired. 'My first thought was some guy in a costume. But, as Hanson never tires of telling me, a law of fingerprints is that it's the oils we secrete that give us away. If it was latex gloves or a false hand of some sort, there'd be no secretions, so no prints. Period.' She paused. 'But there they were.'

'I think we need drinks.'

They went to the Blind Tiger. It was popular with tourists, which made it a good place for privacy. Most people had small shots of Brooklyn lager and guidebooks, or stared around hoping to catch a passing conversation. They found a table at the back.

'To tough days,' Ryan said, raising her glass.

'To them. I suppose you heard.'

'Heard what?'

'Strong broke into Atom's last night, found an eateasy. There was nothing I could do. She never told me. That's the bad news.

It's protected, seriously protected: the city, the feds. No wonder he was so cool. Anyway, she's suspended and I'm heading in the same direction, tracking food terrorists who've been getting up the mayor's ass. That just may be your good news.'

Ryan nodded her head in disbelief. 'At the risk of repeating myself, your partner is grit in the oyster of law enforcement, only she don't make no pearl. I didn't realize that about Atom, though. Interesting.'

Devlin took two sips in quick succession and felt chilled, dry pinot grigio hit the back of his throat.

'She found brown; it matched what was dressing Cupid Frish.'

Devlin told him about Leung's assessment and about Ravenski refusing to acknowledge any significance, insisting that Atom's attorney would blow it out of court, probably two seconds before bringing a harassment suit against the department. He would argue that if a case was to be answered on the basis of a consignment match, it was up to the prosecution to find the rest of that consignment. 'Ravenski's probably right. We'd be tied in knots.'

Ryan turned her glass slowly with one hand and worked a finger through spillage on the table's chipped surface.

'Ravenski seems determined not to see what's in front of him. Probable cause didn't cut any ice?'

'None. But probable cause doesn't cut the ice with Health it does with you. Anyway, he said Atom's operation was a honeypot used by the feds and other agencies, including ours. Strong should have checked. He's not going to throw that by going public with an unsubstantiated murder suspicion, because there's squat to hold Atom on and we'd be blowing a sting operation. Besides, any arrest is down to Homicide. That's you.'

Ryan nodded. 'Well, he could've told you this after you went in the first time and bust that wall.'

'Ravenski climaxes to secrets,' said Devlin. 'I'm not surprised he didn't tell us.'

'You'd think the fact Atom was running an illegal eating den would be enough,' Ryan said. 'There are times when I hate big cities; the deals complicate matters.'

Devlin had parked Ryan in the bay marked career cop, assumed she just wanted to climb the pole, never making friends or enemies, just allies. Cautious, like her handwriting. Outspoken was a surprise.

'I'm learning to feel the same,' he agreed. 'This sure ain't Baltimore. At least nobody can stop me telling you about the match, even though Ravenski tried.'

Why did they ever pull Cupid over and get sucked in? If they'd just told Ryan straight away that they'd busted her. If –

Devlin asked what Ryan had found out from Gotfelt.

'I'm sure he was seeing her professionally, in her capacity, not his. But I can't prove it.' She shrugged. 'Relationships can go bad, especially when money's involved.'

Devlin nodded. 'You run a lucrative Church and a woman you're screwing threatens to go screaming to the *Inquirer*, I can see that might drive a man to murder.'

Ryan was looking around the room. 'I thought that for a while. But I don't see him counting her a risk, that's my problem. Frish was professional, very private. The introduction was made by your boss, the Health Commissioner, which was even more of a warranty. Why else would she be out in Jersey? No prying lenses, I'm betting. And she was making a good living. Sure, she could have destroyed him. But she'd have been ruining herself at the same time. Frish was passed around like rare brown for a reason, and she was getting rich as a result.'

It came to Devlin when they finally walked out into the cool afternoon air, past a vegetable vendor selling packets of dried fruits from an old hotdog stand. 'You said you didn't release any details to the media about the brown Frish was wearing?'

Ryan nodded. 'Just that she was murdered and naked. Why?'

Devlin felt an awkward piece of jigsaw find its place. 'Atom said something when we first saw him: "at least her modesty was protected". I don't recall the exact words. But the thing is, how would he have known that? You didn't tell him, we didn't, and it wasn't on the news.'

Ryan looked at him. 'I don't suppose you got any of that on tape?'

'No. It wasn't a formal interview,' he said. 'To tell you the truth, I was kind of thrown, what with Strong beating the walls with a sledgehammer.'

'I can imagine.' Ryan took out her notebook and was writing. 'Luther Atom has protection from the feds, an attorney on our backs and a line into Fenwick. He seems to be where everything and everybody leads and yet somehow he isn't anywhere.'

'Like all the best illusions.'

'My client is a businessman going about his legitimate activities,' said the small, puce Fury facing Ryan in Atom's office. 'This is egregious. Beyond egregious into some other word. I shall be filing a complaint against the city.'

'Naturally.' But Ryan was barely paying attention. She despised Bo Watz, whose career was spent articulating moral outrage on behalf of the morally outrageous, the lowlifes, the corporate bankers. He was always on cable, his shaved, bullet head bobbing up and down as he vented against that day's infringement of a gangster's civil rights. Always available, always angry, always in a starched collar and wearing a heavy gold bracelet on the other wrist, the one not ballasted by a gold watch.

'I want to ask your client one question, counsellor, and one alone. I need to clarify what he said to Health Enforcement, and it may just make life easier for all of us.'

Watz huffed noisily. 'There's nothing to clarify because nothing he said, correction, allegedly said, on that occasion can be used in a court of law. Those losers didn't have a warrant, never even mentioned his rights. They just bust right in looking for an eateasy –'

'The eateasy,' said Ryan sharply.

'– which we both know has federal protection.'

Ryan felt her stomach knot. Atom was wearing an apologetic expression and a dark suit, as if in mourning.

'I'd like to help you, truthfully I would. Old times and all,' he said, sounding sad. 'But I got to listen to my attorney here, otherwise what would be the point paying his fees?'

'It's your choice, Mr Atom. You can play it his way or wonder how much bad press, how many cops hanging around the entrance scaring off customers, you're prepared to take.'

Watz spoke quietly. 'That sounds like a threat, Detective Ryan.'

'No, it's a fact. People often confuse the two. I don't work for the feds and I don't work for Health Enforcement. Let me spell it out: I'm investigating a murder and that's all I care about, unless you count the Denver Broncos. Things are starting to point in the direction of your client who, somehow, had information that was not made public.'

'Listen, Detective –'

'Hold it, Bo,' Atom interrupted. 'I got nothing to hide.'

'Good. Thank you. I appreciate it. Mr Atom, how did you know Frish was found wearing brown?'

Atom inhaled deeply on a joint. 'In my business you get to hear a lot. People come and go. They talk. Let's just say that word got out about what you'd found and, well, the unusual kink in the whole deal.'

If Atom was lying, he was good, thought Ryan. But then he would be. He was a friend of all those duplicitous City Hall suits breathing down her neck for reasons she didn't understand, but leaving Atom alone for reasons she didn't like.

'You know the Health Commissioner, don't you?'

Atom shrugged. 'I know a lot of people. What of it?'

'Curiosity.'

'Killed the cat.'

'You're telling me that you just heard about the brown.'

'Quiet neighbourhood. Not too many dead and chocolate-covered broads. Natural conversation point.' He smiled, slight and sparing. 'I know what you're thinking. I've been there. But ask yourself this: if I had anything to do with killing her, would I leave the body twenty yards from my business? Do you think having cops wandering around is good for my kind of trade, however much my friends look out for me?'

Ryan slowly noted down the place on her recorder where the interview had reached. 'A procedure nut,' mused Atom.

'If I bid twenty thou under, will I still get the condo in Jackson Hole,' thought Watz. He and his client exchanged glances.

Ryan spoke finally, still writing and without looking up. 'Brown from the body matches brown found here, in your establishment. Well, not here, in the other here. Same consignment.'

'Even if that meant anything, it's inadmissible,' said Watz. 'That freelancing Health Enforcement crazy stole it, unless she planted it. Had you thought about that? The same glory girl who came here with a sledgehammer and destroyed a wall. Are you telling me that you're treating anything she produces seriously? She broke in. A lone agent with a grudge. I live to put attitude like that in front of a judge.' He stopped and leaned forward. 'I also hear she left Homicide in interesting circumstances.'

Atom sounded conciliatory, agreed it was probably a set-up. He understood how frustrating it must be for Health Enforcement agents to find they'd bust the unbustable. But that was the real world. They keep a few little fish like him on a line to catch the big ones. 'I'm still a cop, Detective. In my head. Sure, I make a little living off burgers and brown. But I put back, too. I care about society. Brown comes in batches, a handful of dealers control it all and spread it around. Talk to your buddies in Health, they'll tell you.'

Ryan switched off the recorder, closed her notebook and thanked Atom for his time. Nodding at Watz as she turned to leave, she dropped her wallet on the floor, careful to hold it by one corner after earlier using a soft cloth to polish all the outer surfaces. Atom picked it up.

'Hey, I wouldn't want you to lose this, Detective,' he said balefully, handing it over with a bleak smile. 'Not sure my reputation could take the hit.'

'Thanks. All my worldly debts.'

'Urgh, that is so gross,' said Sylvia, recoiling from the brown paper bag in the kitchen after peering inside. There must have been half a dozen apples, putrefying. A white maggot had half-crawled out of one and was flailing. The bag itself was damp with the juices of decay and they stained the label, which had been expertly printed by a steady hand with Devlin's name.

'I think we should take these back to the store.' Devlin sniffed the contents. 'Looks like grounds for a refund to me.'

They could only have been there a couple of hours and he'd been home all afternoon. Nobody had rung the bell. He inspected the contents more closely. Nothing. Just rotten apples. He knew only one person who wrote that well. The idea was absurd, but quite comic all the same.

'Why couldn't they leave Swiss brown,' said Sylvia through her pulled face. 'Hey, just joking, Daddy.' She laughed and he found himself smiling.

Hanson worked out of a basement with no natural light, preferring the quiet and constancy of artificial illumination, the certainty of where shade fell. It was peaceful, a sepulchre in the depths of Police Plaza. His office was always untidy, the open lunch salad boxes scattered profligately on table tops a testament to long hours spent cutting and poking.

Ryan was one of the few detectives allowed to wander around unescorted; their years together were shared campaign scars.

'Cocktail?' Hanson asked, twirling a speculum around the beaker and its contents. 'Today it's Martini, with a twist of very fine Ecuadorian brown.'

'Sure,' said Ryan. Hanson filled a sample beaker.

Ryan handed over her wallet. 'Dust this, will you? Then I guess we need to talk apes.'

'Yes, we do.'

She watched as Hanson pulled on latex gloves and took out the contents of the wallet, laying them on a table before dropping the old leather into an enclosed glass drum and breaking up a glue bag, releasing the cyanoacrylate fumes that would attach to the unseen amino acids and oils from the fingerprints, highlighting every twist and whorl, loop and ridge, making them ghostly visible.

'Good sets,' Hanson said after a few minutes. 'Sit down. I need to transfer the photos to a plate, then we can both enjoy the show and, if I say so myself, these quite excellent cocktails. I got a good finale, by the way. It's only missing Fay Wray.'

Ryan waited, sipping the drink, which tasted of evidence and probably was. Hanson reappeared after less than ten minutes and went over to a wall-mounted screen, the sort used in hospitals to display X-rays, and inserted three separate images.

'Apart from yours, in the middle, the one on the left is your wallet, the right came from Frish's body, the body you've managed to mislay. Tut tut. You're the talk of the department, by the way.'

Even to Ryan it was obvious the contoured landscape on the other two came from the same hand and she felt a moment of elation. Luther Atom.

'There's no doubt. Look at the radial loops.' Hanson was holding a small baton. 'Identical.' He looked at Ryan.

'You're a genius. Did anyone tell you that today?'

'Just the guy I meet every morning in the mirror. But he's biased and untrustworthy. Don't get too excited.'

'Why?'

'This is the other set of prints I've been working on.' She watched as Hanson put up a fourth negative. 'Look closely. This is from the Montcalm apartment and typical of what we've been picking up.'

Ryan strained her eyes. 'What am I looking for?'

'I said look closely.'

'I still don't get it. What?'

'That's a five-inch-long finger, my friend.'

Ryan stared blankly and Hanson told her to hold out a hand. The middle finger was less than three inches, standard human issue, said Hanson.

'Who has a five-inch-long finger? At first, it made absolutely no sense. In twenty years I've never seen one that long. I figured it might be some mistake. But I had three guys down there and we all lifted them independently of each other and from different places. We all came up with the same configurations. The information from San Diego and the lab at DC is what confirmed it.' He stopped, and took a sip from his drink. 'You know, these are very good.' He licked his lips approvingly and looked firmly at Ryan. 'It's simple,

I'm afraid. In all of creation, only gorillas have a finger bone that long.'

Ryan rubbed a hand over her brow, feeling the deepening crevices.

Elation to deflation in two minutes. It all suddenly made a lot less sense. She could link Atom to Cupid, but not to Montcalm Avenue. Common sense said they were connected. Common sense said there was no gorilla in that apartment.

'I know you don't pop A, Fritz. But listen to yourself; this has to be wrong. Come on. They're fake. There has to be another explanation.'

'A fake, from a plastic or moulded hand in a Halloween costume, say, would leave an impression, not a print. And that's a big distinction.'

'It's Prints for Morons, first page,' Ryan interrupted, so they sounded in unison. 'I know.'

Hanson went on. 'A print needs oils to stick to a surface, the oils and salts that we and our closest animal relatives excrete from the skin, and these have got plenty of both, believe me.'

Outside, thunder ripped open the brilliant orange and ochre sky, a fantasia of chemically diffused colours, sulphates and hydro-carbons and synthetic sulphurs. Ryan lifted the beaker.

'Cheers,' she said. 'Welcome to the world that sense left behind.'

In her office, several flights above, a package had been delivered. It was a brown bag, soft and sealed. Her name was written neatly on a card fixed to one side.

19

Heston Gotfelt knelt at the dining table in the transept and stared at a brilliant and luminous Christ, a thin figure stained into the arched window and surrounded by disciples for the Last Supper. Scholars estimated that the average disciple consumed less than 2,800 calories a day, roughly the same as a meal of fries, shake and cheeseburger in the grimmest days of Abandon. But they walked everywhere, burning off the excess. There was also plenty of fruit, olives, reasonably fresh fish, all deliberately chosen by the Lord God to keep them fit.

'Forgive me, Father, for I have sinned,' he said very, very quietly. 'I have indulged in the forbidden. I allowed myself to gorge –'

He was interrupted by a voice, quiet but persistent, calling his name. Holly Fareham. There were meetings, always meetings. He scrunched his eyes as if that alone would cause her to disappear. It was no good. He was chief executive for Christ and that carried responsibilities. Heston Gotfelt walked this earth for a cause greater than himself. Dust particles caught by the glare of the sun danced in front of his eyes. He thought about the detective. There was nothing he had done, or would do, that was not ordained. Had not the Lord himself been tempted in the wilderness for forty days and forty nights?

Gotfelt did some mental arithmetic. He had only been tempted on twenty-three days and fifteen nights and was, therefore, in credit by any measure. There was no need to seek salvation or forgiveness after all. His credit rating was good with Jesus. Alleluia.

'Alleluia,' he exclaimed.

'Amen, Bishop,' replied his startled assistant.

'It's a new day, Holly. The Lord is with us.' He rose, clapped his hands and beamed 'We have talked and he has told me that my life is in credit.'

'Credit?'

'I have no need to expunge my sins, slight though they are,' he added.

'Well, that's very good news, Bishop. I'm sorry to interrupt; it's just that you're meeting the delegation from Nigeria in less than an hour. You wanted to read the briefing material.'

'I hope Joe has prepared a thorough note.'

'Yes, sir. On your desk. It was great yesterday, wasn't it?' said Holly. 'The President. Here at the university. What an honour for us all.'

'Yes, indeed. Did you see me on NBC?'

'You were magnetic,' Holly said. She had recorded all the bulletins. He was certain to ask for them; the archives were an obsession. Even local television and radio were monitored, collected assiduously by supporters and sent for filing. They helped a Presentation Unit assess opinions of the Church around the country, identify areas where they might evangelize successfully. The days of taking God everywhere, just in case, were long gone. As Regard always said, 'one sinner at a time in an age of globalization makes absolutely no economic sense'.

Gotfelt the Good, beatified by his own congregation. 'One day, the Library of Congress will build a special wing dedicated to Control and I like to think that I, although not me personally, will be honoured for the humble contribution I, that is we, the Church of Christ the Fit, have made to making our nation fitter and leaner,' he told a recent board meeting. The process of bribing senators had already begun. Regard was in charge. His department had files on the most vulnerable members, their vices and eating habits, and he had thanked the President for the extra information that she had been able to supply. It was to be the next mission after the university was completed, a place where future generations would visit the shrine of its founder. There would be a statue. He had approved a design, twice life size and wearing a toga.

The sculptor had warned that suits were expensive to carve and went out of fashion. In one hand he would clasp a bar of brown, in the other an axe that would, by implication, smote the brown into a thousand pieces. 'Class, Bishop. That's what I'm going for here,' said the shrewish figure with the flat Brooklyn accent. 'You could go for your holy book and cross look, sure, but all the religious bosses choose that, no disrespect. The brown and the axe. That's very you, your youselfness, if you'll pardon my presumptuousness. Very you.'

It was, Gotfelt agreed, very him. The public would be asked to contribute. Permanence and immortality.

Ryan. He couldn't get her out of his mind, those steady blue eyes. They weren't mocking exactly. No. It was more than that; a boring into the leaden places of his soul.

He met the Nigerian delegation in a reception room and they exchanged gifts for the official photographs, a carved wooden apple from them and, oddly, a carved wooden apple from him. He would have to speak with Marketing. There was surely no point in representatives giving each other the same gifts, even if it did make sense to centralize operations. The photographs looked ludicrous.

'I see revenue is rising from our churches in your wonderful country, David,' he said to Bishop Instructor David M'Tume, a former refrigerator salesman who had bought the franchise at an infuriating discount after a baffling argument over exchange rates.

'It is a blessing for us, dear friend. The people, they want to comprehend the eating of the Lord and we can make so much off them,' he cackled with laughter, slapping of thighs and twinkling eyes. Heston believed M'Tume blunt, open and frank. These were not useful in religion. 'It isn't about money, David,' he admonished.

'No, sah,' responded M'Tume, winking at him. Winking! Thank goodness the cameras had gone, especially after the last time when the jovial and evidently rotund priest fended off questions about his weight by blaming 'the good feeding of my leader here' during his stay. People had dared to smile, his own people.

The delegations talked politely about expansion plans, campaigns, trading opportunities. Gotfelt promised to visit, as soon as his schedule 'loosened up', which was code for his assistants to kick it into the long grass. He had never liked excessive heat and the Nigerians remained a very large race, big-buttocked like the Germans.

The delegation was to help with the afternoon confession. At least that would keep M'Tume out of trouble. 'The Elevenses service begins shortly, David. Shall we prepare?' His guest, who had secretly done his own preparing by feasting on f*tted goat meats and jellied gongo brought from Lagos, readily agreed.

In the cavernous amphitheatre, Preparers were laying out raw foods for communion. A party of vegans from Oregon was due to give substantial tithes. They were regular donors and the options for Christ's body had been extended to include a lentil and tomato roulade with rice in their honour. The long table was laid out with brightly coloured vegetables and dips, tamales, baked fish and the full sweep of fruits. The confessional booths were busy. Each had a number which lit up when the priest was available. A mechanized voice announced vacancies in a monotone.

'Please go to confessional four.' 'Please go to confessional twelve.'

A steady line of worshippers prepared for their moment behind the curtain. Eating sins were judged on merit: twenty dollars for ice cream; fifteen for profiteroles; one hundred for pure brown, all on a sliding scale. Priests had laminated reminder cards giving the penitence requirement for the full Index of foods, listed alphabetically. Confession was a useful revenue generator and had already paid for the new Scriptorium, where scholars scoured early Christian, Judaic and Aramaic texts for food references. Gotfelt watched from the concealed balcony before they took their places at a randomly selected confessional. There were priests at the dining altar conducting a litany as Gotfelt and M'Tume swept down to the main auditorium, past promotional posters. 'Check out your sins. Special group rates.' 'Have you thought of pre-paid confessions? Buy a pack of twenty for just two hundred dollars, fully flexible: two big sins or twenty small ones. You choose.'

Gotfelt looked briefly at his own lightly tanned and racially ambivalent portrait staring back from the poster, airbrushed to flawless purity. He was holding out the tokens, fanned into a hand of playing cards.

'Atlantic City for the soul,' M'Tume whispered softly to an aide, who laughed delightedly and clapped his hands.

Lumbering poor folk from decent strip housing stood in the line. They fretted about cattle prices, paying for extra school tuition and whether the sun was going to hit the corn crops at the right time. These were his people and Gotfelt experienced the glow of ownership and responsibility.

'Furgive me, Father, for I have eaten,' said one, his defeated, worry-lined face hung limp by a life of disappointment. 'We had some hidden brown, what we was keeping as an investment, and we done ate it in a moment of weakness.' He held a worn baseball cap tightly in his one good hand and looked pleadingly at the Bishop.

There was a moment of recognition. Gotfelt interrupted it curtly. 'Forty dollars to the Church fund for eradicating eating excess in the developing world will absolve you.' He looked around distractedly. 'For a further ten dollars, the Church is prepared to absolve you in advance of any sin involving less than two grammes of brown. It's our early bird special.'

The man reached into his denim pocket and slowly counted off fifty dollars from a crumpled knot of worn notes. 'I might give the extra sin to Nadine for her birthday what's coming up this fall,' he said, brightening.

'Good, good,' said Gotfelt benignly, glancing at his watch and wondering, briefly, what Nadine resembled. Something unappetizing, he decided. Confession was a tedious process. He glanced across. The Nigerians were enjoying themselves. A surprising amount of money seemed to be heading back and forth between M'Tume and a young woman. Surely not? Gotfelt sighed. He would slip away now. He caught the eye of an aide. 'Look after our friends, will you?'

He walked back towards his office, thinking of luminous avocado eyes, fresh lips and the hands that could do such incredible, terrible things and made him feel whole. It was such a puzzling sensation. Her burgers were covered with C and always delicately caressed by Indian spices; the memory of her reckless use of Béarnaise still

153

made him gulp for air. He felt sweat rising, remembering how she would lick the whipped yolks of devilled eggs in careful twists, eyes fixed on him. Devilled. And now she was gone. Forever. It would be hard to find a replacement, someone who loved food as skilfully, someone who understood its powers.

But she had been foolish, overreached herself. It was a shame, he thought, walking along empty corridors to his office. There were ten-dollar gorgers all over, preying on businessmen, tourists, the solitary, the hungry, thrill seekers. They'd work rooms rented by the hour, pour cheap brown, but their tongues were blunt and unskilled. Cupid was an artist with nutmeg, cinnamon and caramels. She would use carnal ingredients: butter from Vermont, cream from Iowa. Good Lord, she could arouse Satan himself with a single skillet of molten brown.

Gotfelt was sweating violently before even reaching the door to his sanctuary, the private entrance that avoided outer-office staff. He went immediately to the daybed and lay down, still, eyes fixed on the ceiling fan turning in slow, flat-lined rhythm.

There was a knock on the door.

'Ryan didn't have the look of a woman soaking up all the sights because she wasn't going to pass this way again,' said Joe Regard, tapping his fingers together.

Gotfelt walked to the fireplace and watched flames lap and crackle around huge oak logs. 'She was shooting blind.' He tried to sound dismissive and unconcerned.

'Perhaps,' said Regard. 'But Cupid Frish was a hooker, someone who gave gorge parties, dealt in brown. I've talked to contacts in the city. She was known. It's going to get out.' He let it hang in the air. 'New York, New York. Not our kind of town.'

'Sinatra?'

'Nearly.'

Gotfelt poked the wood with his foot and aggravated the flames. 'What are you suggesting? That I used her services?'

'I'm just saying things get distorted. If that detective, Ryan, gives an interview to a reporter and somehow your name.' Regard stopped. 'I got word from inside. There's a disc some place. She filmed herself in action, apparently. It's missing. I also hear City Hall has been dropping your name like confetti at a wedding.'

They looked at each other.

'Someone either took the disc or it's hidden and the cops will find it,' Regard said. 'Either way, I need to know whether you're starring so I can do my job, get a strategy together. That's all.'

Gotfelt walked back behind his desk. 'There's nothing.' He looked steadily at Regard. 'Nothing.'

When his adviser left, Gotfelt pulled open a drawer to his desk and lifted out the crushed Bible his father had used. He opened it at Genesis and let the small disc fall into a pale, unsteady hand. 'For God doth know that in the day ye eat thereof, then your eyes shall be opened and ye shall be as gods, knowing good and evil,' he said quietly under his breath and broke it in two, like communion bread, and threw the parts into the fire. 'Goodbye, Cupid. You were the sweetest.'

20

It was a harsh and driving rain whipped by melancholy winds that seemed to come from a distant past, bringing hallucinogenic skies of disgorged matter from ugly places. Devlin was glad to be indoors, the files on food terrorists laid out in front of him. The computer system had collapsed with exhaustion and was arguing with the tech people. He could hear them bickering.

There was security camera footage from Mitchell's. But a group of people in ski masks was about as revealing as a dark hole at midnight. Devlin squinted: large, f*t, short. But mainly f*t. All of them looked as if they'd fail a fergie. He needed help. There were people who worked with the chronically obese, got them legal aid, served as expert witnesses at trials, tried to protect them from discrimination. Susan. He felt his lips tighten and pressed her number into the keypad quickly, before doubt could take over.

They had always disagreed. He felt lower health premiums for the properly proportioned was just fine. She said it was discrimination. They did agree that chasing humonsters in Central Park was bad sport. Even Devlin drew the line when somebody suggested a little league. She once had a fine collection of cookery videos. They'd be valuable now; so many people had burned theirs.

'Hello?' said the voice, at once uncertain and friendly.

It was funny, he thought, when there's so much to say how we say nothing. 'Hey, Suse. It's Matt. How's it going?'

He needn't have worried. She was still open and friendly, a breathless font of news, rarely personal. He'd forgotten that about her. She was married to the job, period. Then she jolted him. She was also married. He was named Aaron. They had a Great Dane and they called her Fi Fi.

'Listen, it's so cool. I'm just getting ready for a rally in Buffalo and I'm hoping we can get down to Louisiana next week to support the legislators there. Kick some butt.'

'Wait. You called a Great Dane Fi Fi?'

She laughed, happy and generous, and Devlin felt warmth and comfort from hearing her voice. But he didn't say that. He said Control was Control and the South should accept the law.

'God, you haven't changed. That's not the issue, klutz. Control is a Trojan horse for federalism, detaching people from the real issues, and we've got to help keep the gates shut.'

'Hey, stop seeing conspiracies. They're not pretty.'

'You are so naïve, Matt. Truly. Helping people eat properly is one thing, using that to give Washington more power is quite another. What about the ozone layer and the crappy air? How come we aren't dealing with that? What about the fouled-up rivers? Industry doing what the heck it likes? Answer: big business lobbyists. God, I'd just love to see a blue sky again. You know there are city kids who think it's supposed to be mauve half the time? This food thing is just a big fucking distraction. And don't be so anal. Fi Fi is fine. Very elegant, in fact.'

'Okay, okay. I surrender. Listen, I need your help. I'm chasing down whoever broke into Mitchell's. I figured you might have some connections, through the practice.'

There was a pause and she took a deep breath. 'I read about that, but I can't pass on client information, to a Health Enforcement agent of all people, Matt. Even one I slept with.'

'Normally I wouldn't ask. But this is serious, serious for me anyway. My job's on the line.'

'Honestly?'

'We cut some corners on an eateasy. My partner's suspended and it was a narrow escape for me. That's life in Hell for you.'

They agreed to meet for a drink that evening. Susan promised, reluctantly, to look through the files, talk to some case workers.

Devlin sat staring at the downpour. He was looking forward to seeing her again, no question. Sylvia was on a school trip upstate to Phoenicia for a couple of days, so he had the apartment to himself but still nobody to share it with. He felt the small, insistent ache of loneliness that came periodically, especially when Sylvia was gone. At least he had the scented candles. But Susan had Aaron and a Great Dane named Fi Fi. The vid rang.

'Hi,' he said, recognizing the number. 'How's life for the leisured classes?'

'Watching the games, bro. In sequence for once. I could get used to suspension. You?'

'Food terrorists.'

'Some day, huh?' she said.

'Yeah, end of summer. Or was it winter? I keep forgetting.'

'Any news on Frish?'

'You've reminded me. I need to call Ryan. She was going to have another crack at Luther Atom.'

'Top of my list. Even beats God's muscle toner.'

'Atom has some explaining to do, you're right there. Good call, by the way. I'm impressed.'

'Lucky break. Listen, I'm curious to see if Detective Genius can break this one. If it is that eateasy, make sure we get the credit. This could put us back on the job again, the old team, not to mention get me out of a dirt hole.'

Devlin was honest and straightforward, Ryan had decided, all the things it was surprising to find in men. He was sensitive about calories, too, but balanced; probably didn't spend the whole time worrying vainly about moisturizers and skin-care routines like some of them. Didn't talk about them either, which was a relief.

'Hi,' she said, the first to speak. 'If I said the Blind Tiger, thirty minutes, would I be drinking alone?'

'Not after my day. I'm in for the season.'

'Good, because I've got news.'

Cupid Frish. Her death and Devlin's life connected by a random stop on the expressway. It was odd the things that brought people together, he thought, ordering a beer for himself and a white wine shot for Ryan.

She was ten minutes late but quickly told him about the finger-prints that matched and those that didn't.

'Think you've got enough to go for Atom?' Devlin asked.

'I'm not sure. I wish his prints were around her throat. But they weren't and it worries me. Still, she was on the game and he's a player. They probably knew each other and they sure as hell walked those same streets, Lust and Temptation. I'll bet she went to his place, did a little business. He lets them; takes a cut, I hear.'

'Any sign of the body?'

'No. Morgue seems to be some kind of all-you-can-steal buffet. At least we got Atom's prints from the scene.'

'But who would take her? They'd have to know which computer to hit to find where she was taken, which of the morgues. Someone in City Hall?'

'It has crossed my mind. Somebody doesn't want her reaching autopsy, that much seems obvious,' said Ryan. 'But why? And who'd dump a body in a public place, just to steal it right back? You can't just walk into morgues, either, even during strikes. We talked to the doormen; they swear nobody without ID got in.' She raised both her hands, palms up in surprise and surrender. 'Does this make any kind of sense to you? Don't answer.' She sipped the wine. 'But, hey, thanks for Atom. Those prints and that brown mean we can sweat him again, which seems to be my new leisure activity these days. He definitely knows a lot more than he's donating to the cause. I can drink to that.' She raised her glass and smiled; it was slight, but certain.

They moved off the subject and she asked about the militant investigation, how Strong was taking suspension.

'Your girl still using?' Ryan looked concerned.

'No, at least not in an insulting way,' said Devlin. 'She's got a boyfriend. I'm kind of hoping that might be an alternative.'

'Mine are the same, if it's any comfort. Listen, the way I see it, they got to experiment. It's natural. With me it was dope and amphetamines, before they were legal. Probably the same for you, too. Jake's eleven, Kieran's nine and I'm not dumb. I told them, "If you're using, do it at home. Want a street cheeseburger, make sure

159

nobody's looking and put it on the grill next to the chicken. I don't want you being cautioned by Health patrols." No offence.'

'None taken. We haven't the resources to ticket many backyard barbecues anyway. Those ads with the vans and all that tracking equipment are just to scare people.'

'Well it works. In the end it's about relationships. I'm lucky, got a good one with the boys. Since their father died, we look out for each other.'

'I'm sorry, I didn't –'

'Don't be. He blacked out one day in the bedroom. Brain tumour. Bang. That was it.' She clicked her fingers. 'Check-out time. Never regained consciousness. Kids were at school and found him when they got home. That was the evil of it. I just wish I'd got there first.' She looked at the wall.

Devlin felt awkward and took a sip of beer.

'Someone you love dies, gives you tolerances, I guess,' she said. 'Everyone has family, friends, loved ones that get left behind.'

'Cupid Frish?'

'Except her, actually. She came over from Russia as a baby named Pavlina Rubinskya. Only child. Parents went back to Odessa when she was sixteen, just after the Communists got back in. She stayed to finish high school and was supposed to join them, but changed her mind. Far as we can tell, her folks are dead, killed in the fighting. We can't find any other relations, but it's hard to get sense out of anyone over there, with the harvest failures and water riots.'

Devlin shuffled his glass absently around the table. A lot of people were sure America had invaded southern Canada for the water. 'She was so cool when we pulled her over. No nerves or distress that I could see.'

Devlin wondered if Cupid was looking down, filing her nails, bored by all the confusion she'd left behind, the memories stirred in a Homicide cop. Probably not. She'd be feeding brown behind the clouds to a fallen angel.

'Did you find the disc from the camera in her bedroom, or office as I guess it ought to be called?'

'No,' said Ryan. 'Could be there wasn't one, of course. We're still dusting for prints. Nothing. At least nothing unusual except King Kong and your partner.'

'ET had a big index finger.'

'And I'm certainly not ruling him out at this stage. Little green men on bikes sound pretty good to me right now. I'm thinking ET's evil twin.' Outside, rain and storm winds sighed and groaned, baiting vehicle alarms that filled the air in dismal harmonic counterpoint.

'You ever think about Control?' Ryan asked, returning from the bar with two glasses of beer. 'I do,' she answered herself. 'I wonder why we deny the pleasure of food. I don't mean we don't still enjoy it, but we've turned it into some kind of boogeyman. The Constitution says we're about pursuing happiness. Yet here we are running away from it. I think it's some human condition. Whenever a pleasure comes along we absolutely want, it gets banned or criticized. We've been doing it forever. One way or another somebody says, "whoa, hold on. It'll kill ya." Like we aren't heading for a hole in the ground anyway. I don't get it.'

Devlin wondered if she was drunk. 'You sound just like Strong. She thinks it's all crap, too, a denial of the pleasure zones . . .'

'A denial she plainly enjoys subverting at every available opportunity,' snapped Ryan.

'Me? I think it's about making it all last as long as possible, because nobody knows what comes next. It's about being in charge of life,' said Devlin. 'In control.'

Outside, winds rattled the windows and Ryan smiled. 'Hear that? Still think we're in charge?'

'Taking charge, then.'

'We don't seem to be doing much of that either.' They sat silently for a while then she changed the subject. 'There is a favour I need to ask. Can you get a fix on the brown?'

'I'm not on the case. You need to approach the department formally.'

'Your commissioner's taking too much interest in Frish. It doesn't make me comfortable, especially after finding his name in her address cards. I don't want every step of this investigation leaking through him to City Hall.'

'I doubt Fenwick's tight with Finch,' Devlin said. 'In fact, it seems incredibly unlikely. There's tension between federal agencies and city ones. Hell, it's practically in the ordinances.'

'What about Ravenski? He could be playing both sides against the middle. I'm not comfortable. We're being pushed at Heston Gotfelt. Yet the only evidence that points to anybody is from an eateasy, and not just any eateasy.'

They sat in silence for a few minutes. 'I'm trying to find links of my own. All these leads, rolling up like targets on the range. It's just making me nervous,' said Ryan. 'I want to find something myself, preferably that makes sense. It might help if the brown matches any recent consignment you guys have seized, one with a name attached.'

Sense said stay away, thought Devlin. If Ravenski discovered he was still poking around, end credits would start rolling. Back to the drawing board. Back to Baltimore.

'I talked to Tibor Gunduc. He supplied Frish and says he knew about Gotfelt being a client, that's all. I'm inclined to believe him, based on past dealings. I'll ask our path guy, Leung, if he's had any other samples brought in that look similar. I've got a contact in the candy store.'

'Candy store?'

'For seized brown. A warehouse out in Red Hook. It all goes there for storage. They keep it for trials, investigations and so on.'

It had stopped raining, which seemed to be a cue. 'Interesting. Thanks again for Atom,' she said as they got up to leave.

'That was Strong, by the way.'

'Still trying to outwit Homicide.'

'Maybe. But you should give her a break. I think in her way she's trying to help.'

It was starting to cool outside, an unexpected autumn bowling a sharp wind down the brick-buttressed canyons of Manhattan. Cold and snow had dropped by already, but they only stayed a few days before hurtling unexpectedly to the Gulf Coast. Atom sat hunched behind a pale oak table, Bo Watz beside him and alert. They went through formalities for the record: name, address, occupation. 'Restaurateur and political donor,' Atom said without a trace of embarrassment. Watz leaned and whispered in his ear.

'And philanthropist,' Atom added equably.

Ryan nodded. 'Okay, gentlemen, we'll head right in. Mr Atom, it's another simple question: can you explain why your fingerprints were on the body of Cupid Frish? You have said that you didn't know her.'

'You don't have to answer that, Luther,' Watz interjected with a punishing zeal.

Atom dismissed him with a drop of his hand and lit a joint, inhaling deeply. 'I wasn't completely straight with you, Detective. More –'

'– curved?'

'Yeah, more that way. Fact is, I was in the downstairs part talking with my chef, Henry Bouche, going over menus and that kind of thing. I told him we'd got a new consignment in the storeroom, needed sorting out. We do this every week. So, he goes in and the next thing I hear is this dawn-of-the-universe scream. He's standing there. Well, obviously, I see it's a woman covered in brown.'

'Covered?' said Ryan.

Atom inhaled deeply again. 'Look, I ain't saying I did the right thing, okay? But I run a business and she obviously didn't have a need for it no more. It was top-grade shit so I told Henry to crack some of it off and put it in store, but leave her, you know, decent.'

'Good of you,' muttered Ryan.

'Yeah, I know. Anyway, I got to wondering how the hell she made it into my store on account of it ain't the city morgue.' He started to laugh, an organ wheezing to its crescendo, but stopped himself. 'And from what I been hearing, that's just as well. No offence, Detective.'

'Well, I knew it wasn't good for business having her around and I didn't want the heat, rivals maybe trying to drive me out. I'm in a competitive occupation and it stank of a set-up. You got to understand, protection comes with discretion. That's my side of the deal. If I stopped offering that, I'd stop being valuable to the feds, to City Hall. I'd be out and someone would just take my place. Everybody'd be worse off.'

Ryan walked over to the window, staring outside. 'Then what happened?'

'We put her in the cooler.'

'For the record, I'd like it noted that my client acted in full compliance with regulations governing the storage of fresh meat,' added Watz.

'Sure. I didn't want dead bodies near to fresh meat or vegetables; cross-contamination is a serious risk,' said Atom. 'Anyway, soon as the last guest left, maybe four in the morning, I carried her out to the alley. Henry helped, but it was me mostly. He's French, so the whole dead thing was freaking him out, sending him below the waterline. Muttering and moaning all day.'

Atom sounded detached and steady, making the story seem as interesting as a stomach bug.

'We just left her there. She didn't arrive with any clothes or nothing. I figured she'd be found quick enough. Actually, come to think of it, Bo, it wasn't the cooler. We put her in the chill section, so she was easy to handle and not too rigid. Like a lettuce or –'

'Did you recognize her?' Ryan interrupted.

'I don't think so, but that ain't to say she didn't visit my place.'

'Was she there over the weekend?'

'Like I told you, I can't say either way.'

'Is Bishop Heston Gotfelt ever a customer?'

Atom let out a loud laugh. 'The food nut? You got to be kidding. No way. Never. Listen, if he turned up I'd know the revolution was won.'

Even Watz grinned.

'But the Health Commissioner is a regular,' said Ryan dispassionately. Atom's face retreated to its blank indifference. 'Upstairs, yes. Downstairs, no. It'd leak out. He ain't that stupid and neither am I.'

'But he knows about the downstairs?'

'He's a grown-up and, like I said before, we're on government business.'

'I've heard eateasys claim a lot of things, but that's a first,' Ryan observed. 'I'll make sure I'm there to see you get the Congressional Medal of Honor from President Bryant. Concealing a crime is a felony, Mr Atom. You're looking mighty unbothered for a man looking at ten to fifteen in Sing Sing,' Ryan said.

'I'd say we uncovered it, Detective,' Atom replied, focusing watery eyes on a far wall. 'We left her in a public place and made sure the cops were called. I did my duty. Check your logs, trace the vid number. You'll find it's registered to Bouche. But I had to protect my joint and the operation we got going. Civic duty.'

21

As Heston Gotfelt lay cocooned and restless on his daybed, eleven people – six men and five women – sat in a New York apartment three states away and nurtured revolution. Not one of them was less than two hundred and fifty pounds in weight, so it wasn't a very active revolution they had in mind.

Anna and Grace were knitting at the back, absorbed in cross-stitches and drops, thinking about their families.

'The action against Mitchell's was a resounding success, fellow eaters,' said Hyram Drigger, lawyer, militant eater, Friend of the Metropolitan Opera and convenor of the New York chapter of the Pursuit of Happiness Mission. He sat facing the group.

'Media coverage was excellent, beyond what I dared expect. Every newspaper carried a report and we were on National Public Radio.' He held out the *New York Post*, the *Daily News* and the *New York Times* one after the other. 'Now we have shown that we will not be ignored, we will eat as free as our forefathers,' he said with passion.

'Amen,' said Anna, eyes fixed, puzzling over the sleeve of a sweater she was creating. It was emerging where the neck should be.

'Uh huh,' said Grace, Anna's cousin, although they looked identical. It wasn't quite the right response. But more often than not they got to be so absorbed in their stitching that they quite forgot whether they were pursuing earthly Happiness, which came with chips and dips, or Eternal Salvation at the First Baptist Church, which did not.

Drigger continued, encouraged by the show of fealty. 'My family did not flee persecution in Europe just to be told how to live their lives here in the land of the free.' In fact, his family never fled persecution at all, but emigrated quietly in the 1990s aboard a comfortable cruise ship, selling the small leather goods store they owned in Baden Baden to seek a split-level, condominium life in Westchester County.

'Of the free,' intoned Anna mechanically, dropping a stitch and cursing gently under her breath. 'Uh hm,' matched Grace.

'And neither did yours, my friends. It has fallen to us, the significant of size, to seize the banner of freedom, to fight for the right of all Americans to consume whatever they want, whenever they want it, wherever they find it. A right we had, but which was stolen from us by politicians pandering to multinational insurance companies and the infernal health lobby.'

James Benson, a security guard, interrupted. 'And ain't it the case that in ancient Rome, when they was ruling the world, they had the great feasts with tables piled high with a whole deli load o' shit, pastrami sandwiches, mayo, ketchup and so forth. They was lying around all day on their couches holding up bunches of grapes.' He turned to the assembled group. 'I seen the pictures.'

Drigger discouraged interruptions, but was happy if they deferred to his wisdom and allowed him to widen the lecture.

'Good, James, that is quite correct. The emperor Clodius Albinus, for example, could park five hundred figs, a basket of peaches, ten melons, twenty pounds of grapes, one hundred garden warblers and four hundred oysters. Although, I can't vouch for the condiments,' he smiled knowingly at the sea of blank faces hoping for signs of wry amusement. There was none and he coughed absently. 'They were, indeed, of great importance. And you may wonder "how is it that the most powerful nation on earth today does not allow its citizens to celebrate with food like the ancients?"'

Nobody had thought to ask that question, but they liked the sound of it anyway. There was a murmur of approval.

'I will tell you why,' said Drigger, grabbing a handful of potato chips and holding them aloft for dramatic effect, but being careful not to break them and compromise any resale potential at the auction later. 'It is because this nation of ours has been taken over by food fundamentalists. People who want us to live without life.'

He watched the reaction, gratified to see he had the attention of

167

everyone in the room. Even Grace and Anna looked up briefly, the steady click-click of needles momentarily stilled. This was the bit they enjoyed, when Mr Drigger made like Rev'unt Fogerty, spitting and sweating and cussing the iniquities of the world.

'Yes, my friends, these are people who want to tell us how to lead our brief spans, who insist that life is an end in itself, that they alone should dictate what makes for quality in that existence.' Drigger pointed his hand dramatically at the sky as Mrs Solkowitz in 610, just above, hit the floor with her broom handle to complain about the noise, which she had been listening for carefully.

On plates before them were challenging delicacies: tortilla chips, doughnuts, pastries filled with colourful, gelatinized fruits, cheese whips, refried beans and a large jug of home-made lemonade sweetened with real sugar from the pharmacy.

Most of them were like James Benson, humonsters, struggling against convictions for obesity. He had done time at the state f*t farm. Three months' hard aerobics and he hated those mothers; the jogging, the salads, all them classes telling you what was good, what was bad, green leaf this, fruit that. Sheee-it: everything he liked was in the bad column. Carrots and celery and tofu. I mean, what kind of food was that for a working stiff?

Compulsory stomach-shrinking surgery was next if he got stopped again; the judge had given him seven months to shed his co-f*tteral. He was lucky not to be in Los Angeles where three strikes and your hypothalamus was out. Zapped. All appetite gone at the cut of a laser.

Them Health Enforcement agents was ev'ywhere, he told Shawana. Now he had to drive and could only work nights. They never went out, except to the eateasys in Harlem, where the old guys played hip-hop and big, heavy-breasted women served sixteen-ounce burgers, wading through seas of hot eaters, jiggy hips, sexy, food people. Man, he loved the eateasys.

'I like a prisoner in my own body,' he blurted. Others stared. 'Sorry. Didn't mean to shout or nothing,' he said apologetically. 'It's just like you ain't worth shit if you're over your limits. Know what I mean? You get judged. Like you stupid or lazy.'

Drigger was pleased to have roused passion among his followers. 'You are so right, my friend. But there is a comfort. The greatest people through history have been f*t. Winston Churchill, Franklin Roosevelt, Oliver Hardy, Napoleon and the great twentieth-century musician Meatloaf. Rapacity, now that has always come in thin form.'

A man in the front row with short, dark hair and rimless glasses interrupted quietly. 'Not Roosevelt.'

'I'm sorry?' said Drigger.

'Roosevelt. He had problems with his legs because of polio, but he wasn't overweight.'

'Not physically, I grant you,' replied Drigger, scrambling. 'But Roosevelt would have been significant if he had been able to use his legs and given the chance. In fact, he would have been a champion for largeness; it's clear from reading his speeches.' Drigger moved on quickly, fearing somebody might ask for the precise references. The man in the front row looked as if he was about to do just that. 'Anyway, now we must decide what to do next. We are all very busy people.'

'We are busy people,' intoned Anna under her breath. 'Uh hm,' Grace added.

'And I ain't getting laid,' James Benson blurted out.

'Excuse me?' said Drigger.

'I said, "I ain't getting laid." I mean, having sex when you weigh two hunned and eighty pounds ain't easy.'

'Ain't easy,' murmured the knitters together.

'I think we should discuss that, man, set up some self-hep thing.'

Drigger stiffened. He had always been adamant that Pursuit of Happiness would not be drawn away from militancy.

'James, I sympathize with you, I do. But we're the silent majority, the masked crusaders.' Drigger spoke patiently, as if lecturing a child. 'You understand that, don't you? We're the people who break this cruel law, not ones who work within it. That's the whole point. It's what sets us apart. Batman, the Lone Ranger, they all wore masks to fight for justice. We talked about that last week, didn't we?'

He sounded kindly and James Benson squirmed on his two creaking, hardback seats, shuffling from one buttock to the next, f*t waves rippling, a tidal ebb and flow against bulwarks of belt and buttons.

'Guess so,' he said reluctantly. 'Still, I'd like –'

Drigger interrupted, raising his hand for silence. 'Talk to me afterwards,' he said, firm, insistent and avuncular. 'There are organizations, people you can see.'

'We could do a lonely hearts,' said another voice.

Preserve me, thought Drigger, surveying his army, people he had first met at his one-man obesity law practice Downtown, heavy souls with little prospect of winning court cases and weight extensions, or of paying him for that matter.

Most of them were on welfare, unable to work because of their size. They shuffled and waddled into his tiny office near the Woolworth Building, hoping for a miracle after hearing his advertisements on Hispanic and black radio stations. He was cheap. He could get exemptions. ('Hyram Drigger, attorney-at-law. Why weight and see?')

Drigger understood prejudice through the prism of his own life. To be short was bad enough. To be short and bald was worse. To be short, bald and refused entry to the Yacht Club and the brunette divorcee who worked there was intolerance of the worst kind. Or so Drigger supposed as his law practice had struggled to keep its purchase against soaring rents.

Resentments grew and he saw slights and snubs at every turn. 'Go away, little man,' they all seemed to say. Ulcers formed and bile filled his ducts, poisoning his soul as he ploughed through suits against the city brought by chancers who slipped on the sidewalk, neighbour quarrels and the other debris that washed ashore at night court.

Then Timothy 'Jim' Beam wheezed into his office one day, easing apologetically sideways, a small, round head balanced on enormous bulk and two legs, lower limbs bowed by the weight they had to bear. Jimmy Bean was his first attempt to use anti-discrimination laws to spare a client the rigours of f*t farm or compulsory surgery. It failed. But f*t Jimmy came from a wealthy family of storekeepers in Poughkeepsie and Drigger found patrons and a vocation.

James Benson was a rarity, despite his frustrations. At least he worked, albeit labouring at night and leading his public life in private places for fear of being arrested or taunted. Few humonsters could find jobs. Insurance premiums were high for the overweight and employers baulked at taking them on, even with the weight exemption certificates given to key workers.

They were all in debt to Drigger financially, tied to him through efforts to get exemptions, their inability to pay his fees or the loans for surgery and counselling programmes that he offered, but only at unfavourable rates.

'We are making our presence felt,' said Drigger, feeling the eyes on him and enjoying the attention, the energy. He had respect, at least here.

22

Devlin met Susan in a coffee shop on the Upper West Side and they embraced, holding each other tight, but not with their lower bodies. Fi Fi was slumped under the table.

'You're looking so good, Suse; beauty unbound.'

She smiled and stuck out her tongue. 'Still reading the romance manuals, I see.'

Devlin laughed. 'Don't knock self-improvement. But, professionally speaking, you're an Enforcement agent's nightmare. I bet you've never failed a fergie. Too many of you and we'd be out of bonuses.' Devlin felt the private protective affection that lovers give each other. 'Hey, congratulations, by the way. Aron, isn't it?'

'Aaron.'

'Aaron, yes. Sorry. How long have you guys been together?'

'Two years now, hence Fi Fi.'

Devlin reached down and patted a hairy head that had raised for formal acknowledgement.

'Where'd you meet?'

'We both do exemption cases, although he's more corporate, and we were both at a convention in St Louis.' She paused and let out a short laugh, as if expelling surprise. 'It's surprising, but I'm happy. I mean, he's got acceptable neuroses, a rent-controlled apartment and a sense of humour.'

'Those are good,' said Devlin. 'And I guess going out with an attorney is better than catching some other, more nasty disease.'

'Matt Devlin!'

'Hey, I'm kidding. Attorney is good. I'm glad you're happy.'

'But how are you?' she asked, suddenly leaning forward and concentrating. 'You look tired.'

'I'm fine. It's just been a difficult few days, that's all. And does anybody manage to sleep properly in this city?'

Once, she would have reached over and stroked his face or touched his hand and he noticed that she didn't ask whether he was seeing anybody. Perhaps she didn't need to, it was so obvious.

Hyper-skimmed lattes arrived and Susan, still a genetic project of wild hair and nervous energy, got down to business via a small siding, where they talked about Sylvia and she said that Devlin should stop worrying. He wasn't the first single father in the world or the worst. It was healthy for teenagers to rebel.

'Okay, there is a guy, Hyram Drigger, runs a pro-choice group. I know him vaguely through his legal work. He represents the weight-challenged at hearings, mostly court-appointed. But he also does *pro bono* stuff, some of which we send his way.

'Anyway, rumour is that he has this group, radicals, that meet in his apartment and talk about how to bring an end to Control. I don't have more than that. It's probably just a load of arbuckles sitting around and moaning. But he'd definitely be worth checking out. He's connected to the whole angry eating scene and has some pretty militant attitudes himself, least so I hear. Listen, he's prickly and pugnacious. Be careful.'

'It's my new resolution, believe me. And thanks. I won't mention where I got the name.'

'God, don't. I have to work with these people.' She shivered and her thin shoulders hunched. Case loads were now in double figures every month, she said, stirring abstractedly at the cold coffee. 'It's getting to be a big problem. Every time they make a food ban, not-for-profits get the consequences. A lot of people are just giving up on it all, middle-class people. It's weird. But we're getting professional types who just can't cope. I don't think Washington realizes what a crutch food is, a real stress buster. It isn't just about health and money and big principles, I mean.'

'It's conditioning, Susan, that's all. In the old days everyone just accepted what they were given, no questions, no thought.'

Susan nodded her head in frustration. 'No, no, no,' she said, restraint and passion tightening her voice. 'It's only about power. What's the difference between accepting things without question and doing what you're told without question? Not much, I'd say. Matt, I think you're blind to what's around you.'

'Fine, okay, I'm a deluded sap.'

'I didn't say that.' Susan sounded sad and Devlin regretted being drawn into their oldest, most corrosive discussion.

'I'm sorry. It's just hard for me to think outside the job. I guess I just feel that people need to be protected from their appetites and always have done. Food is no different.' He smiled. 'Besides, we still got fructose and it isn't rationed.' Fruit.

Devlin told her about the rotten apples. 'It's probably nothing,' he said, shrugging.

She frowned. 'But you don't think that, do you? Maybe somebody you arrested, a looney out there with a grudge.'

'It's possible. But I don't get a connection. It seems too kind of childish somehow and what could it mean? I'm rotting. I don't get it.'

Susan pursed her lips. 'Dead things rot, Matt.'

They paused and stared seriously at each other. Then they drifted on, dropping in and out of each other's lives. Susan had vet bills and a husband, Devlin had a daughter. 'At least you can put Fi Fi to sleep.'

She looked shocked.

'A joke, Suse. But that girl's like some kind of radio I just can't seem to tune into.' Susan made the sort of sympathetic noises a childless dog owner can make to a child owner: ones with an undertone of relief.

'Listen to yourself, Matt. Get some perspective and stop being so anxious. You need to get a date, give yourself another life. I bet you're working too hard and not seeing anybody at all.'

'It's top of my list, believe me. Well, second, after getting the leaking windows fixed. I'm sorry we didn't –'

She took his hand and smiled. 'Don't say a word; it was the best thing. What's so cruel is how loving a person isn't always enough, especially if the chemicals that say "this person", or "that person" have a different idea. Nature's very contrary.'

'Like the new weather?' he said ruefully. 'Hey, thanks again.

I appreciate your coming out and it's been good to see you, catch up.'

They hugged and promised to keep in touch. But he knew they wouldn't and he watched her leave quickly, bundles of papers under her arm, without turning back.

'Fi Fi is fine,' he shouted after her. But she probably didn't hear and he felt emptiness.

'No kidding,' said Strong, drawing heavily on the first of five laid-out beer-shot glasses. Devlin had caught the subway to Brooklyn after seeing Susan and they were sitting outside a ramshackle bar with views of the dismal, decayed old navy yards. 'Are we surprised Atom has an explanation? Come on.'

'I don't know,' Devlin said. 'With his underworld contacts? It's true, isn't it? He wouldn't need to dump a body in his backyard. He's an ex-cop. Why leave fingerprints? It doesn't stack up.'

'Double bluff. Like hiding in plain sight. He comes out with a story that covers all the angles, stops Ryan snooping any more. Big-shot detective is all relieved because she doesn't have to run up a guy with City Hall connections and put a crink in her own neat career.' Strong raised her hand like a jet taking off. 'How'd the body get in the eateasy if it wasn't Atom or someone he knows? Did anyone ask that?'

It was a good question, Devlin thought. Someone with knowledge and access. 'It would help if we had a body,' he said.

'We?'

'You know what I mean.'

'You and Ryan getting close? In a work sense, naturally.'

If she wasn't going to let Devlin into her life, there was still no deal. He moved to more neutral territory and asked what she'd been doing. Fishing, she said. Bought herself six months of a motor boat moored out near Breezy Point. Devlin had no idea she fished.

'Helps keep me out of mischief until Internal Affairs are done. I can sit out there, in the deep. Nobody bothers me. Not even the fish.' She laughed. 'Come on, tell me; are you and the detective making out yet?'

'Jeez, where did that come from?'

'I heard she even sent you some fruit. Kind of sexy, don't you think?' She winked.

'Sorry to disappoint you. Somebody did, but not her, buddy. It was all rotten. I think that'd be sending out the wrong impression, don't you? Like a bouquet of dead flowers.'

'Shame. Maybe somebody we got sent to a f*t farm. Razors, scary notes, anything like that?'

'No, just mush and maggots. Not pretty. But not deadly either. No big deal.'

'You report it?'

'What's to report? This is New York, Wal-Mart of weird, so the guidebooks tell me. I'm not losing sleep.'

Devlin told her about Drigger, but sensed no interest. He wished the reunion had been better. But it was a desultory hour. Strong became distant, sniping and teasing, and he wanted to get away, feeling her Furies rage, tightening around them both; wounded animals circling each other on a shared, arid plain, probing for information neither wanted to volunteer. He resented her attitude to Ryan and, by implication, to himself. Grow up, he wanted to yell. Sort your life out. Think. Or was he talking to himself?

Hyram Drigger had an office Downtown, but it was after hours and Devlin decided to surprise him at home.

After leaving Strong, frustrated by the gulf his visit had exposed, Devlin went back to the Upper West Side, past streams of men and women running or stretching on the outdoor exercise equipment, newly installed for adults in what had been the Riverside Park children's play area.

The bicycle lanes on Henry Hudson Parkway were more congested than the narrow blacktop left for vehicles. People pushed children and elderly relations in jogging buggys, so the taxi ride was less than twenty-five minutes. He was dropped outside an old brick apartment block, the stone steps to its front door chipped, worn into concaves by feet that couldn't quite afford to occupy a better neighbourhood.

Devlin searched the buttons and found Drigger's name neatly written in small capitals. He ran his fingers over the letters and recalled the apples, the neatly handwritten card.

It was a fifth-floor walk-up, good for thighs at least, maybe ten calories if he took it two steps at a time. He saw mail scattered on the hall table. A letter from the revenue service, a holiday brochure and this month's *What Weight?* magazine. The cover had a photograph of a model and promised to give up the secrets to her all-you-can eat lifestyle.

Hyram Drigger was short and trim, wearing casual blue chinos and a button-down white Oxford shirt. His bald head seemed to gleam and there was a strong smell of cologne. There were no signs of nerves or surprise or excess weight, thought Devlin, as he was led into a cluttered sitting room.

'Sorry to arrive unexpectedly, Mr Drigger. I was in the area – '

He lifted a hand. 'Spare me. I'm in the business. You're investigating a food crime and my name came up.'

Devlin nodded.

'Please, sit down. Many of my clients have difficulties with Enforcement. I'd be very surprised if my name doesn't warrant a considerable amount of space on your files. Can I offer you an apple juice?'

'No. Thank you. I'm investigating a break-in at Mitchell's, the food emporium, and was talking with a contact who said you might, through your pro-choice group, be able to help with some names.'

'Is that all?' he said, amused. 'Forgive me, Agent Devlin. But I'm not in the business of throwing out names and connecting them to a crime about which I have no knowledge, apart from what I read in the newspapers.'

'Can I see a list of group members, Free to be F*t, isn't it?'

'Pursuit of Happiness,' he corrected. 'The others broke away. You should update your files, or your contacts. And the supporters' list is confidential.'

'I'm on Health Enforcement business, Mr Drigger. I'd advise you to cooperate.'

'Please, don't threaten me. It's time-consuming and pointless. Others have tried, including the mayor and the Anti-F*t League. As you can see, I'm still here.'

'With secrets?'

'With beliefs, Agent Devlin. The state pursues those who choose to exercise their right to eat freely and, freely, not to exercise. It's what keeps you employed.'

'And you, Counsellor.'

He leaned forward. 'I pursue the state. There's a difference. Let me tell you who they are, these people who make up our world, yours and mine. They're sad and pathetic, some say; but to me they merely want the comfort of food in this dying, drained planet we inhabit and are so successfully destroying. It is – was – the one power they had, the right to eat fast food and brown and f*t-filled cakes oozing with sugars; unlimited portions of unthreatening, uncomplicated sensations served in bright, cheap places where a light always shone. Not religious light, Agent Devlin, but real artificial light. It made up for the drab boundaries in the rest of their lousy, complicated lives; the hopeless communities they never manage to leave; an escape from a world watching itself die on CNN.'

'I just enforce the law, Mr Drigger. I'm looking for names, not a cause.' Devlin looked at him. 'If I suspected you of anything I'd have come here hard, with a warrant and crew of agents. I'd be tipping this place upside down instead of delivering your mail. This is a friendly visit,' Devlin added in an unfriendly way, thrusting over the letters and magazine. 'I need friendly in my life at the moment.'

Drigger stood up, nodding his head in some sort of silent dismay. The meeting was over. Lawyers were good at judging that moment, Devlin thought, a time when the bill reached a round number, or a conversation was becoming dangerous or unwanted.

As he walked out, Devlin recalled the name plate. 'Do you know where I live, Mr Drigger?'

'What?' He was obviously puzzled, startled by the question. 'Of course not. I don't even know you, my friend.'

Devlin nodded. 'Good.'

'One more thing, Agent Devlin. Confidentiality is important to what I do and I'm an expert in the food laws. I'll tie you up in court for months, believe me, if you step into my life again.'

23

The text was anonymous, untraceable but carrying enough information for police sent in response. 'Roosevelt Island. Fifty yards from crossing. A body.'

There wasn't time, for a dollar in quarters, to add that it was past rigor mortis and pliable again, nor that weather and rats can be uncharitable to the naked form, so they should hurry.

The first officers to arrive scanned the eyes and knew straight away who it was, which badge to call.

Ryan had been cooking a tuna and zucchini bake. She left her children playing the latest hologram game, a vicious dynastic struggle between the Helgarths of Nirtana, in the third galactic empire, and their rivals, the sugar smugglers from Dorn.

It was a slow ride into town, with traffic creeping up the parkway. Gales blew through the empty exercise pods, turning pedals and wheels in ghostly pursuit, as small clouds harassed pedestrians rash enough to ignore the weather warnings.

She saw the squad cars before crossing the narrow bridge that linked the sliver of island to Queens. An early evening light was rich scarlet reflected off the United Nations building, and a small, brightly-lit tent obscured the forensics team moving around in silent, absorbed industry. It was a shadow show for death near the Octagon building, the last fragment of an old lunatic asylum. They moved aside when she arrived, pushing her way through blooming myrtle trees, banyans and flaming azaleas. The air was damp and heavy and an alligator thrashed on the river bank. Ryan looked at Max Meyer, one of the older, more experienced scene-of-crime investigators. He didn't need to be asked.

'Three, four hours at most.'

Ryan took a while to realize what was missing. Then she knew: smell. From the bacteria, protozoans and nematodes that stay dormant in living bodies, but revive with death, like prisoners on discovering that every guard has gone. The body didn't seem swollen or decayed either, despite the rotting subtropical heat.

'Tell me, Max; how can a person be dead for five days, but look like they died five hours ago?'

'Freezing. I do that with all mine,' he dead-panned, sweat pooled under the arms of his shirt. 'She was dumped recently. There's no larval infestation or swelling.'

'Or a cooler, a chill cabinet,' said Ryan, picking at her lower lip and thinking about Luther Atom and the precision with which he knew how, exactly, he had stored Frish; his knowledge about meat decay.

'That'd work,' Meyer agreed.

But at least there was a body again. 'Let's get her to the morgue.' And under her breath, she added: 'This time I'm following.'

Ryan was met by Jack Krebs, a semi-retired pathologist and widower who worked the shifts nobody else wanted. As nobody wanted him, the arrangement suited everyone.

'Hi, Jack. Long time,' Ryan said, shaking a steady, liver-spotted hand.

This sort of night made it worthwhile for Krebs, a change from insulin overdoses. A real murder. He had read the file, such as it was. No pathology to speak of, just some skimped scene-of-crime analysis, fingerprints, and photographs of the body in its curious, mocking costume.

He coughed, hard and wracking. 'I'll tell you, Nathalie Ryan, the damn air these days doesn't agree with me.'

'It's chemicals,' said Ryan disinterestedly as they walked along strip-lit corridors in the basement. 'In the clouds. I read about it. Nature getting mad or even. They don't know for sure.' The morgue was close to the outside incinerator, although the temperature cooled as they approached.

They reached a room of shining metal vaults and handles; a clean place with grey linoleum. Krebs pulled out a trolley. It moved soundlessly on oiled castors carrying a shapeless mass concealed by pale plastic sheeting.

He pulled back the cover. 'You don't know how she died, correct?'

Ryan nodded, staring at the body as if willing it to speak, offer up a clue, hold out a cue card. 'She disappeared from the morgue. We did preliminary at the scene, but not enough. She was a hooker.'

'I may be able to tell if she was working immediately prior to death, but as for dating it exactly, this one's too far gone.'

'Anything. Stomach contents, drugs, brown especially.'

Krebs promised to work on her overnight, depending on what else the city brought him, how many other lives extinguished by design, despair or bad judgement were due to discover that the road to eternity can begin not with a brilliant, beckoning light, but a grizzled pathologist whistling a medley from *Cats*. The strike was causing more chaos than the weather, bodies were shunted around, paperwork disappeared. Krebs had never known anything like it. Ryan left for the certainties of life, such as zucchini bake and the sugar smugglers from Dorn.

Krebs rubbed his hands and turned on his old recorder, placing it beside his sandwich. He used a spatula to gently open the jaw, pleased that at least this flesh was still held by connective tissue and not yet collapsed into pulpy, spongy strips. 'Oy, oy,' he muttered, wondering how a Homicide detective could have missed what he was seeing.

'Face undamaged, no abrasions, bruising,' he said briskly, a subduing echo capturing fragments of his flat, incurious voice as he moved the head. 'Band of bruises, grazes and interdermal haemorrhaging evident on front of neck and extending symmetrically; oval grazes each side of voice box; multiple small bruises right side of neck, fingertip bruise below left angle of jaw, more bruises on left side of lower jaw.' He switched off the recorder and rubbed his eyes.

The damage was too obvious, surely, to have escaped even the least experienced scene-of-crime forensics and Ryan was not that.

182

He went back to the original report and frowned. No mention of what he would have expected even a rookie to note: Cupid Frish was strangled with extraordinary ferocity, the breath squeezed out of her like the last juice from a fruit.

He examined her hands, waxen and cold, and took a small scalpel between the nails. He was rewarded by the index finger on the right hand, which yielded a tiny length of coarse, black animal hair.

The Bronx zoo was tired and worn. Everyone was so caged in crowded tenements, co-ops and gated communities, that it made no sense to visit the same. Moulded concrete buildings patched with weed and mosses were surrounded by project housing; encroaching hells of booming music and gunshots that loomed over the lonely enclosures where animals paced, tails tucked, bored and cowed and listless, or leapt, suddenly agitated, on to gnarled wood that they pretended not to recognize. Giraffes reached inquisitively. Birds flapped hopelessly in netted atriums, testing the limits of half-remembered freedoms. Ryan drove through the entrance gate to her appointment with Dr Leo Franklin, keeper of primates.

'Apple juice?'

Ryan declined.

'This is an excitement for me, Detective,' Franklin said, pouring himself a glass. 'It's not every day a murder visits, so to speak. Mine is a very sheltered existence.' He sounded entertained, his voice dancing, hinting at an alternate past in some other country.

'It's not every day an investigation brings me to the zoo, believe me,' Ryan replied. She followed him into a cluttered office; books were scattered on the floor, some half-open.

'My apologies. I'm researching primate eating habits for the federal government and the bibliography is large. The Department for Health Enforcement want advice on dietary instincts, from an anthropomorphic perspective.'

Ryan took in the scattering of open documents. 'You're on the system. It's how I found you. Not a problem I hope.'

'I'm certainly not grumbling at helping a murder inquiry.' He laughed softly again and sat on an overstuffed chair, pointing Ryan to its twin. She sat and began, eventually reaching the precipice where sense tumbled into a void. She told him about the fingerprints and the black hair, the overhead fans and the fruit, and where it all seemed to be leading.

Franklin laughed loudly, uproariously, rocking back and forward, his sharp eyes kindled with pleasure.

'This is funny?'

'Forgive me. It's just, well, firstly, gorillas don't swing from trees, let alone ceiling fans. They can, but choose not to. It's a common misconception, so don't feel bad. In fact, chimpanzees are not too keen on it either; uses a lot of energy and is, of course, very risky. Only in Tarzan movies, I'm afraid. But chimps are like us, they'll do anything for a good agent. Incidentally, we share 98 per cent of their DNA. The smaller species, such as squirrel monkeys, now they spend their whole lives in arboreal canopies. But that's an entirely different matter based on genetic predisposition. The ground is terrifying for them.'

Ryan sighed. 'Can you offer a better explanation for what we found? There was gorilla hair in the engine mechanisms of the fans.' She handed over a sheaf of photographs taken at Montcalm Avenue. Franklin studied them carefully before grimacing.

'Happily, that is not my job,' he said, leafing through. 'All I can do is tell you about gorillas and their habits.'

'Go.'

'Well, as I said, they simply don't swing, nor, by the way, do they sing that they're the king of the swingers, a jungle VIP. My children love that cartoon.'

'Mine too. What about the prints, the fruit?'

'I can't help there, either. Gorillas certainly cannot, would not, peel an apple.'

'Could you train one to do it?' Ryan asked.

'Not in a million years. No dexterity, you understand; although they share with us opposing, revolvable thumbs, there is little sense of how to use this great gift. Holding a knife with any artistry requires many, many little skills that we take for granted, the evolutionary heritage of *homo sapiens*, that interesting place where the body is the action of the brain. It's rather beautiful, philosophically, don't you think?'

Ryan shifted awkwardly in her chair. Franklin looked sympathetic, a consultant to his patient.

'I can't offer you an explanation, I'm afraid, just what science knows. Please, come with me.'

Ryan followed through a back door, past enclosures of white foxes and half-familiar feral wildlife, a raccoon, a lemur and, incongruously, a goat. In the distance, a police siren wailed in counterpoint to a lion's yawn and the yelp of howler monkeys, who leapt noisily around their domain of hanging tyres as Franklin passed.

'Don't mind them. Sociable creatures. They normally range over several miles, so this isn't ideal. Given our evolved ambulatory laziness we should swap: give them Manhattan and take over the cages. Life is very unfair.'

Soon, Ryan was facing an enormity of haired musculature with small, alert brown eyes, a squatting Buddha.

'This is Baku, a lowland gorilla. He's twelve years old and three hundred pounds, which is rather small, actually. We've reared him here, Detective. But apart from recognizing his name, cognitive skills are practically zero.'

'Meaning?'

'Meaning that it simply isn't possible for a gorilla to have carried out the attack you've described. It's an absurd idea. They can't use tools of any description, let alone wield a knife. In fact, they are unlike chimpanzees in that respect, which are capable little creatures, able to observe and replicate human activities. Orangutans on occasion. But not gorillas, and that print you showed me was most definitely from a gorilla, there is no doubt. The length of the index finger alone makes it obvious.'

Ryan stared at Baku, who stared back through impassive, soft eyes.

'There's extensive research into what gorillas can attain as skills. The great apes never use tools, even when they've mixed with chimpanzees that do; further evidence of a poor learning capability, by the way. They might learn to use a stick to rake over some food, if you're lucky. But that is all. Basically, Detective, we're talking about a creature with the skills of a slow two-year-old human, not some sophisticated beast capable of being unleashed as a selective killing machine. I'm sorry to disappoint you.'

'Cutting up fruit is out of the question?'

Franklin smiled. 'Completely.'

'And you're saying that under no circumstances could a gorilla kill a human?'

'They will kill, yes. But training them to kill? No. And I have to tell you, a three- or four-hundred-pound gorilla in an apartment would have caused a lot more damage than those photographs show. It would have been indiscriminate, loud, wanton and profligate. It would have defecated and urinated. Tell me, do you have any complaints from neighbours about noise? How did it get in? It's a doorman building, yes? Did it use the elevator? How did it know which floor to press? What are the answers to those questions?'

'Unsatisfactory.'

'A gorilla going bananas, if you'll excuse that rather tedious phrase, is a very raucous affair, believe me. They are not quiet creatures when gripped by frenzy. It is simply not possible that nobody heard.'

Ryan looked hard at Baku, who stared back, giving nothing away.

'He's got an alibi,' Franklin said, before they turned and started walking back to his office. A light yellow snow began to fall and Ryan pulled up her collar.

'Tell me, is there nothing, nothing at all out there, that might support evidence pointing conclusively to a gorilla, with or without an accomplice?'

'You could be on the cusp of an article for the scientific journals.' Franklin was laughing. 'I'm sorry to tease. It is just extraordinary for me, you see. Gorillas may look fearsome, but they are very gentle creatures, more likely to run away from conflict with us than seek it. They are, if you will, vegetarian pacifists trapped in the bodies of prizefighters. It's why we make such monstrous presumptions about them. Perceptions. But ours, not theirs. Look at your evidence again. Whatever else it is telling you, it isn't that there was a gorilla in that apartment.'

He walked Ryan to the door. 'One other thing, Detective. Only humans are cruel enough to kill for reasons other than food, procreation or protection.'

'But this was about food. Gorillas are vegetarian, right?' Ryan found herself saying.

'Food is many things to us, Detective. More than it is to other animals. They could teach us a thing or two about priorities.'

As she drove back into Manhattan, Ryan ran through the evidence and was gnawed by another remark Franklin had made: only humans feel the need to explain themselves. It tugged at her, demanding attention.

The evidence still all pointed to a gorilla, even on the freeway, and she tried to think of accomplices. Fritz Hanson said so. The science said so. The hair in the ceiling fans, in the mouth of Cupid Frish and scattered on cushions said so. It was animal hair. The fruit in the kitchen told the same story, as did the terrible, excessive crushing of throat cartilage that she had somehow missed. How had that been possible? Food. It all came back to food. When she arrived at her office there were four messages marked urgent from Public Relations. They needed to put out a statement urgently.

Secrets in New York soon leak. A measured piece from the *New York Times* Metro section headlined 'Primate May Be Implicated In Unusual Murder' was on Ryan's desk together with 'Ape Goes SxxT!' from the *Post's* front page, illustrated with a photograph of King Kong straddling the Empire State Building holding Fay Wray. 'At least Hanson'll be happy,' she muttered.

The calls had been coming in from all over the country – the world – said her assistant, adding that the commissioner wanted a briefing urgently. A Japanese television crew had already flown in with a blow-up Godzilla, seventy feet tall, and caused panic near the Holland Tunnel. An armed response unit had been sent and it had got messy.

Ryan flipped channels before taking the elevator up to the

commissioner's office on the eleventh floor of One, Police Plaza. There were experts everywhere. 'Who knew we had so many gorilla watchers in Manhattan?'

'We need to contain this,' said the commissioner, pacing his office. 'It's making us look like idiots. Damn it, we're scaring people.'

Commissioner Reynolds always considered the moment when a Japanese television crew turned up with anything inflatable to be a tipping point.

'This has gone international, Ryan, and I've got the mayor's office on my back. They seem to be obsessed with this Frish woman.'

Reynolds looked out of the window and folded one arm behind his back, a gesture he had seen in a movie about Napoleon. 'If there's a murderous gorilla loose in this city, I want it stopped, understand? It's working for somebody. I don't need John Finch with an opportunity to chew me over about priorities, not with the strikes stretching resources.'

'Listen, Chief. I've talked to experts. I don't think it's possible –'

'I don't care what's possible, I care about headlines and about the mayor. I've already ordered up extra patrols and cancelled all leave. We need to reassure people that there isn't some rogue creature out there. It's bad enough with the damn clouds menacing anything that moves.'

On Fox News a woman was pleading and looking around in mild panic. Live. On air. 'I was booked to talk about Fashion Week.'

'But there's an ape loose in the city,' said the male interviewer, sternly. 'It's killed.'

'Oh sure, you're so right,' said the young woman from *Vogue*. She composed herself into Serious and cleared her throat. 'I think we can expect a lot of *faux* fur next fall, whenever that is.'

'It's due in the next few months,' prompted the interviewer.

'Well, black and brown are real difficult colours, a little frightening. I think the big design houses will wait a little, just to see what the street picks up.'

'Frightening indeed. Linda Smith, thank you. After the break, is there a gorilla in your neighbourhood? The five signs. And Patty will be here with your full weekend entertainment and weather alert round-up.'

Reynolds pushed mute. 'It's everywhere, the biggest story in the city, Ryan. The country.'

'It can't be an ape, sir,' she said. 'No way. They can't be trained, they make a noise –'

'Yes, yes, I know all that,' Reynolds broke in impatiently. 'But Hanson has the prints and Krebs says the life was squeezed out of her with, I quote, "an animal force". We're not talking a Pekingese here.'

'There's no animal DNA at any of the scenes, Chief.'

'– apart from the gorilla hair,' Reynolds interrupted accusingly.

'Apart from that, sure,' Ryan conceded. 'But there's no mucus, saliva or blood, or shit or piss. We've been back. There's no sign of a struggle, just mess.' Her voice began to rise. 'If Frish was murdered, she would have fought back, scratched, kicked. There'd be matter under her nails, her long nails. But none of them were even broken. I would have expected blood, much more hair, something more. Something from her.'

'So, it's a difficult crime scene. Let me give you a piece of advice. Prints don't lie. Evidence doesn't lie. You're a good cop; start thinking like one. Focus on what you know, not what you don't. It makes life a whole lot simpler.'

24

'Me too,' Devlin said as they sat in his apartment. 'Seven of them. I thought for a moment it might be you. The neat handwriting.'

Ryan snorted. 'And they say women have suspicious minds. I would've made sure to scrawl, by the way. But this is good, a break.'

'More a purée.'

'I'm serious. There has to be a link with Cupid Frish,' said Ryan. 'She's the only thing that connects you and me. Whoever it is obviously knows we're working this together. Still.'

'What do you mean?'

'These have arrived since you were taken off the case, officially anyway.'

The vid rang and Devlin reached across. 'Hey,' he said. It was Strong and sounding contrite. 'Look, I just wanted to apologize for being so shitty at the bar, compadre. I guess I've got a lot on my mind and was just lashing out.'

'Don't worry about it,' Devlin said and meant it. 'We all get bad days. Anyway, it wasn't just you. I've been scratchy, too. I wish we'd never stopped that woman.'

'For what it's worth, you're probably right about Atom. It doesn't make sense for an ex-cop to dump a body in his backyard. I mean, even I wouldn't do that. Tell that to hotshot next time you see her, by the way. She's probably got me on her suspects' list by now.'

'I will,' said Devlin, laughing despite it all. 'She's here with me now, matter of fact.'

'Of course she is,' said Strong, not a trace of surprise. 'I never doubt office gossip.'

'It isn't like that,' Devlin replied. 'Look, I have to go. Thanks for the call and, well, you know.'

'Yeah, I know.'

He closed the vid and told Ryan.

'Strong apologizing? Now I do believe in the tooth fairy. So, what we got here? Seven apples, not five nor three. Seven. Deadly sins? Days of the week?' Ryan ruffled her hair.

'Seven is one of the big numbers,' suggested Devlin, pinching the bridge of his nose. 'Genesis. God took seven days to create the earth. Apples represent the fall of humanity. It's communion blood for us, of course. At the church.'

They threw it back and forth, what they knew, trying to find invisible wires connecting the Bible, a prostitute and a gorilla that they could tug. And all without the help of hallucinogenic drugs because the pharmacy was three blocks away. Whoever it was seemed to have personal knowledge: home addresses, for example, private agreements to work together.

'Heston Gotfelt,' Devlin said. 'There's a guy who thinks he's got God on his side and apples are big in the Bible and get used a lot in Christ the Fit promotions, like a kind of logo. He could find out where people live. You and I both went to see him and he knows I'm on the church roll.'

Devlin drove on, reluctantly, because his mind was only illuminating the next few moments ahead, and it wasn't a journey he wanted to make.

Ryan nodded. 'Let's say you're right. What's in it for him to draw attention to himself? Not too much, wouldn't you say? Okay, let's try and throw out a motive: Cupid blackmails him, he comes to New York, sets up a meeting. They fight. He kills her in a moment of madness or as part of a premeditated plan.'

It seemed plausible, but only for about twenty seconds.

'With a gorilla?' said Devlin. 'Wouldn't it be easier to use poison, a knife or a gun? I mean, an animal is kind of a peculiar choice of weapon, or am I just not up on the latest slaughter techniques? And what about Luther Atom? Now there's a guy connected to everybody in the city. He can find out things, knows how to fake a crime scene. Slippery as a greased pole. Besides, you said the zoo guy thought the ape thing was crazy?'

'He did. But I also read in *National Geographic* about scientists in Los Angeles teaching them to speak or write.'

'Yeah? Or was it the other way around? An ape teaching Californians how to communicate?'

'Now that will never happen,' said Ryan, opening her notebook and flicking through its neat pages. 'Frish was strangled by someone with abnormal strength. Her voice box was crushed. Gotfelt's a fit guy.'

'But a gorilla would be fitter,' Devlin countered.

'He has a zoo,' said Ryan quietly.

The apples had offered much, but given little, it seemed to Devlin. There was no real contact with what seemed likely or possible. After an hour or so he suggested a break. There was a bistro at the end of the road that stayed open late.

'Will you be requiring an eating counsellor tonight?' asked the waitress chirpily once they were seated at a corner table.

'No, thank you. We'll be fine,' said Devlin, poring over the menu and ordering his usual boeuf bourguignon sans boeuf.

'Count me in,' Ryan said.

They both used the scratch and sniff dessert menu cards. Devlin smelled tiramisu; she went for the ice cream. In the intimate glow from a damask-covered table light they searched for distractions and talked about other things: children, the weather and about how the romance had definitely gone out of the name Cupid and from somewhere else, too: their own lives.

'It's hard on relationships,' Ryan confessed over coffee. 'The hours are insane.'

'Mine, too,' Devlin replied. 'Health is the death ray to love affairs.'

But Ryan was still half in another place, frowning and tossing a coin, still circling restlessly around the case. 'Heston Gotfelt, Luther Atom, Heston Gotfelt, Luther Atom,' she repeated with each spin. 'It still seems too coincidental, don't you think? A major league holy roller turns up in town, very publicly, and a connected prostitute, one he knows very privately, dies. Then there's

City Hall. They fear what we might find, but I don't understand what.'

They worried in silence before she continued. 'A body covered in expensive chocolate. It disappears. It turns up again. But this time with incredible injuries, ones we missed first time around. Makes us look like idiots. Fruit being sent every which way and there's a gorilla in the mix. I've dropped acid, but this beats it. We're being played. I can feel it.'

Devlin wished Strong was with them on the case. This was her kind of insanity. Ryan was scowling.

'Let's follow the apples,' she said. 'Somebody is sending them and it's probably connected to Cupid Frish.'

They were close to Devlin's apartment and he asked her back for coffee after the meal. Sylvia was out seeing a movie.

Only she wasn't. 'Hey, monster mine, what are you doing here?'

'Don't sound so freaked. This is my home, in case you'd forgotten,' Sylvia said. The real reason emerged shyly from the living room.

'Damon,' said Devlin.

'Hey, Mr D. We got a project on old eating habits to work up. I figured you'd probably got some books we could use. Hope that's okay?'

Devlin narrowed his eyes suspiciously and might have been convinced if any volumes were open or even off the shelves, but let it pass. Damon was the kind who thought adults all fell off the ship named Naïve.

'Of course. Meet Nathalie Ryan, guys. She's a Homicide detective, so no killing tonight.'

'Pleased to meet you, ma'am,' said Slick.

'Hey,' said Sullen.

'Hey to you, too,' Ryan replied as Sylvia turned to a portable hologame. 'Oh, Dad, there's a delivery for you in the kitchen. Kinda smells so I'm not having it whatever, okay? We'll eat out.'

Ryan and Devlin looked at each other and she followed him. The odour was sweet. Devlin reached out to the grocery bag.

'Hold it,' Ryan said suddenly.

Devlin pulled back. 'What?'

'It moved.'

'Say again?'

'The bag. Look.'

A small indent gently pushed out at the sides, slowly, as if the bag itself was flexing a muscle.

'Got gloves?'

Devlin passed them over. Ryan approached cautiously and, gently, slipped a hunting knife, that had appeared in her right hand, along the sealed opening. This infuriated the bag.

'Careful. I don't want a Homicide detective killed in my kitchen,' Devlin said. 'It could screw the household insurance.'

The blade scythed swiftly through the tape and Ryan gingerly teased back the brown paper and moved her head, slowly, to inspect the contents.

Devlin eased forward as well. It was thin and green. A head turned towards them, but it was otherwise motionless, coiled on a bed of softening apples. But that was only half the surprise. It had no eyes at all.

There were many things Health Enforcement prepared agents for: snakes in the grass, snake eyes, snake oil, snake charmers. But live snakes home-delivered? For a moment they looked at each other then Ryan asked for a solid container, 'with a lid and holes. I don't want any more dead evidence.'

The vid rang again. 'Hey, I hate to bust into your romantic, sorry, working, evening again, but guess what I got delivered in a very upscale grocery bag?' Strong said.

Devlin felt his heart quicken. 'I might win this dollar. Thin, green, no eyes?'

'Hey, how'd you do that? Peeking in my shower again?'

'In your dreams. I got the same. Can you put it somewhere?'

'Done already. It's flushed.'

'What?'

'Down the john. Snakes just don't go with my decor, clash with the curtains. You know how it is when a date goes wrong.'

'Congratulations on trashing evidence. Again. Way to go, partner.'

Strong said sorry, she was suspended and not thinking straight. Devlin said so was her professional judgement. But he felt some sympathy all the same, knowing that for all her front, Strong could have been no less startled than him.

'Someone sends me snakes, first thing to go is the snake,' said Strong defensively. 'Anyway, you still got yours. Maybe it'll talk when it hears that the great Nathalie Ryan is on the case.'

'Funny. Look, we got our own situation here, I'll call back,' Devlin said urgently, hearing the snake hissing in its new home. Ryan had punched holes into the top of the plastic food container and made the transfer with the help of a long spaghetti spoon.

'Count yourself lucky,' Devlin told it. 'You'd be hurtling through the bowels of Brooklyn if you'd drawn the Strong residence.' The snake hissed back, unimpressed.

'Give it a name?' said Ryan. Just at that moment, Sylvia walked in with Damon.

'Gross,' she said with feeling.

'Did that come with the groceries? You should send it back, Mr D,' said Damon slyly. 'That meat is way too fresh.'

'Who delivered it?' Devlin asked Sylvia.

'Some guy, I think. The buzzer went a couple of hours ago. But it was kind of fuzzy; said there was a package on the front door. I asked did I need to sign and he said "no". That was it. Damon went down and picked it up. It was a Balducci's bag, so I figured it was just groceries.'

Ryan was already on Sylvia's computer looking up snakes.

They left Gross in the kitchen. Damon and Sylvia went out and Ryan said she'd get an expert on to it in the morning. They collapsed, drained, on the sofa drinking shots of wine, lots of them.

Devlin had no idea how it happened, or even why. Probably they both needed to escape, just for a while, and to feel shy again. Maybe just to feel.

He rubbed the back of his neck; it was just a tic, but she reached over with a hand and squeezed the tightened muscle and he said thanks. Instead of taking her hand away, it stayed squeezing, rhythmic and consoling.

'That's very good, Detective. You're in the wrong business.'

'My late husband. It was his business. Here.'

She half-turned him, put down her glass and began massaging his shoulders. Devlin felt the tension drift to some place that wasn't him and they started kissing, awkwardly and silently at first. It didn't matter. Soon, they were in the bedroom. It had been a while since he had let an intimate touch into his life, felt its power and purpose and possession. They made love and talked and told secrets through the heat they generated. The sex burned about five hundred calories, he estimated later.

25

'The Texas blind snake, *Leptotyphlops dulcis*,' said Murray Murtry, closing up his shop as soon as Ryan came in and opening up the box. 'About as rare as a please in this town. Completely harmless, though.' He sounded disappointed.

'Got a mean hiss,' said Ryan.

'All talk. Eats insects, termites mostly. Looks weird without eyes, don't it? Evolution sure cut them a tough hand. You got an average-sized one, maybe seven inches.'

Murtry was holding Gross confidently, stroking its skin and cooing.

'I usually carry one or two, matter of fact, when I can get hold of them. I'll be glad to take it off your hands.'

'Keep it. Just don't sell to anyone without contacting me first.'

'Sure. You'll need him in the witness stand, right? Check his movements?'

'Somebody delivered him to a Health Enforcement agent. In a bag.'

But Murtry was in love and barely paying attention, Ryan could tell. He was stroking the snake like a second date. He curled it around an arm and shrugged. 'Well, I guess it's how God would've delivered the rattler in Genesis. They didn't have UPS deliveries back then, you know.'

'I'd guessed. Sold any recently?'

'Two. Special order. Same guy. Said he was holding a party night, wanted snakey shit to go with the temptation theme. These here fit the bill perfectly. Like I said, all hiss and wind.'

'This buyer got a name?'

'A big one. Luther Atom. Hey, but the best of it is, I even get to put up a sign: "Reptiles by Murray Murtry, Biblical Animals, wholesale and retail." Worth the 20 per cent discount to get myself in that place, believe me. He's the king of eating.'

'He's illegal.'

Murtry put the soft end of a pencil in his ear and turned it vigorously. 'Is that bad?'

Devlin, who barely noticed Ryan leave, was in a post-coital funk when the vid rang, tugging at his subconscious. He reached out an arm.

'You were right,' she said, restrained and immediate. 'It's Atom. He bought the snakes from a dealer. I'll call you back. Oh, good morning, by the way.'

He felt exhilarated and then angry. Luther Atom. Revenge? Or a warning? At that moment, he didn't care how powerful or connected that man was in the city. Strong was right, and Devlin was impressed, again, by the firmness of her instincts.

Finch was reading the sports section and eating a doughnut. His wife had given him a wallchart for his birthday. It matched what you could eat with how much exercise was then needed to keep within weight permits. It was meant for children, he complained. You eat like one, she retorted, then had him work out to an exercise hologram, one she'd picked up at a theme park in Arkansas, where people went to fire paint pellets at humonsters they chased through scrub and brush. He'd be sure to respond with a catcher's mitt for her next big day.

Finch was five-ten and a hundred and sixty pounds. It was always tight. But he worked out most days, pounding the running machine at level one for fifty minutes, burning off seven hundred calories, or so his eating tactician said. Still, jam doughnuts, even the baked ones at one hundred and sixty calories each, were a throw of the dice. But he was nervous and when he was nervous he ate. Right at that moment he was eating.

The share in Dangerous Passion, which was fancied for the 2.30 at Saratoga that afternoon, was making him nervous. Cupid Frish was making him nervous. But at least she wasn't running later. His two-year-old hadn't won a thing yet and Finch was anxious, especially after paying racing writers a thousand a month. His politics was based on giving people potential, that's what *Time* magazine said. But so far, potential was costing him and could become embarrassing unless it secured a place in the winner's enclosure.

'Forget about it. Politics is only the illusion of progress and potential, on account of people needing to feel their lives are moving forward to some purpose,' Lonergan said one evening in Madame Jolly's as the cooking act was finishing on stage. 'But, you know, time marches on and it isn't going anywhere in particular.'

It wasn't the money for sure. Finch had a million ways to make millions of dollars. This was about demonstrating his nose for a deal. The fact that the share was payment from Luther Atom was neither here nor there. Nobody but Tom Lonergan, who also had a share, could know that, anyway.

Next door, Lonergan was quietly replacing the receiver on his vid. The call had come from a contact in police Dispatch. Detective Nathalie Ryan had ordered back-up. She was planning an arrest after 'linking' Luther Atom to the Frish murder.

It wasn't the most worrying word to hear, linking, but it was up there.

Lonergan pushed his chair back and looked out of the window, throwing pistachios into his mouth, one at a time. Brilliant black and green clouds rolled across Lower Manhattan. He hoped it wasn't going to be another yellow day. He hated the yellow rains and the snow, which smelled of sulphur and stained leather, making him want to piss all the time.

Arresting Luther Atom wasn't the plan. Ryan was supposed to be on her way to West Virginia by now and pulling in Heston Gotfelt. Apples. Snakes. It was meant to be a no-brainer, a biblical candy trail that even the dumbest cop would follow. Unfortunately, Ryan wasn't the dumbest cop.

He wondered about calling Atom directly. But it wasn't worth leaving a trace for some sharp-eyed detective to find. Somebody like Ryan.

'Tommy,' shouted Finch. 'Where do we stand on Saratoga? Is the race going to be thrown by Evil Software, or what? Get in here.'

Of course it was, he said to himself. Jockeys were easy to bribe, always needing to stay within weight permits to keep their jobs. Health Enforcement officers were easy, as well. Ridiculously so. As a voter, Lonergan thought that this was outrageous. They should pay them better.

'It's done,' he shouted back, tired and annoyed by the doubt. 'Listen, give me a moment. I've got a call to make.'

He pressed in the number and waited for the reply. 'It's me. You've screwed up. The cops are going after Luther Atom' were the first words he said. 'Call Atom on a secure line, a payvid. Do it now. I'll hold Dispatch as long as I can.'

Devlin bumped into Sylvia, who defied the laws of adolescent nature and gave him a huge sleepy hug through bleary, morning eyes.

'Hi, Dad.'

Two surprises together.

'Morning, sweetheart. Listen, I've got to run. You okay for school? Swear to your maker you won't skip anything today?'

'Daddy?'

'What?'

'Your detective. She's fine. For a cop, I mean.' She stared at Devlin, who looked at her suspiciously. 'You're mellowed out, is all I'm saying. I'm glad you're seeing someone, makes you less grumpy. Believe me, it is so much easier being with a grown-up without issues.'

'Thanks. Well, enjoy the moment. The detective isn't mine, by the way.'

'Bet she could be,' Sylvia said, shuffling, yawning, her mind already wandered elsewhere.

He grabbed his gun and keys. He would drive to Strong, surprise her. It was early. She was bound to be sleeping off whatever indulgences had filled the night before; and he thought about his own.

Mine? Devlin smiled. It was good, unexpected, to have earned the approval of his daughter and he felt the possession of Ryan all over again, her soft contours, muscle and energy. That was good, too.

Ryan requested the address from Dispatch and ordered uniformed back-up. You never could tell with people and arrests, she always thought. Some were cool, others pulled a gun or an attorney. Guns never bothered her.

She waited at the Park Avenue entrance, admiring the glass inlaid door and checking her watch. What was keeping them? Twenty minutes so far. The door was a mild diversion: a Bible scene cast in an elaborate, exquisite mosaic of coloured glass. They were fashionable five years ago, in the early days of Control. Every upmarket apartment block seemed to put one in the lobby, huge plates of translucence depicting scenes of dietary restraint or excess. The Burger King collapse was a favourite motif, bloated humonsters rising to a heaven adorned with halos, another was devil's helpers in grease pits poking the fouled deposits of burgers with forks. Victims in most of the tableaus were usually seen carried by teams of beatific, toned angels using sensitively cast hoisting equipment, strong golden ropes passing through gilded pulleys. This one was the Sermon on the Mount, another favourite. Ryan peered closely, squinting at the detail as a squad car pulled up. There was Jesus, sipping a low-calorie juice, and laid out before him were loaves, fishes and – what was that? – looked like chocolate cake and one of the seven dwarfs. She smiled. It was good to see a little sedition.

'Detective Ryan? Saunders and Holman, ma'am.'

Ryan looked at the two men walking towards her, gym-jawed and clean shaven. Rookies. Leather holsters like their faces, unsplit or blemished by age and experience.

They went inside the building, flashing identity badges at the doorman. Atom had the penthouse. Of course, thought Ryan.

In West Virginia it was a short service from the Book of Common Exercise, one designed to prepare the digestive system for the lightness of fruits and whole salads; that is to say, no spilling of essences by knife.

Heston Gotfelt was leading through the various running levels of the service. Disco played in the background as congregants, many of them guests who had paid hundreds of dollars to stay overnight and fast, were excoriated through loudspeakers for their lack of Control. Images of humonsters through the ages flashed on the screen behind the exeraltar, great hanging plates of flesh, or arrogant and uncreased protrusions. Spurred by the sight of a massive woman from Houston blabbering about her rights (a favourite scene from the *Vid of Flesh*, scene forty-nine; by scene sixty-three she's being chased by an enraged mob through a mall) Gotfelt was sweating hard, pumping out the foulness of excess, purifying himself for the day, feeling toxic matter being forced through his pores, the triumph of outer beauty.

He saw Holly Fareham out of the corner of his eye as he ran for purification. She nodded at him. He summoned a Preparer, who handed him a sacramental towel, and he indicated to a junior prelate to take over before making the sign of the cross, stretching in obeisance to the altar, and walking away.

'We've had a call from New York,' she said as he approached. 'Mr Lonergan from the mayor's office. He said it was urgent. Asked me to mention somebody called Cupid Frish. Does that name mean anything to you?'

He stumbled.

'Bishop?'

'It's nothing. Low blood sugar. Liturgy level nine doesn't agree with me. I'll be whole after my fruit.'

Lonergan knew. Then the mayor must know. The police had already come once. Now he understood why. It was collusion, but for what purpose? Nothing had been made public. Nothing had been on the news. God knows they hated him in that city and would buy tickets to see him brought down; an instant humiliation. 'Get Joe.'

The walk across the campus to his office was one he usually enjoyed, a lion amidst his pride. Not today. Cold sweat seemed congealed on his back, rather than a lubricant to his limbs. He felt his love handles, a habit since childhood at times of stress.

In his chambers there was order and certainty. Everything was where it should be. Seven apples, each peeled and severed into quarters, lay splayed on a white plate, vulnerable and exposed. Gotfelt stared at them before eating greedily, crushing the pulp, savouring the bitter liquid of his favourite fruit, the acrid taste of oral pleasures that it represented. He thought of Cupid Frish.

The disordered streets around Williamsburg were still barely understood by Devlin. He preferred the comforting symmetry of Manhattan, so it took a while to find Euclid Avenue, where Strong lived.

It was wide, with neat, white clapperboard houses and tidy front yards, a respectable street without a particular past or any defined future, anonymous and timeless. Children played, screaming and noisy, on the sidewalks. Strong told him once that her home was a ground floor and basement, chosen because of a perfect outside deck for barbecues; those barbecues to which Devlin was never invited.

There was a chain, which he pulled, hearing an answering chime inside. Nothing. He looked at his watch. Nine-thirty. She should be up, suspension or not, like him or not, hangover or not. He hit the door hard. Nothing.

He walked down the side of the house, around the back, and peered through the kitchen window as he rang her vid. He shouted, knocked; then tried the front-door, which, to his surprise, yielded. No wonder Strong lost her cop badge. Devlin put his head around the opening, but kept his feet on the porch. It felt less of an intrusion.

'Hey, Kate? It's me. Public enemy number two.' He definitely smelled toast and tried again. Silence. Hell with it, he thought, entering noisily as his vid sounded. Ryan, but he was too edgy and guilty for a call, which didn't seem to fit with trespassing into somebody's home.

No reply. Ryan flipped the vid shut. She wanted Devlin at Police Plaza when the questioning began. Maybe he was stuck in traffic. The rookies had looked surprised when asked what kept them.

'We got here real quick, five minutes tops,' said Holman. 'We were only three blocks away.'

Three blocks? Standards were slipping. She'd called it in at 8.45 a.m. and back-up arrived thirty minutes later. Ryan hit mute on her vid and fifteen on the elevator.

'You got neat writing, ma'am,' said Holman, watching as Ryan studied the notes in a pad. She hated it when they flirted.

'Just some order in a mad world. Now, listen up. Let me do all the talking. You guys hang back and stay alert.' They looked nervous and eager and very young. 'Either of you done this before?'

'No, sir,' said Saunders. 'Never busted a celebrity, except on the simulator.'

'Well, it's different in real life. And this time there won't be any media. They're like everyone else, except with a publicist, and I don't anticipate one of those today. This is a surprise visit.'

Atom was leaning against his open door, waiting for them and holding a tray with three cups of coffee. Ryan was taken aback, but caught a sweet odour from whatever he was smoking.

'Is that tobacco?' she asked, eyes narrowing.

Atom smiled wearily. 'Rest easy. It's just marijuana with a tobacco smell.'

He was wearing a purple, quilted jacket over his suit. There was piping on the sleeves and a crest of some sort above the breast pocket.

'The elevator. Slow, isn't it? Like so many things in this town.'

Like getting back-up, thought Ryan.

'Coffee? Fruit?'

'This isn't a social call, Mr Atom. Can we go inside? Saunders, stay by the door. Holman, hold that elevator.'

The apartment was small, with low ceilings, but seemed to be filled with green, thanks to plate-glass windows and views over Central Park across to the Dakota Building. The furniture was fiery gold and twirled French, Louis Quinze chairs inlaid with fine wood marquetry; complex stitching was poodle-delicate. There were no plain surfaces.

'Kind of over the top, aren't they?' Ryan commented, rubbing a hand across a chair.

'You see any onyx?' Atom replied, annoyed that his taste could be questioned, and by a cop.

There were food artefacts in glass disyplay cases. Ryan saw a copy of *Joy of Chocolate*. Atom caught her eye.

'A first edition. Take a look. Please. Be my guest.'

'It doesn't do anything for me.'

'Really?' Atom laughed indulgently and indicated a chair, before sitting down himself. 'I find it very sensual, Detective, a little reminder of our past. It isn't so long ago. People were quite brazen once, eating chocolate in the street, cooking –'

Ryan interrupted. 'I don't need a history lesson. This mean anything to you?'

She held out a photograph of Gross.

Atom looked closely. 'I bought two just like that a week ago. Don't tell me; your latest suspect in the hooker case?' He arched his eyebrows in mock horror and raised a hand to his mouth.

'Where are they now?'

He shrugged. 'In my restaurant. I got them as a little fun for my guests.'

'Word is you've got some party coming up.'

'Another word is bullshit, Detective. You mustn't believe everything you hear. For instance, I heard you lost a corpse. Imagine that.' He sipped his coffee. 'Look around. I collect rare things. There are sugars in my cellar, for instance, rare shit from way back. Samples. All licensed, by the way. You can check the locks. I got devices used to keep f*t in a skillet, they'd make your hair curl. A customer mentioned the snakes to me. Amusing diversions. Blind. Don't see what's in front of them, Detective.'

'They whistle Dixie?' Ryan asked to see them.

Atom shrugged. 'Sure. You can feed them larvae, which I consider quite amusing, except for the larvae. They're not fussy. About who feeds them, I mean.'

Ryan stared steadily at him. 'You ever own a gorilla?'

Atom raised an eyebrow.

Devlin decided to wait. She obviously wasn't far away. The coffee was still warm and a piece of toast, liberally buttered and smeared with strawberry jam, was half-eaten and abandoned on the draining board. It smelled of about one hundred and seventy calories and he felt a small yearning. He should have waited outside, but found himself snooping idly. The fridge was huge, but empty. No shelves either.

He closed it and walked around. A baseball bat was tacked to the living-room wall, a photograph of some Mets line-up. The chairs were battered, yet the desk seemed ordered, unusual enough for Devlin to want to see close up, just to make sure. The computer was switched off. He ran a finger over its keyboard and looked out of the window, absently picking up the vid.

The front door opened and he called her name.

'Devlin?' Strong replied, sounding surprised. 'Scared the hell out of me. You should have called.' She looked at him, waiting for the words of explanation.

'I've got good news, the sort you like to deliver in person and the door was open. Your friend and mine, Mr Luther Atom himself, is being busted right now. He sent the snakes. Ryan found out he bought two of them.' Devlin looked at her expectantly.

'Yeah? So, we bust an eateasy operator who keeps reptiles. Big deal.'

'Big deal? It means Ryan has found a thread that connects all of us. I'd say that was deal enough, wouldn't you? It also gets you off the hook with Ravenski; shows you were right all along about going into Atom's.' Devlin looked at her. It was obvious. She had to see it.

'And why would Atom want to do that?' Strong asked, looking quizzical. 'Get us all woo-wooed up to make connections, rattle his cage?'

Devlin's brain raced, but not to a finish line. 'Well, I don't think he expected Ryan to make the link with the snakes. Anyway, who cares? I think you should give her some credit here. It's not her fault you screwed up at Homicide.' He regretted the words in an instant, but they just came out thoughtlessly, a mass evacuation of resentments now that newer loyalties had posted a claim. 'Look, I'm sorry. I didn't –'

'Forget it. Look, I don't mean to be rude. But I got things to do. I'll call you,' she said, turning away.

'Listen, Kate, I –'

'Depositions for Internal Affairs are due next week. These are things that may keep me employed. But for what it's worth, I think you're wrong. My money's on Gotfelt: motive and opportunity, at least that's what they taught us in Homicide back in the day.'

Devlin was puzzled. 'But you thought it was Atom?' he said to himself, walking to the door. He'd expected triumph or happiness, not the worst kind of brown, the sort that was brittle, dry and left a bad taste.

Atom was unperturbed enough not to call Bo Watz during the drive to his club through light traffic and small attack-clouds, which darted between the lanes. Just juveniles, said the happy weather guy on ABC. 'Everyone can ignore them.' He made it sound like a party.

'They're out back during the night,' Atom said, leading the way when they finally arrived at the elegant brownstone on Perry Street. 'You ever try rigatoni with mole?'

'No,' Ryan replied tightly.

'Me neither.'

'Mole poblano de guajote?'

'What?'

'It's mainly nuts and brown with turkey and chilli. Nice.'

'I don't need the small talk, Mr Atom.'

Ryan followed with Saunders, leaving Holman at the door. They were soon in a storeroom, shelves stacked with foods, cans and bottles. In the corner, Ryan saw a long, empty glass tank, wire mesh pulled tightly over the top, its interior of rocks, snake and sand dimly lit. 'Where's its friend?'

Atom poked around the rocks with a kitchen spatula. 'Here somewhere.' Ryan watched him steadily and made a decision when the absence became clear.

'Could the other have gone to a Health Enforcement agent involved with the Frish investigation, Mr Atom?'

He laughed. 'Without saying goodbye? Without packing?'

'You think I'm kidding around?' Ryan thought about the earlier interviews and made a decision, reaching for wrist restraints, the new issue with soft, mock-fur rims and aloe vera lubricant. 'Luther Atom, you're under arrest for the murder of Cupid Frish.' She spoke the liturgy of seizure without emotion or drama.

Atom let his jaw fall open: disbelief, anger, amazement, all found a moment as the metal softened by the Forty-Fifth amendment to the Constitution clicked into place, locking his hands together. 'Maybe I do want my attorney.'

'Do you understand your rights?' Ryan persisted.

'Yeah, yeah. And they include my attorney.'

'You can call him from the precinct. Let's go.' Ryan wished she knew what would happen after that piece of geographic certainty had been reached. A snake had entwined around them all and the arrest was its temptation. But she didn't know that and called Devlin, telling him to join them at Police Plaza.

Joe Regard sat in contemplation. This wasn't the first time things had been hidden and Gotfelt was an admirably accomplished liar. It was a significant strength, Regard thought; part of what made publicity so easy.

'Yes, I saw her. Yes, we played around. I should have got her to come to the hotel. But she wanted to see me, said it was important.'

He was pacing the room. 'I took a taxi to Hoboken. We did some brown,' he said, adding quickly: 'My god did forsake me and the flesh was weak.'

Regard nodded neutrally. 'Yeah, he can be unreliable.' There would be time to lay down a sympathy track later.

'She asked for money. A great deal. Even gave me bank

account details in Switzerland. There were pictures, she said. I had to act.'

Homicide was on the eighteenth floor and Ryan met Devlin at the elevator. She smiled with pleasure and relief. 'We've got him in an interview room. Follow me.'

'Did he kill her?'

'Watch through the one-way. Best seats in the house. We're about to find out.' She sounded high with determined expectation, but confident.

The room was small and narrow, bare except for a table with recording equipment at one end, and chairs. Accuser faced accused and his representative. Bo Watz stared intently, an umpire looking for fouls, his face contorted into an expression of perpetual, but billable, fury. Devlin, watched with other, senior, police officers from a long bench, and felt like a blood sport spectator, but one invisible to those about to do verbal combat.

Ryan seemed calm. So did Atom, finding corners of the room to stare at, time to stretch, yawn, sip coffee, fire up a joint.

Ryan took him through the snakes. Atom heaved his shoulders, said he had no idea what happened to the second one. Must have escaped.

'The owner of Biblical Animals has positively identified the snake that I found in the apartment of a Health Enforcement agent last night as one of two he sold to you.'

Atom looked at Watz, whose eyes had widened, an involuntary reflex. Devlin stared intently, barely breathing.

'I own a snake and it disappears. Happens all the time. Bodies from morgues. Animals. They slip away. Get stolen. These are difficult times. I got employees with light fingers. Canadians.'

Ryan pressed on. 'Don't you think it's an unlikely coincidence? Detectives and Health agents investigating a murder, that apparently took place twenty yards from your eateasy, start getting your creatures delivered.'

'Hey,' interrupted Watz.

'Correction, twenty yards from your legitimate eating establishment. Am I supposed to believe that a man with your connections, a former police officer, can't find home addresses?'

Atom turned a watery eye to the ceiling. 'And why would I do that?' he asked quietly. 'Like I need the attention.'

Ryan persisted: 'To throw the investigation; give us some holy shit to confuse everyone. I bet you knew all about Cupid Frish's client list. We've got brown matching.'

'I already explained that; got it off the body. Of course the brown matches. Throw an investigation? Like I'd care. I got all the protection I need,' said Atom, suddenly leaning forward. 'Or haven't you noticed yet?'

Watz found an opening. 'So, what exactly is it you're claiming here, Detective? That a snake kept by my client found its way into the homes of a Health Enforcement agents and, let me get this straight, such a thing implicates my client in a murder? Come on. You think a judge will even entertain your breathing court air with that line? As for the brown, it's everywhere, or hadn't you noticed? Somebody gets hit with a brick, so you arrest everyone who lives in a house? Give me a break.'

The lawyer raised a pudgy hand and began counting off one ringed finger at a time. 'No opportunity, no motive, no witness, no DNA; and prints linking my client to the scene are fully explained. He's already told you what happened –'

Atom interrupted quietly. 'Wait up, Bo. Something isn't adding up here. Ryan you said agents, addresses.'

Ryan looked at him. 'Devlin and Strong were both sent snakes, Mr Atom. They arrived at the same time. They both interviewed you.'

Atom blew a circle of smoke towards the sky. 'Yeah? Well, you need to do your math.' He watched the ring float and expand before breaking. 'I had two. Only one is missing, as you saw.'

Ryan suddenly looked thrown and sat rigid, as if suddenly paralysed. Watz gleamed, triumph in his eyes. 'Can I assume that this interview is terminated?'

Ryan's hands were flat on the table, lips tight. She looked at the wall clock and recorded the time.

'You'll keep your client available for questioning, Mr Watz,' she said, flat and deflated.

A middle-aged captain with jet-blue hair named Diamond nodded unhappily when Ryan came into the viewing room. 'Ryan, that this case needs more work might get an understatement of the month award. Snakes? Good God, it isn't even circumstantial, let alone connected to the murder of Cupid Frish. And you've still got a gorilla to figure out.' He looked squarely at her and there was anger in his eyes. 'I don't want to be this embarrassed again before my retirement party. Is that understood?'

Ryan nodded and looked at Devlin and, for the first time, he was seeing beyond the eyes. At least she had sense and stayed quiet despite the flaying. He could see pain, which is what you like to do in a relationship. And then he felt stupid. It was only a night together and he wasn't sure about adopting other people's frustrations. He had plenty of his own.

Hanson was waiting outside the interview room. 'We need to speak,' he said to Ryan, quietly. 'We've found other prints at the Montcalm apartment.'

'And?' said Ryan, looking at him.

'They match Heston Gotfelt's.'

26

The F*t-Free Duck was a ten-minute walk from Police Plaza. They were having lunch.

'It's true about the snakes and I can't put Atom anywhere near the body or at Frish's place,' Ryan admitted. 'The plain fact is they didn't seem to know each other –'

'But, the snakes, the brown?' Devlin cut in.

'I'm certain they're to throw us. Temptations. I don't know. But they seem to have a humiliate-me clause attached.'

'Meaning?'

'Listen, what do we know? Cupid Frish is strangled, although we seem to miss it. We've got fingerprints that make us feel stupid, because they point to a gorilla. The media is laughing at us.'

Devlin stared at her. 'But the zoo guy –'

'He's laughing, too. Said he'd never heard of a gorilla killing methodically, so quietly and under, for want of a better word, control.' She looked up suddenly. 'We're being taken for a ride.'

'And Gotfelt?' Devlin said. 'You said he keeps gorillas. He had motive and opportunity. The fingerprints show he was lying. She was blackmailing him; they fight. He kills her, big powerful guy thanks to all that prayercising, the snakes are a warning, he got his supporters –'

'I'll buy he was seeing her. I mean, I'd guessed that much. But how does he get the body out from the morgue? Why does he dump it in an eateasy? How does he even know about the eateasy, let alone how to get inside? No. This is too deranged.'

Joe Regard had reached a similar conclusion. Gotfelt screwed around, but he wasn't a killer. Regard knew about Cupid Frish, despite pretending otherwise. He'd been tapping Gotfelt's calls since the institutional shareholders began paying him a retainer for monthly reports. They discovered their chief executive's adultery through due diligence and needed it under control, guided towards Church members, women who could be relied on for discretion. But he wanted to hear what Gotfelt had to say, to test the words against a known truth; Gotfelt had visited Frish that weekend and she was certainly alive when he left, because he knew. A paper surveillance log from the detective agency was the proof.

He was glad he kept them; paper was more secure than electronic records, harder to tamper with and easier to read in the bath. 'Aug 15: Subject left C at 4.35 p.m. Driven off by Sunrise Taxis. Op Two followed. Op One saw C follow six minutes later. Not followed. Suggest car bug for future surveillance of C. Check other contacts.' It was signed and dated.

'We spent time together,' Gotfelt said, sipping at a glass of freshly pressed apple juice. 'I was going to tell her it was over. But she tempted me and I was weak. She had film of me, of us. We argued. She was drunk, dizzy, swearing, and I slapped her and took the disc. That was all. I didn't kill. It's bad –'

'No, that's not bad,' broke in Regard, rubbing his chin thoughtfully. 'That's prime-time, fallen woman taking advantage, temptation; useful marketing. Bad is somebody setting you up for a fall, somebody powerful enough in New York to kill, move bodies, get the cops to go where they want them, which is in your direction.'

'Finch,' Gotfelt said, almost inaudibly. It seemed improbable but possible all the same. This was a big-city politician, friend of the eateasys and the criminals who supplied them; a man woven into corruption, to its charity fundraisers, a world he could never hope to access, but one he threatened. Gotfelt stared out of the window, at a palette of fluorescents, turquoise flashes and chemical orange clouds that seemed to drift with grace and purpose. Quite beautiful.

'What do you think they plan next?' he asked Regard.

Lonergan went to Atom in person, which was the way it had always been since the early days, when high-rolling gorgers were blackmailed into funding the first Finch election campaign. Nobody knew of the liaison and, with judicious disguise, it was possible to escape tracking by street cameras. Retinal monitors were everywhere. 'I'll be at the gym,' he'd tell his secretary, Miss Harple.

'Okay, Mr L. I'll tell the mayor's office. Stretch a muscle, now,' she'd shout, pretending to believe him and wondering if he would ever invite her out.

Atom was in his second-floor office, which was a colourless counterpoint to the restaurants, a retreat into drabness. It had small, round windows veiled with grime. Old filing cabinets lined one wall and brown leather armchairs were weary and torn, offering minimum comfort to visitors. An overhead fan turned without consequence. Three lines of crushed brown lay across a small mirror, flat on Atom's heavy wooden desk. He sucked at each row in turn, noisily, through a straw. Lonergan watched and winced. It was too early for him.

'First, this broad's body turns up, which is unsettling, gives my chef palpitations. So, we move her a few blocks. Get her out. I didn't need to lose her, Tommy. It was nothing to do with me, see. I figure, let her be found, just not in my premises. But I got to thinking: she came in through the kitchens. Not many people know about that entrance. Me, the chef, the twins. That's it.' He paused. 'Oh yeah. And you.'

Lonergan smiled. 'Now what are you suggesting, Luther? That I set you up?' He laughed softly. 'My retirement fund.'

'Whoever it was knew how to get in here through the L train subway stop at Fourteenth Street.'

'Let's take a walk. It isn't just genetically modified fruit got ears these days.'

'I have this place swept every ten hours.'

'They come every eleventh.'

As they took to the littered streets, crouched against assaults of trash barrelling down the canyon of Eighth Avenue, Lonergan talked.

'The mayor had a problem and Cupid Frish was the solution. We came up with this thing. Then she got, got –'

'Greedy,' Atom volunteered, nodding his head.

'No,' said Lonergan. 'Careless.'

Atom looked at him.

'Brown addiction requires skills, measurement skills to deal with the sugars. You know that, Luther. But she was so high, couldn't tell an insulin unit from an insurance form after gorging and filling herself with champagne. When she needled down, just in case she was pulled over, dumbass took three times the safe dose, went into, what is it, that thing?'

'Hypoglycaemic shock. I see it all the time.'

'That's it. Heart gave up. Ruined a perfect deal, Luther. We had a plan, and she syringed it away.' Lonergan slapped one hand into the other. 'We were going to bring down two joyless bastards, Heston Gotfelt and the Health Commissioner. Her weeping testimony was all we needed. It was going to be perfect. But she couldn't control herself, that's the real human tragedy here.'

'Control, it's a sweet thing,' said Atom. 'My sympathies.' He heaved his face, briefly, into an expression of sadness. 'Moving on. Why'd you have her dumped at my place?'

'I didn't. As you can imagine, we were thinking fast. Had to. I only needed to make sure Ryan was watched, led where we needed her to go, so we had to dress the death up; catch their eye, make sure Health Enforcement was drawn in. This way we got the Health Commissioner sweating and on the defensive, too. But your place was not my idea, believe me. This person we used is a hothead, flew solo, had an agenda. By the time I found out, it was too late. Still, I figured you could handle it; man with your connections.'

Atom grunted. 'If I'd known, I would've called in expert removal myself. Stuff like that happens, you worry. I got enemies, too. Needed her out fast.'

'I understand. It was unfortunate,' said Lonergan. 'But we did get the commissioner strung out, which is good for all of us, my friend.' Lonergan slapped his companion on the back. 'Look, I knew Ryan would work out you couldn't possibly have murdered Cupid Frish and that Fenwick wouldn't have the guts. She's only got one other suspect and that's the guy we need to cripple most of all,

Heston Gotfelt. It'll work out. Fenwick we can bring down any time just for brown gorging. Besides, he's more useful to us now where he is.'

They were at Forty-Second Street and stopped, sheltering inside a doorway, as a powerful wind blew paper and people along the sidewalks. 'This trash is getting dangerous,' said Atom, dolefully, as a can flew past at chest height. It hit a cyclist, who tumbled into the road forcing a car to swerve into a lamp amid a terrible, anguished rending of metals and screams from shocked pedestrians. 'And somebody ain't recycling.'

'We need to find out who's playing God,' Ryan said, pausing for a moment. 'There's only one person who deals with the Almighty on a regular basis in this mess. We need to see Gotfelt again.'

'You think?'

A vid sounded. It was Ryan's. She looked at the name flashing up. 'I'd better take this.' Devlin looked at her as she listened intently and he tried not to see her as beautiful, just as a detective. It seemed more businesslike.

'Are you certain?' She sounded excited and perplexed all at once. When the call ended she sat completely still, staring at the ceiling, before speaking.

'Krebs, over at Pathology; a part-timer, but very methodical and experienced,' Ryan said after the call ended. 'He's analysed hair he found in Cupid's nail.'

'Don't tell me, another gorilla?'

Ryan was looking at Devlin evenly through unmoving eyes. 'Sort of. Man-made.'

Ryan was already on her feet and moving quickly.

She whistled up a cab and was on her vid, passing out instructions. 'Every theatre costume supplier, every fancy-dress place. Halloween store, student frat house. Anyone who hired a gorilla costume in the past two weeks.'

Everyone has a face, one that appears when all muscular command is shocked, paralysed by the raw and unbidden. Devlin's appeared three hours after they left the cab. Ryan was bouncing a basketball through a hoop built into the corner wall of her cramped office. 'Gives you an edge, walls work for you, help focus the eye,' she explained. He nodded, his own eyes on the squad room. In the end, the name came in a banal way from a bored cop. Devlin thought how foolish and impetuous and typical to use a credit card.

Ryan was shocked, too, and they just stared at each other in silence. It was the shock of realizing that she was right, strings had been pulled, this way and that, attention deliberately misdirected, forced down corridors to chase shadows that disappeared, laughing, around a corner before they could be reached. It was the shock of knowing the knave had played them for a fool.

27

Lonergan took the call on his private line from a contact in the police department and replaced the receiver quietly after listening. His fingers hovered over the number pad. Too dangerous.

Instead, he suggested to the mayor that they should go for a walk, a code both understood. They went uptown in Lonergan's car and parked near to the East River, under the vaulted shadows of the Fifty-Ninth Street Bridge. The abandoned, derelict lands nearby were used by joggers and drunks and fundamentalists of all beliefs, but offered a sort of privacy. A small encampment of eco-warriors was the latest of its occupiers to be hosed into the river. Neighbours in the nearby environmentally friendly apartment block had complained about smell and smoke. The remains of reclaimed wood huts were still visible, stricken but defiant.

The most powerful men in the city walked beside each other, muffled against the cruel, cold summer wind, and unrecognizable to the few other New Yorkers also braced against gusts that were sudden and ferocious. They stood beneath confused trees that had shed leaves after spring. The spindled branch tendrils, twisted, arthritic and forlorn, reached, pleading, to the skies.

Lonergan spoke first after blowing into his chilled hands. 'We can be saddened, but should stay aloof. It'll be a case of obstruction, paid for by persons unknown.'

Finch nodded slowly. 'There's no link to us? You're absolutely certain?'

'None. The money went through third parties.' Lonergan omitted to add that the money had come from the same third parties, brown smugglers anxious to see the back of both Heston Gotfelt and the Health Commissioner. Two for the price of one hit, Lonergan argued when the ruling council of the five families had met in a Manhattan hotel as the charitable Friends of F*t Midwesterners.

'When the committee met to discuss –'

'The thing,' interrupted Finch impatiently.

'Yes, the thing; Tibor Gunduc offered us Cupid. He supplied her, so knew her clientele. I think he gave her a discount for information. Anyway, he told us she was professional, could be relied on not to screw things up. It's a damn shame. Maybe she was drinking heavily because of nerves. It probably clouded her thinking.'

Lonergan felt his vid vibrating and reflexively reached inside his jacket. It was a West Virginia number. 'Yes.'

'Lonergan? Joe Regard. Can you talk?'

'Sure. What's on your mind, Joe?' They were in an abandoned exercise area, sheltered from dancing flakes of snow. Lonergan turned from the mayor, just to make sure he was out of any camera shot, but Finch had instinctively moved away. The less he knew, the safer things always were. He kicked at a stone, staring at the ground, deep in thought. Somebody always knew.

'You called the bishop this morning during morning service,' said Regard.

'I wanted to let him know, in case he was interested, that a detective investigating the death of a woman named Cupid Frish was circling. Could be nothing, of course. Just thought you'd appreciate a head's up, so to speak. Your man being such a big supporter of the mayor. It was just a professional courtesy.'

Regard nodded slowly. 'Why?'

'Why? We heard Gotfelt and the victim were friends, close friends. In the fullest sense.'

'Then I'm sorry to disappoint you. They knew each other, but that's all.' Regard allowed himself a small smile. 'Fortunately, I have him followed everywhere. He was nowhere near her place when she died. I can prove that, by the way.'

Lonergan realized the king on his chessboard was toppling.

'They say film –'

'They're wrong.'

'Good, that's very good. Naturally, the mayor will be delighted that this potential slur can be –'

'Stopped,' Regard interrupted steadily. 'There are fundraising events that the Church will be glad to organize. For you or your rivals. It doesn't matter to us. Do we understand each other?'

'Always.'

'Good. Then I can consider this matter closed?'

'In the vault.'

'You and Jane will be over for Thanksgiving?'

'Wouldn't miss it. Your wife still makes the best chocolate mud pie east of the Mississippi.' Lonergan closed the vid and glanced at Finch, who was watching the icy river, a man momentarily powerless and paralysed. There was still one other person and one question: would they talk? Lonergan tried to call. It was worth the risk, given the stakes. No signal.

Something gnawed at Devlin as they drove across the city. 'It was nylon hair, right?'

'Yes.'

'So it was definitely a fake costume.'

'The real hairs on the fans at Montcalm were probably taken from the zoo here in town, or some taxidermist. Wherever. They wouldn't have been hard to get.'

Devlin waited a second or two. 'So, how come there were fingerprints? Your Path guy, the one in the apartment. He said there were secretions, didn't he? Secretions means pores, means flesh, means. First lesson –'

She looked at Devlin. 'What are you saying?'

'Hell, I just don't see how a person in a suit is going to leave prints, that's all?'

Ryan smiled. 'No?'

'Is this glass half full?'

'Yes, it is. You should learn to be more optimistic, unwind a little. Life is surprisingly good when you get into it.' She seemed happy, almost skittish.

Devlin frowned. It took a while to drive through the traffic. Ryan had ordered back-up and a signal seal on the area, just to make sure nobody could call with a warning. There were unmarked cars on every corner, she added. Nobody was getting in. Or out.

'I still can't believe we're doing this,' Devlin said as they stopped a block away. He could see the house and thought it would look different, somehow; guilty and complicit. But it didn't. The snow was swirling and confused. Like him.

Ryan was checking her gun.

'You won't need that,' Devlin said, appalled. 'I know this person.'

'No, you don't.'

Strong was watching an old cookery show on hologram. 'Hey, two visits in one day. Does it get any better?' she asked, holding open the door and looking at Devlin as a bowl was whisked in the background. She was wearing tight jeans and a tattered green sweatshirt.

'Can we come in?' Devlin asked.

'Sure.' Strong led the way, half-turning to him. 'And thanks for asking, by the way. I know how you prefer not to.'

The three of them sat down in the living room and a woman with a British accent talked about double cream. Devlin felt himself retch. He had no idea Strong was so into cooks, none at all. Maybe Ryan was right.

'Turn it off, please,' said Ryan firmly.

'I always start my day with her. Gets me all tingly.'

'Turn it off.'

The cook disappeared at the press of the remote.

'This isn't a "how-you-doing" call,' said Strong. 'I can tell because I'm sensitive that way.'

Ryan pulled out her notepad. 'You said you flushed the snake, correct?'

Strong looked at Devlin. 'It was a spur of the moment thing. I didn't know it was harmless.'

'What makes you so sure now?'

There was a pause. 'Because you guys are still here.'

Ryan nodded, noting it all down in her pad.

'The bag?'

'Trashed,' she said easily.

Ryan nodded. 'Then I'd be correct in assuming there's nothing left, no evidence at all that a snake was in this place?' She looked around.

'Nothing. Gone. Is that scary for you?'

There is a moment in every chase when hunter and hunted are looking at equal odds; a trip, a lapse of concentration and one develops an edge. It's like a date.

'The only supplier of the Texas blind snake that we could find in the five boroughs had two in stock.'

'And your point?' said Strong.

'They were both sold to Luther Atom. Devlin got one,' said Ryan, nodding at him. 'The other was still at his eateasy. I checked.'

Strong rested her head on the palm of her left hand, a student deep in concentration, and stared at Ryan as if trying to work out an equation. She wrinkled her freckled nose. 'I'm just not following you, ace.'

'There was no third snake for you to flush, Strong, is what I'm saying. So how could you possibly have known that Devlin had been sent one?' She paused. 'Unless you sent it.'

'Wow,' said Strong in tones of amused disbelief. She looked at Devlin. 'You'll learn, partner. This is how Homicide gets even. We made you look slow, a bit off the ball, didn't we? My friend here and me.'

'Spare me the idea that I give a shit about you, Strong, or your fucked-up career. But let's try it another way, just for old times' sake. The elevator at Montcalm Avenue, a Donny, third generation. It was an upgrade I'm willing to bet you didn't think to check. It made you. We examined its retinal records. The Threes have them. You were there,' Ryan stopped for a few seconds and stared out of the window, as if partially bored, 'the day Frish died.'

Strong started to make defensive noises, those ones without words. Ryan raised a hand to silence her. 'Here's the play. You have connections with the mayor's office, deep ones that go way back, and they ask a favour, the sort of favour that could be rewarded with a job back in Homicide, that detective's badge you want returned so, so badly.'

Strong nodded her head in disbelief.

'They have a problem so Cupid Frish has been enlisted to blackmail Heston Gotfelt and Commissioner Fenwick. It's a sweet sting, isn't it? Finch or somebody close to him catches two fish and only has to cast one hook. Well, one hooker. Only it goes wrong.'

Devlin felt a weight in the pit of his stomach, as if all the illegal food he'd ever eaten had returned. He opened his mouth, a sound tried to come out, but thought better of it.

'Look, you believed she had all the answers to the city,' said Ryan, turning to Devlin on some instinct. 'By the way, she knew that and exploited it.'

'What do you mean?'

'You were tempted, just as I was. In my case, by Luther Atom. Think of Strong as another snake in all of this. The Old Testament kind that promises you all the good things.'

'A snake?'

'It was Genesis from the start, just the politically correct version. You were a male Eve.'

'Equality sucks,' Devlin said.

'She tempted you with your own ambition, worked your inexperience, lack of contacts, loneliness. How do you think you ever got to be on the Cupid case? I'll tell you, Strong arranged for you to be the nearest unit, knew where you would have lunch that day. It was her choice, if I recall. Regular as clockwork, tick-tock, my restaurant or yours. Isn't that how you worked it? Her idea, wasn't it?'

Devlin opened his mouth.

'All that shit at the Montcalm apartment, the holograms; it was all meant to send you, proxy for me, towards Heston Gotfelt. The only reason you ever stopped Cupid at all on the expressway, by the way, was because your partner needed to pass on instructions, in person, not over anything electronic that might be bugged. My bet is she was telling Frish to hand over the film she had before Gotfelt met the mayor.'

'I don't get it. Why?' Devlin was confused. 'It was a random stop-and-weigh,' he whispered.

'It was a pre-arranged meet. Big people want Gotfelt shut down, and the Health Commissioner, too. Cupid was a shared weakness, their temptation. Cities run on connections and greed and black-mail. Strong was tapped into all of them, which is what made her so perfect. Why do you think she could lose her Homicide beat, but so easily find another job? It was a favour being banked and Cupid was somebody calling it in. I doubt your partner even knows who was paying her. Then Cupid went and died, spoiled everything.'

Devlin's head was swirling. 'Wait. You're saying Strong didn't kill her? And it wasn't Gotfelt –?'

'Nobody did,' Ryan interrupted. 'Frish pumped herself full of insulin, overdosed, to get down after a gorge. Krebs found it with toxicology tests, amounts so massive they were still there. Incidentally, I think that was why your friend Tibor Gunduc couldn't resist being sceptical when you said it was murder. He knew. But on the day, Strong was supposed to be picking up the disc of Frish and Gotfelt, only by the time she got there Gotfelt had already been and taken it. The gorilla suit? Now that was a smart idea: completely obscured Strong on the vid and any other standard surveillance equipment out there. The black figure?'

'The ghost in the machine,' Devlin said almost inaudibly.

Ryan looked at Strong, who sat impassively. 'Another maximum ten from the judges. Except for the elevator, Strong, it was pretty slick.'

Devlin broke in. 'It said "nice to see you" when we went to Montcalm that first time. You interrupted it.'

'Yes, it did. The missing word was "again". The camera stored a retinal scan, routine, like I said, for an upgraded Donny, and the one thing Strong didn't think to find out. A straight match to records when somebody had the bright idea to check. Took a while.' Ryan looked over.

'Here's the play. Strong goes into the apartment to collect the film, finds Frish already dead or dying. Now that was very bad news and threatened everything, especially her payments. Worse, she had no disc, nothing to turn the screws on Gotfelt or the commissioner. The disc had gone, remember? Gotfelt had certainly taken it. Maybe Frish was blackmailing him separately, but it's not important. He found the camera, his prints were all over, carelessly so. Even a ten-year-old knows you wear gloves at a crime scene, especially if you're about to create it. The point is that he had no reason to think like a criminal; Frish was still alive at that point.

'But she's slipping. When Strong arrives and realizes that, she improvises, comes up with a plan to make it look like a murder and points the blame at all the people she needed freaked to keep her paymasters happy. She was clever, a few clues, the holograms, diary. But the gorilla was a master stroke, compelling and puzzling; stopped us thinking about anything else.'

'But the fingerprints,' Devlin said. 'They were real. Your forensics guy checked.'

'Feel my face.'

'What?'

'Go on. Give me your hand.'

Devlin reached over.

'Now, rub it along. Go on.' She waited. 'Oily, isn't it and I'm not wearing make-up.'

'I don't get it —'

'The body secretes the same oils on the face and hands. All Strong had to do was rub her gorilla hands with the long fingers along on her face and then dab all over the walls to mimic a print. She knew enough about detective work, not to mention pathology, to realize we'd be looking for corroboration, especially for such an apparently bizarre murder. But the more we found, the deeper the hole we dug for ourselves. The fans, ripped books that even looked chewed, jewels everywhere, but not taken. The kitchen. It goes on.'

Ryan turned to face Strong squarely. 'But you didn't understand frenzy, did you? Fritz Hanson does and he could tell that everything done in that apartment was carried out with an equal, considered amount of pressure. No rage. No anger.'

'What about dressing Frish in brown?' Devlin wondered, although it barely seemed to matter.

'She got that idea from the print in the bedroom. There was plenty of brown at Frish's place, after all, and what there wasn't you supplemented from the – what is it called? – the candy store.

'The hair wouldn't have been hard. But the problem was, she didn't have it there, to complete the effect at the time –'

She looked at Strong again and clicked her fingers in rapid succession. 'Because you were improvising, thinking fast, and knew there'd eventually be a DNA test. You needed time.'

Strong nodded her head, smiling still. 'You got a big imagination, especially for a cop.'

'Oh, I'm not done yet. You needed to get real gorilla hair, didn't you? And the opportunity to place it. Atom's gave you that. You also knew that an autopsy would probably throw up the true cause of death, the insulin overdose. So you needed her to disappear until traces disappeared with decomposition. I wonder where you put the body?'

'In the fridge,' Devlin said quietly. 'All the shelves are missing, there's plenty of room.'

Strong opened her mouth, but Ryan raised a hand.

'So, you used the strike as cover to get into the morgue, re-trieve the body. How did you do that, by the way?' Ryan clicked her fingers. 'Of course, you've got a badge. Who'd stop you, especially in all the chaos? My guess is you got real gorilla hair from the zoo. Am I right? Baku. But you forgot that, in her final moments, Frish reached out, touched you and a small piece of the other hair caught under her nail. Or when you moved her. It's not that important.'

Two uniformed police were at the door, watching. They moved forward as Ryan nodded to them and she made the arrest after asking Strong if she understood her rights.

Devlin was trying to catch up. 'But what about the eateasy, the brown clothing. I still don't get it. Why?'

'That was all to guarantee media interest, which was crucial to the plan because it kept us on the case. The last thing Strong wanted was some story buried in the local news; read today, forgotten tomorrow. A hooker dies. So what? She needed big heat, the intense kind that has you rushing all over, cutting corners, anything to make a bust and get some cool from the reporters roasting your butt. It worked. The chief was practically alight.

'But you got a bit ahead of yourself, too. Got City Hall rattled because you couldn't resist humiliating Homicide, or trying to, on the way. Oh, and you always knew where the entrance was to that eateasy. But you needed an excuse to go back alone, unofficially, to make sure I wasted time with Luther Atom. I doubt your paymasters were very happy with that, by the way. But then, reckless is your middle name, isn't it?'

'You're good,' Strong said. 'I can see, truly, why you're the cat's whiskers.' She shrugged and smiled and seemed sad. 'Sorry, partner. I guess you should have stayed in Baltimore after all. I'm not sure New York is your kind of town.'

'Tell me,' Devlin called, as Strong was led out of her house. 'Did you have any respect for me at all, any ounce of it?'

'Respect?' She laughed, surprised. 'You mean, did I think you'd find out? No.'

'That's not what I meant.'

'Oh, did I like you? Interesting question,' she said. 'Don't sweat it, amigo. You'll see, it's just New York. Like is okay, but use is better. You were useful, so I liked you. Yes, I liked you.' She smiled. 'I was even going to invite you to my next Strong night, by the way. I got Leung along. Then all this –'

Devlin nodded. 'Thanks, appreciated.'

He watched her being led to a squad car and shouted, 'Was it money?'

She turned. 'Man, you ain't been paying attention. Open your eyes. It's only ever about appetite. Life. We talked about that. You have got a short memory.'

'I know, that stuff about sin being a calculation, not an impulse.'

'Hey, you were listening. Yeah.' She looked thoughtful. 'I guess I made the mistake of letting impulse take over.'

★

227

Mayor Finch was re-elected that November. Even thick fog failed to keep people out of the polling booths. As usual, he campaigned with Heston Gotfelt for a f*t-free future. Cupid Frish was recycled, scattered over the collection of rare cocoa plants that grew in the city arboretum. It seemed fitting. Devlin and Ryan were the only witnesses.

Strong was jailed for ten years on obstruction charges. Stubborn to the end, she never plea-bargained or said who she was working for. Maybe she never knew.

Nathalie Ryan and Devlin started dating and Devlin definitely felt better, especially about food and about life's priorities, particularly those of tolerance and pleasure; accepting humonsters as normal people, for example. He had got it all in perspective. Last night they had sex. It burned three hundred calories. Not as many as their first time. But that was often the way with relationships.

Epilogue

Listening to Irving Dunworth and ditching the angels had been a mistake, God could see. Earth had less than fifty years, but nobody paid any attention to the clouds or seemed to understand what they were trying to warn them.

Selected Extract from the Book of Indulgence

The angels visited the descendants of Terah and said unto Isaiah, the cousin of Lot and uncle of Aaron, who was related to Esau, but only by marriage, with a warning. 'The people of Balah are wicked sinners, in great excess and become slothful.'

The Lord had sent the angels, who were perfectly proportioned, to guide Isaiah and his family from the city before it was destroyed.

Now the elders of Balah, which lay in the land of the Anihalites, mocked the angels with Friendliness and invited them to Eat with them.

The angels did not break bread. They said the people of Balah were great Sinners and must Repent of their ways and the Lord would be merciful.

But the elders feasted that night, even as the Lord ranged his heavenly Trumpets and sent such great Fire from the sky. They did consume one thousand f*tted sheep and small birds of the air and honey and figs. Perizzites and Canaanites from Sodom and Gomorrah were honoured guests.

They came bearing birds of the air and fish of the sea and unleavened breads.

The weight of molasses and sugars was the burden of a multitude of asses. They brought with them a hundred virgins for the elders of Balah to know.

Even as winds hurled stones and tempests through the streets and dark places, the tables were bent asunder by wines and cheeses and meats and sweet creations to steal the souls.

None were spared for the Lord was angered and even as they fled the falling temples, the elders of Balah were turned into ash, and it was unseasoned. God then sent demons and tempests and creatures with hooves and cloved feet to destroy the city of Balah and all trace thereof.

(Ind. 8–19)

Man was given choices: he chose forbidden fruit and the madness, the unhappiness of seeking unfettered joy. The natural state of all God's creatures is to live within boundaries, to consume only that necessary for life and to want many things. The emptiness of material fulfilment, the cruel exploitation of happiness, is what has brought us to where we are today, weak and lowered and seeking the illusion of progress through products. The Book of Indulgence offers us the true word.

Revd Heston Gotfelt
Extracts from Commentaries on Pleasure
(Harvard University Press, 2015)